AN
ISOLATED
INCIDENT

AN ISOLATED INCIDENT

EMILY MAGUIRE

Lightning Books

First published in Australia by Pan Macmillan in 2016.

Published in 2018
by Lightning Books Ltd
Imprint of EyeStorm Media
312 Uxbridge Road
Rickmansworth
Hertfordshire
WD3 8YL

www.lightning-books.com

ISBN: 9781785630835

Cover by Ifan Bates

British Library Cataloguing in Publication Data
A catalogue record for this book is available from the British Library.

Printed by CPI Group (UK) Ltd, Croydon CR0 4YY

To my sisters

Monday
6
April

It was the new cop who came to the door, the young fella who'd only been on the job a couple of months. I thought that was a bit rough, sending a boy like him to do a job like that. Later, I found out that he was sent because he'd gone to pieces at the scene. That's what we all call it now: the scene.

'Miss Rogers?' he said, as though he was about to confess to reversing into my fence.

I nodded, waiting for the blow I knew was coming. I knew it was coming because Bella had been gone days and because no cop ever came to anyone's door to bring them cake or wine.

He rocked on his heels and cleared his throat.

'You found Bella?' I said, to give him a way to start. To show him it was OK.

'Yeah.' He blinked and I thought, *Jesus, he knows her.* 'I mean, there's been a body found. Matches her description. We need an official ID. Um, need you to come to . . . to do that. To confirm.'

Someone who's been hit as much as me should've known that seeing a blow coming, asking for it even, doesn't make it hurt any less. Probably hurts more, I reckon, because you're thinking *yeah, yeah, get it over with* and you think you already know. So I stood there nodding, thinking how the poor kid knows my sister and what a rough job to give a new fella and then I was shaking so hard it was like a demon had got inside.

The whole way to the hospital I wanted to ask him what had happened. I was hoping she'd been hit by a car or had a brain embolism or something. I wanted to ask those questions I'd asked when Mum died: 'Was it quick? Did she suffer?' But I couldn't speak. Never happened to me before, no matter what drama I've been chucked into. But there in that car it was like . . . It was like when you're so sick with some damn stomach thing that you don't even want to say 'no' to the offer of ice chips to suck, don't even want to nod, because the tiniest movement will bring the spewing on again. Like that, but I didn't feel like spewing. I just felt like any sound or movement would start something that would hurt and be impossible to stop.

The cop, Matt was his name, told me that he knew her from school. 'She was two years ahead of me, but it's a small school, ya know?'

I knew. I went there myself. Bella was twelve years younger than me, which made this boy twenty-three – so not a boy at all, technically, but his clenched jaw was dotted with pimples and his hands on the wheel were smooth and unscarred. I asked him if he'd seen her since school and he nodded, smiled like a love-struck dork and said he'd seen her a few times at the nursing home where she worked. 'We get called there a bit,' he said and it was clear he never minded being called to that stinking place by my sister who, even in that blue polyester uniform and those clunky white nursing clogs, was the prettiest thing anyone in this hole of a town was ever likely to see.

At school we had an expression: Strathdee-good. It meant that something was tops by Strathdee standards but not much chop compared to anything you'd get outside of here. So if you had a particularly good pie or whatever, you'd say, *Man, this is good. Strathdee-good, obviously, but yeah*. We did the same thing for people. None of the blokes at our school could compete with boys from Sydney or Melbourne, obviously, but there were a few who were definitely Strathdee-hot and so they were the ones we'd go for.

Bella was, if I'm being honest, Strathdee-pretty. I was always telling her she could be a model if she wanted, and I still think that was true, but it'd be modelling in the Kmart catalogue not *Vogue* or anything. I'm not putting her down. Like I said, she was the most beautiful thing anyone around here had ever seen in the flesh, but she was five foot nothing in high heels and had a size 10 arse on a size 6 body. Her skin was like fresh milk, and her light blue eyes so goddamn lovely it made me jealous as hell when we were younger. She could've done cosmetic ads, for sure, except they'd have had to do something about her hair, which was thick and frizzy and grew out and up instead of down. I used to tease her, saying that she was actually an albino African and that Mum had just adopted her because she felt sorry for this poor kid who all the other Africans thought was a freak. When she was twelve or so she started getting up really early to go through the rigmarole of oiling and flat-ironing her hair before school and then I felt bad for tormenting her. I told her that her hair looked hot, that it was way nicer than my bog-standard mousy-brown mop, but she never believed me.

One good thing about getting older is you make peace with the things you can't change about yourself. Not that Bella ever got old, but she was always mature for her age. By nineteen or twenty she'd stopped straightening her hair every day and just let it frizz out over her shoulders. She had to tie it back for work, of course, and I loved it like that most of all; the front all smooth and sleek and out the back a giant blonde fuzzball.

I never had to make peace with my hair – it was never my problem. My problem was my tits. I was too young when they sprouted and then they grew so fast. Eleven, twelve, thirteen and becoming used to feeling naked, feeling rude because of the way that boys and men – old men, teacher men, family men, strange men, friendly men – looked at me and found reasons to touch me and press against me and every now and then go for a sneaky grope. It set me apart from the other girls and made their mothers narrow their eyes and suggest I put on a jumper when it wasn't cold and made the boys my age laugh and call out *slut* and *showusyertits* as I walked past. These giant tits that told everybody I was a *scrubber* and *easy* and *trash*.

For the first few years I tried to ignore them. I mean, ignore the effect they had on people. The things themselves I packed into bras which my mum bought grudgingly (I kept outgrowing them and then wearing through the nylon). Once she said, 'Try and slow down, Chris. I'm not made of money,' as she tossed a Target bag on the bed, and although I knew she was joking I felt hurt and shamed like there might be some truth in the suggestion that I was growing these things on purpose.

At around fourteen I picked up the idea that I could diet them away, but a smaller arse only made them look more super-sized. I tried to keep them covered, but, you know, a mountain range covered in snow is still a mountain range. Then I gave in. Not to the men who tried to corner me, but to the name-callers and whispers. I pretended to be the thing they all thought I was.

And now, well, now, I wear low-cut tops and bend forward more than I need to if it's been a slow night for tips and I barely notice when men speak to my chest, women shoot death-stares at it and people of both sexes treat me like I have brain damage. Now, I've learnt to live with the fact that most blokes who come home with me will be breast-men and that once in bed they'll spend more time nuzzling and squeezing than getting busy down below. I spend a lot of money on good bras and keep my thigh muscles strong so I can bounce up and down forever. Give 'em what they want.

I didn't choose to have an enormous rack, but you have to accept the things you cannot change, don't you? So I do. I accept that having big boobs makes me a popular barmaid and an excellent root. Not excellent-excellent probably, but Strathdee-excellent for sure.

I've gone off the track. I do that. I have to, you know? This track is not an easy one to trudge down.

It was a quick drive. I mean, there's no such thing as a long drive in this town – you can go from highway exit to highway on-ramp in the time it takes to drink a large takeaway coffee – but the drive from my place to Bella's body seemed supernaturally fast. As we pulled out from my driveway I noticed that there was yet another stripped-down car on Carrie's lawn, making it four in total. Then suddenly we were at the three-churches intersection downtown and a second later we were swinging into the staff car park behind the hospital.

Matt led me through a door I'd never noticed and into an elevator which seemed to take about as long as the drive had. When the doors opened there was another cop looking right at us. Senior Constable Tomas Riley, I knew, because he spent almost as much time at the pub where I worked as I did. He told me he was sorry to see me under these circumstances. He walked me and Matt through to a reception area where he said something I didn't follow to a woman behind a desk. The woman asked me for ID and I was confused for a minute, started to say I hadn't done it yet, the ID-ing.

'No, no,' Riley said. 'Do you have some identification? A driver's licence?'

'I don't drive,' I told him, rifling in my bag for my wallet. 'I've got Medicare. Bank cards. Responsible Service of Alcohol.' I piled all the plastic onto the counter. The woman smiled and grabbed up a couple, scanned them through a machine, handed them back. She printed a form and passed it to Riley, who signed it and then touched my arm and led me down another hallway.

My skin tingled as the air-con dried my sweat. I hadn't known I was sweaty until then. I don't think it was even hot that day. It was grey out, I remember that much, but we do get those grey days so humid you can hardly bear to wear a stitch, don't we? It might have been like that. I don't know. I just know that walking down those empty blue hallways with a cop on either side, my skin started to cool and dry. I did a fake stretch and had a quick sniff under the arm. No BO that I could detect, so that was something.

'Rogers your married name?' Riley asked me, but in a making-conversation way, not jotting it down in his notepad or anything like that.

'No.'

'Oh. Your sister –'

'Bella has a different dad.'

Bella's father was a real classy bloke, which is how come she had such a pretty name. Me, I was named by our mother who was not of the soundest mind at the time, given how she was eighteen years old and newly delivered of a giant baby whose dad she'd not seen since he fled to Tassie on hearing he'd knocked up the checkout chick he'd been rooting behind his wife's back. Mum was pissed off she couldn't give me his surname so she gave me his first – Chris. When I was younger I pretended it was short for Christina, but now I don't bother. Just Chris, that's all.

We stopped outside a set of dull silver doors. 'Chris, have you ever viewed a body before?'

I shook my head. He said some stuff I don't remember. I couldn't listen. I was suddenly sure that the dead girl through those doors wasn't Bella. I was sure. I started practising in my head how to sound sad and sorry for whoever she was even though I was lit up with joy because she wasn't mine.

'Are you ready?'

I nodded. It'd all be over soon and I'd be back on my way home, trying her mobile again, leaving her another annoyed message about driving us all nuts with worry.

Funny thing is that even when they pulled the sheet back I thought for a minute it wasn't her. I thought, *Jesus, what has happened to this poor kid, this poor girl, someone's darling girl, how do you do that to someone, someone's precious beautiful girl, this poor little thing with hair just like Bella's.*

And I didn't think of this right away, but later I realised how lucky it'd been I couldn't speak on the car trip. Can you imagine if I'd asked that poor young cop whether Bella had suffered? I mean, Jesus. Can you imagine?

Matt drove me from the hospital to the police station back in the centre of town. He didn't try to make conversation, just told me there were tissues in the glove compartment and asked a few times if I wanted to stop and get a cup of tea or something.

I didn't cry or feel anger or anything, but I shook and shook so much that it made me giggle, which made Matt look at me like I'd screamed. Honestly, it was like I was on one of those vibrating chairs in the shopping centre. Like I *was* a vibrating chair.

At the station they offered me tea again. I said no and let them lead me to a room with a white formica table and a couple of sweaty vinyl seats. Riley was there, along with two men in suits; detectives from Wagga, they said. They wanted to know when I'd last seen Bella. I had to think a minute and then it took me another minute before I could say it.

'Wednesday night. She dropped into the pub –'

'The pub where you work?'

'Yeah, the Royal. She dropped by as we were closing. She'd worked late to cover for a sick colleague and since she knew I was due to finish soon she thought she'd swing by and offer to drive me home, maybe have a hot choccy and a catch-up before bed.'

'And how late did she stay at your house?'

'She didn't . . . I told her I had to stay back and do some admin stuff. Said we'd catch up on the weekend.'

'Alright, Chris. Take some deep breaths. I'm sorry but we need to get a bit more information from you before we take you home. Deep breaths, that's the girl.'

They asked me a bunch of stuff they could've found out from the phone book and then some stuff about my family, Bella's family. They wanted to know about the men in Bella's life, but there weren't any. I mean, there were the men who worked at the nursing home with her and there was her seventy-eight-year-old neighbour whose dog she walked and there was her dad, who she'd not seen since she was twenty, but who she exchanged emails with every so often. But no boyfriend, not for a while now.

'Girlfriend, then?' one of the men in suits asked.

'She's not a lezzo if that's what you're asking. She's got women friends, of course. The girls at work for a start. There's a group of them who go out together when their off-shifts match up. And she still keeps in touch with a few mates from school.'

'All women?'

'I suppose.'

'She didn't like men?'

'Bella liked everyone. It's just that she didn't trust men very much.

They had to prove themselves first, you know.'

'Why d'you reckon she didn't trust them?'

'Because she knew what they were capable of,' I said, and then one of the suits said I needed a break.

You know, I've often been told I'm too trusting, too generous, too open. I used to think these were compliments, but recently I've come to realise that they are not. They say 'trusting' and mean 'stupid', 'generous' and mean 'easy', 'open' and mean 'shameless'. All of those things are true and not true. It depends who you ask, doesn't it? Ask old Bert at the pub if I'm easy or generous or any of that and he'll say no. He'll say, 'The little bitch slaps me hand if it so much as brushes against her.' Ask my ex, Nate. He'll tell you a different side.

Look, what I'm saying is, sometimes I am trusting and generous and open and stupid and easy and shameless. What I'm saying is, who isn't?

Bella. Bella wasn't. She was older than me from the time she turned thirteen. I don't know what happened to her then, maybe nothing important, but I remember she changed. She stopped being a kid and started being a proper adult. She'd come around to my place after school, find me still in bed, usually hungover as hell. She'd haul me up, make me coffee and eggs, give me an ear-bashing. At sixteen she moved in with me on account of a personality clash with Mum's new boyfriend. I used to complain about what an anal, nagging little cow she was, but when she turned eighteen and took off on her own I missed her like you wouldn't believe.

Sally Perkins, whose dad sat in the pub and drank himself almost into a coma the day his little girl graduated from the police academy, brought me some unasked-for tea and a couple of sugary biscuits. The suits watched me not drinking or eating for a few minutes and then asked if I was right to continue. I said yes, because while

I'd been sitting looking at the tea I'd remembered this one man Bella'd mentioned a couple of weeks ago. It was my night off and I was about to get to bed when she turned up. After eleven it was. Unusual for her to come over that late and without texting first to see if I was home and awake. I opened the door and there she was, eyes all shiny. I thought maybe one of her favourites at the home had passed on – they're not meant to take it personally, but that was Bella for you. Then I saw she was dolled up, cute little heeled boots and a bit of eyeliner and that, and I rushed her inside, feeling a bit worried about what might have happened.

It was nothing really. She'd been at a trivia night with some mates and when they announced the lucky door prizes at the end, her number got called. So she went on up to collect her prize – a basket of chocolate truffles and candied fruit and the like – and this bloke who'd won another one of the prizes started chatting her up. He asked her how she'd get the great big basket of stuff home and she said it was no problem, she had her car with her. He started in on a whole sob story about how he'd walked right across town to be there that night but now he had this great big basket to carry and taxis were so expensive after 10pm it would take most of his grocery money just to get home. Bella wondered why he'd come to a trivia night so far from home when every pub and community group in town held one seemingly every damn week, but she didn't say that, she said, 'Oh, dear' or something, and went to carry off her loot. He stopped her though, a hand on her arm, and asked her which direction she was heading. She felt a bit scared then, she told me, and so she lied, told him she was going straight to her sister's place which was around the corner. 'It's just I could really do with a lift, at least up the main road,' he said, still holding her arm. 'Ah, well, ask around some of the old fellas in there. I'm sure one of them can help you out,' she said and then – her voice was kind of disbelieving when she told me this bit – then she tried to move away but he moved with her. She had to actually *pull* her arm away from his.

When she got to her car she locked all the doors and started crying a little bit. 'Stupid, I know,' she told me that night (because although she hadn't planned to, she did as she'd told the man and came straight to my place, round the corner). 'He was just an awkward bloke, didn't know how to take a hint and nothing happened, but I just felt so *rude* and I hate that.'

I made her a hot choccy and we talked about other things and just when I thought it was all forgotten she said, 'You know, if it'd been a woman I would've offered her a lift no question.' I think she felt bad about that.

The older suit asked me if Bella had described the bloke at all, but she hadn't. The younger one asked me if I thought she'd been upset over nothing and I don't know why but I wanted to punch him then. No, I do know why. It's because I *had* thought she was overreacting and I told her that. Gently, but still. What if she took it to heart? What if the next time she was approached she went against her instincts?

'I mean,' the young suit went on, 'from what I hear, you yourself are known as a trusting kind of a woman. When it comes to men, I mean.'

'Alright,' the older one said.

I couldn't speak just then. I couldn't.

'Alright,' the older one said again. 'Thanks for your time, Chris. We'll keep you updated. And you call me if you think of anything else, yeah?'

Sally Perkins drove me home, warned me that the story would be all over the news soon.

'I'll keep the telly off then.'

'If there's anyone who you think should know . . . I mean, hearing something like this from the news is pretty tough.'

'Her dad. I suppose I should call her dad.'

'The detectives have his details, they'll get in touch with him. And they've been to her work already. But if there are any other friends, distant relatives . . .'

'Yes,' I said. 'I'll have a think. Call around.'

'Journos might try and talk to you. Probably not today. Your names are different, so with any luck it'll take 'em a while to track you down. Anyway, you don't have to deal with them, alright? We've got people to do that for you.' Without taking her eyes off the road she pulled a card from somewhere down her right side and passed it to me.

We drove past the park where I used to take Bella when she was a tiny thing. I'd never take her there now. I mean, I wouldn't take a little kid there now. The old fort she used to climb on was covered in graffiti and deliberately gouged splinters of sharp wood. The swing where I would sit and watch her disappeared years ago but the frame's still there, FUCKING CUNTS scrawled up its side, the scrubby grass beneath caked with old chip packets and cigarette butts. I walked past it most afternoons and again late at night, but I never thought about me and Bella there.

This is my life now, I realised. Just, you know, remembering Bella everywhere she'd ever been and wouldn't be any more. I thought how even this weird day, seeing the inside of a morgue and the back of the cop shop, was made even weirder by the fact that Bella would never know about it.

'Chris? This is the one, yeah?'

We were out the front of my house. It's one of the neater ones in the street. I keep my lawn mowed and my mailbox cleared and the driveway free from oil splatters. Only Frank on the corner, who trims his lawn with nail scissors and cleans his gutters daily, keeps a neater street front than me.

'Chris?'

I thanked her for the lift, got out of the car. 'Take care of yourself,'

I said and she smiled. She wasn't a pretty girl, but her smile was lovely.

I did as Sally had said, called a few of Bella's friends, asked each of them if they'd mind calling some others. It was strange. I thought they'd scream and cry and say, 'No, it's not possible,' but everyone just kind of accepted it. Everyone said sorry to me. Everyone asked what they could do. It was like they were more worried about me than about Bella, which is logical, I know, but also terrible. Maybe I just sounded that bad.

By late afternoon, my phone was ringing every time I hung up from making a call. The news was out and people wanted to know if it was true and what they could do. I told them it was and that there was nothing.

Around six, there was a knock on the door and I started shaking all over again. I told myself there was nothing to fear now, the worst had already happened, but my nerves wouldn't listen. I braced for another blow, opened the door.

Nate. Love of my life, smasher of my heart. There he stood, my mighty tree of a man, with tears splashing down into his bushranger beard.

'Babe,' he said.

'Yeah.'

'Oh, babe.' His body surged forward. He wrapped his giant arms around me, squeezed all the shaking out. He carried me inside and put me down on the kitchen chair. Knelt at my feet and hugged me some more, rubbing his wet, scratchy face against my neck.

'Heard it on the midday news, no details, just a woman found near Strathdee. Then next update they said an aged-care assistant. Tried to call you, but couldn't get through. Then the next update had the name. I had to call base, get 'em to send a relief driver. Caught a cab back to my car and drove straight down.'

'Thank you.'

'You should've called me.'

'I was going to. Everyone's been calling me.' As if to prove it, the phone started ringing again.

'Oh, babe.'

'Yeah.'

'Poor Bella. That poor little thing.'

And I lost it then, because no one had said that. Not anyone.

I'd met Nate at the pub, of course. Where else would I ever meet anyone? I was twenty-five and never short of offers but I was getting tired of it all. I'd been thinking that it might be nice to get serious with someone, set up home, maybe even have a baby. Most of the girls I'd gone to school with had a few kids by then and, though I wasn't jealous of their lives, I was starting to feel a tug deep inside when I'd see them in the main street with a pastel bundle strapped to their chest, a curly-haired munchkin clinging to their hand.

So, I was in a suggestible state you might say, but honestly I know I would've fallen for Nate even if I was married to Prince Harry and had a pair of ginger twins cooking in my oven. I would've fallen for Nate no matter what.

This was before the bypass went in, when Strathdee was still the main truck-stop town on the road from Sydney to Melbourne. So I was used to serving blokes who looked like they could lift their rigs with one hand, but I'd never thought of the place as small until Nate walked in. Right away it was like there wasn't enough room for anyone else. All those other boofheads, they were pushed to the corners, and even though I was back in the kitchen looking out through the little service window, I felt he was pressing right up against me. It was like the mass of him had shoved out whatever air we had in there, because I suddenly couldn't breathe real well.

He ordered a burger and chips and an orange juice. I'd never seen a man order an orange juice. Not sure I've ever seen *anyone* order an orange juice without vodka in it. But it's not like Old Grey behind the bar, or anyone else for that matter, was going to have a go at this mountain for being soft. Jesus.

When I called his number and he came and got his burger my dirty mind wondered if those giant paws might actually be able to cover my tits and I shivered all over and was sure he knew what I was thinking.

I hung back and watched as he rammed a handful of chips into his gob and then licked his lips. It was indecent, that wet pink tongue peeking out from these thick red lips hiding in that tangle of black beard.

Just as well I got called back to cook some steaks before he started on his burger because I might have gone ahead and wet myself if I'd seen how wide that mouth could open just then.

As it happened he left after his burger and the pub filled back up with air and space and I settled down, even had a little laugh at myself for getting so worked up over a juice-drinking ape-man.

And then the next week he came back and it was just the same: the walls closing in, my mind full of filthy thoughts about his hands and mouth. But this time he stayed by the service window and talked to me between orders. God knows what I said to him. When I look back I imagine a hot mist of desperation spraying from my mouth every time I opened it. But I guess that was just what he was looking for, because he offered me a lift home and had my knickers off and my knockers bouncing before the windscreen of his coach was even half fogged-over.

Nate had been a truckie once, but by the time I met him he was driving tourist buses up and down the east coast. Most of the passengers were oldies wanting to see the country but too scared or frail to brave the distances on their own. Nate was like the cheeky but dependable grandson they all wished for. And for his part he got to be on the road but without the pressure that turned so many truckies into pill heads. 'Australia at a leisurely pace' was the catchphrase of the mob he worked for.

Once him and me hooked up, though, he gave away the long-haul route and picked up the day-trip run from here to the small towns further west. I didn't ask him to. He wanted to be home with me every night. Incredible. Man like him, girl like me . . . I knew how lucky I was, believe me. Didn't stop me from fucking everything up though.

But I mustn't have burnt every last bit of his love for me to the ground, because here he was in my kitchen taking care of me like the last decade had never happened. He checked that I'd made all the calls I needed to then turned my phone off. He made me a cheese sandwich, which I ate almost half of, and a cup of tea, which I drank. Then he dosed me with what he called 'ten-hour guarantees'. I told him I could never imagine sleeping again but I let him put me to bed anyway. He got in beside me and there was no need to talk about that. I backed up into his plank of a chest and he pulled me in with those enormous arms and I sank into sleep like it was five years ago and there was nothing to worry about except whether he'd still be here in the morning.

Tuesday
7
April

AustraliaToday.com

'BEAUTIFUL BELLA' VICIOUSLY MAULED

May Norman
7 April, 2015

A 'terribly mauled' body found yesterday by a traveller taking
a roadside cigarette break has been identified as that of Bella
Michaels, a 25-year-old aged-care worker from Strathdee, in
south-western New South Wales. Ms Michaels had been missing
for almost 48 hours when emergency services received a call from
a distressed Melbourne man reporting his gruesome find.

'The gentleman stopped at an expanse of grass and scrub
just past the Strathdee exit heading south. His intention was to
stretch his legs and have a cigarette while his kids were sleeping in

the car. It's a lucky thing they didn't wake up and decide to come look for Daddy,' a police spokesman said this morning.

Local police arrived at the scene to find a body which an officer who had known Ms Michaels recognised as her's. Official identification was later made by Ms Michaels' sister.

Police are so far declining to reveal how Ms Michaels died or whether she had been sexually assaulted, but unconfirmed reports from those on the scene suggest she was, in the words of the man who found the body, 'terribly mauled'. Detective Sergeant John Brandis, who is leading the investigation, would not comment on whether this mauling may have occurred after death, but locals point to the presence of many wild dogs and cats in the area and the fact that the body may have been out in the open since Friday night.

Ms Michaels was last seen leaving Strathdee Haven, the nursing home where she worked, just after 5pm on Friday. Her car was parked less than a three-minute walk away, but she never reached it. Staff and residents at Strathdee Haven are 'in shock, just absolutely stunned', according to manager Cathryn Charles. 'She was an essential part of the team here, always going above and beyond and always with a smile on her face. It beggars belief that this could've happened to her, and right here on our doorstep it seems.'

Det. Brandis said that so far door-to-door interviewing in the area Ms Michaels disappeared from has turned up nothing, but that the canvassing will continue. 'It was a very short walk, in daylight, along a quiet residential street. If there was a struggle or commotion of any kind, someone must have seen or heard it.'

Police are also appealing for motorists who may have noticed stopped vehicles or any suspicious behaviour between Gundagai and Holbrook on the Hume Highway between 6pm Friday and 6am Saturday to contact the Strathdee police or Crime Stoppers.

■ ■ ■

I didn't sleep the promised ten hours but I slept almost seven, which was a damn near-miracle given the circumstances. As soon as I was conscious I was thinking about Bella and what they'd done to her. Yeah, *they*. It was never a question to me. Not after I'd seen her, you know?

When my mum died it took months before I woke up knowing she was dead. Every morning there'd be this sweet, sleepy moment in which the world was as it always had been before the truth crashed in. It was like that after Nate left me, too. I'd wake up and for a second be sure he was beside me. But that didn't happen with Bella. I woke and straight away I saw her face as it'd been in the morgue.

(The first time I ever saw Bella's face I told Mum it looked like she'd been bashed because her skull was all lopsided and she had scratches on one cheek and there were patches of blue over her weird little bald brows. Mum laughed and said that being born is the roughest thing most of us'll ever go through.)

I dragged myself out to the kitchen. Nate was at the table drinking coffee, reading from the screen of his phone. He flicked it off, shoved it into the front pocket of his jeans, came and kissed the top of my head, cradled me like that for a long, lovely moment. Without asking whether I wanted it he went ahead and made me coffee and it was exactly the right temperature, exactly the right milky sweetness.

He waited until I'd drunk about half and then covered my hands with his. 'So, what's the story? What have the cops said?'

His hands seemed to muffle the grief and horror a little. I felt like the weight of them on mine would stop that terrible shaking demon from taking me over again.

'She left work on Friday a bit after five. Said bye to everyone inside and off she went, just like normal. Three hours later a nurse arriving for her shift noticed Bella's car on the street. She thought it was weird and tried to call her, got no answer. On her break, around eleven, the nurse went to her own car to grab something and saw Bella's was still there. She tried her again and had such a bad feeling about her not answering that she looked up Bella's emergency contact, me, and called to see if everything was OK. I was at work and then didn't bother checking my messages before I crashed out – and – and –'

'Hey, hey.' Nate stroked his thumb over my hand. 'Breathe, babe. Come on, big breaths. Good girl, that's it.'

'So I never got the message until the morning. There was another one by then – from her boss – Bel hadn't shown up for work. I went round to her place, but there was no answer. I called the police. They said wait. I waited. I kept calling her all day. Called her friends. At the end of the day I called the police again. They filed a report. Told me she'd probably turn up, red-faced about causing all this trouble when she'd just gone off for a weekend with her fella.'

'Who's her fella?' Nate asked and it was only a split-second but I saw it, the violence. It was good to be reminded. I took my hands out from under his. I did it casually, picked up my coffee cup and took a sip and left my hands wrapped around its hard warmth.

'She doesn't have one. They just assumed. Talked about her like she's some other girl. Some idiot who takes off from work without telling anyone. As if she would.'

'World's youngest grandma,' he said, smiling.

We used to call her that, me and Nate, back when we'd get pissed and make messes and she would bustle in, clean up and lecture us about responsibility.

Nate touched my hand. 'And then what?'

'Then yesterday morning there was a cop at my door . . . They said she'd probably been out there since Friday night. It rained so much over the weekend. Nobody stopping by the roadside for a piss or a picnic.'

Nate sucked in his breath. I knew he was imagining her, lying out in the rain, knew he was worrying about how cold and scared she must've been and then remembering she wasn't feeling anything by then. The quick double-punch of horror and gratitude.

'Do you know how ... On the news they said she was ...' He held out his hands, helpless.

I told him what the police had told me. I didn't spare him any details, because they had not spared me and I suppose I wanted to share the pain of it. But now, well, I am reluctant to repeat it, to tell you the truth. Bad enough to have heard it all from my own mouth that morning. Bad enough that I saw what they left behind, and heard what the coroner made of that mess. Bad enough to glimpse the newspaper headlines as I rush through the shopping centre on my way to the supermarket. Bad enough to guess at what the blokes in the pub are whispering in between saying, so loudly, 'How you doing, love?' Bad enough that when I try to sleep the images come so hard and fast they feel like memories. Bad enough I can't go a night without dreaming some of it, all of it, the things being done to her and the men doing it almost almost almost showing their faces so that I hope for these horror shows to come again because *this* time I might catch a glimpse, see whose fists and cocks and knees and forearms they are. Worse, worse, worse than bad, the goddamn vivid guesswork of my mind, which has spent too many hours watching crime shows, too many nights reading true-crime stories. Bad enough I must see inside my own mind flashes of suffering that look like fucking *NCIS*, sound like *Underbelly*, feel like a boot coming down on my chest. And if that sounds good to you then go ahead and read the goddamn coroner's report and look up those obscene photos for yourself. I'm not your pornographer.

Nate was still and silent through the worst of it, but when I told him the police had no suspects, he cracked his knuckles, clicked his neck back and forward. 'Hope I find those fuckers first,' he said. 'Gunna do worse to them then they did to her.'

'Please don't.'

He cracked his knuckles again. 'You think they deserve to live?'

'I think I deserve not to have a husband in jail for murder.'

He looked at me then, properly. 'Babe,' he said, 'I'm not your husband.'

'You know what I mean,' I said. 'You know I need you to be . . . OK.'

He looked at me for a long time. I don't know if he was thinking of the past, or of Bella, or of his woman up in Sydney. 'I'm sorry,' he said. 'I'm OK.'

There were a lot of visitors that first day. First full day I knew she was dead. Each sat at the kitchen table with me, looking out the window to the driveway, saying *goodbye and take care and call if you need* as the next car pulled up. I don't think they'd coordinated it or anything; it just happened that way. It shocked me a bit, how many people came. Nowadays I have to think of it more darkly. I have to think that half of them were rubbernecking or trying to get in on the tragedy. Weird how many people do that. Makes me sick that I know about it, that looking back I have to assume that's what was going on. But at the time what I kept thinking was, *Miss Popularity, aren't you, Bella! Look at all these people coming around. Listen to all the sweet things they're saying about you.* I remember saying to Nate that I hope she knew how many people thought she was the shit.

First was my neighbour on the right, Carrie Smith. Carrie was my age, and a grandmother twice over already. She'd had her eldest,

Emma, at sixteen and Emma had her first at fifteen and her second a few months ago. The kids and grandkids and various partners and friends lived with Carrie sometimes and sometimes not. Hers was like a different house from week to week. One week there'd be plastic scooters in the drive and blinding-white nappies flapping on the line and alternating baby cries and toddler giggles from inside, the next, red-eyed slurry teenagers slumped under a smoke haze, hip-hop blasting from stereos of cars parked but never turned off.

Carrie asked how I was and I said I was fine, and then she made tea and showed me pictures of her grandkids on her phone and asked if she could smoke inside and asked if I needed anything and asked if that was Nate's car parked out front and asked, oh, I don't know, a bunch of things that had nothing to do with why she was fussing around my kitchen at nine on a Tuesday morning instead of down at the club flushing her pension down the pokies as usual.

Next was Lisa from across the street. Lisa was in her fifties, an accountant who dressed and spoke like a north-coast hippy. She had a daughter Bella's age and a son a few years younger. When she swept through the front door her green, floor-length skirt got caught on the door jamb and we both ignored the sound of it ripping as though it was a loud, wet fart. Lisa had brought me a loaf-shaped cake on a glass platter. She placed it in the centre of the kitchen table and then wrapped her scrawny, sun-leathered arms around me, pressing my head down into her shoulder.

'I didn't know what to do,' she told me when I had extricated myself. 'I called my friend Di – she's just the calmest person you'll ever meet and she's got the gift, you know, like second sight – and I asked her and she told me – listen, I know this sounds far out, Chris, I *know* that, but she said that people who die violently can have trouble finding peace and so you might –'

'Not now.' Nate must've been listening from the bedroom. From the doorway he filled the kitchen. 'Chris doesn't need talk like that right now.'

Lisa stood, her face flushing pink, her hands fluttering up to the beads looped five or more times around her throat. 'Nate! Oh, it's *such* a relief to see you, to know that Chris isn't on her own over here.'

'You made this?' He bent to the cake, sniffed it. 'Orange?'

'With fruit picked from my tree this morning.' She returned to my side, patted my hand. 'And just this once I said to hell with the toxins and put a nice full cup of white sugar in there for you. Situation called for it, I thought.'

'You going to have some?' Nate asked, but she shook her head.

'I'll leave you to it.'

'Thank you,' I think I said.

'Of course, and if you need *anything* . . .' She shot a look at Nate, who was busy cutting the cake. 'Or if you want to talk to Di about –'

'Actually, there is something you could help with. Cops want Chris to speak at a press conference tomorrow and –'

'Oh, I don't know. Chris, honey, are you sure you're up to it?'

'They say it'll help,' I told her. 'People more likely to come forward.'

'It'll help. And they said she can read from a prepared statement and they'll deal with questions and all that,' Nate said. 'So what would be good is if you could help with writing something, 'cause I don't have a clue, to be honest. It needs to just say stuff about Bel – personal stuff they said – and just ask for people to tell the police anything they know.'

'Oh, of course. Consider it done.' She rubbed the top of my arm lightly. 'I'll put something together and then you can just make any little changes you like tomorrow before the thing. Does that sound OK?'

'Yeah, appreciate it.'

'You're a legend, Lis.'

'Alright. I'll get to it.' She squeezed my arm and left.

Soon as she was out of sight Nate shoved a piece of cake in his gob. He chewed, swallowed. 'It's good,' he said, but didn't try to make me have some, which I appreciated.

There were a couple of other neighbours after that. I don't remember the details of their visits, just that from each of them, or at least from the combination of them, came thick waves of warmth and worry and curiosity and a pity so heavy I began to feel that I was the one who'd been brutalised.

Then in the early afternoon one of Bella's co-workers, Vicky, came and I snapped out of it. I'd only met Vicky a couple of times: once at the nursing home when I went to see Bella and once when Bella popped around here on the way to some function, and Vicky sat in my living room and chatted to me about her cat while Bella went through my shoe collection searching for a pair to match her new black-satin capri pants.

On the day after they found Bella's body, Vicky sat in my kitchen and told me that when she was sixteen her nineteen-year-old brother had been stabbed to death after intervening in a street fight down in Melbourne. I don't think she said it as blunt as that. I don't remember the words she used, just the change in atmosphere. She didn't say much else I don't think. Maybe told me about how missed Bella would be at work. It didn't matter. Nothing about her mattered except for the fact she was another person who knew what it was like to find themselves in the middle of a living nightmare. I could've sat and looked at her all day and night – this plain, pale-haired thirty-year-old who had survived that, walked out of those pages, gone on long enough to have become ordinary again.

Around eight, a couple of hours after the last guest had left, I started crying and couldn't stop. Nate rubbed my back for a while and then he gave me a couple of the pills that'd worked so well the night before and tucked me into bed.

Next thing I knew I was dying. That's the only way I can say it:

I woke up and I was dying. It was pitch black – blacker than I've ever known night to be – and there was something on my chest crushing the life out of me. My arms and legs wouldn't move. I couldn't scream. It was like my body was dead already, just waiting for my mind to catch up.

I don't know how long it lasted, but I know when it stopped because I could see the green fluoro 4.42 and hear Nate's gurgling snore and feel that my skin was wet. I rolled over, locking Nate down beneath my arm and leg. I forced my breath into the rhythm of his. I slept and woke and slept like that until daylight.

Wednesday
8
April

'Thank fuck for that,' May muttered, spotting the Strathdee exit sign. Her body and head had ached even before the five hours on the road. Three nights of sobbing instead of sleeping will do that to you. And then the torture of the drive: nothing to see but endless grass, sometimes with cows or horses scattered over it, road trains alternately tailgating and slowing to under forty kilometres per hour, and all of it in her shitty twenty-year-old Hyundai that revved out and shook whenever she went over a hundred.

Her motel – the cheaper of the two options in Strathdee – was less than a minute's drive into town. The 'Air-con, FOXSports, Tea & Coffee, Inspection Welcome' sign was draped with black crepe paper. May checked in, used the toilet, put the kettle on and then listened for the twentieth time to Craig's voicemail and almost, *almost* deleted it this time. 'Fuck you, fuck you, fuck you,' she said to him and herself and the slow-boiling piece of shit plastic kettle. She started to dial into her message bank again, but the kettle clicked off and saved her. She dumped four of the hotel's coffee sachets in her travel mug, filled it with water and headed back to the car.

She drove past a pub whose car park was a quarter full despite it being not yet 11 am, a car rental office, a service station with a single fuel pump. Next to the service station was a preschool and across the road Strathdee Medical Centre. From there both sides of the road were lined with fibro houses with front yards twice the size of May's Sydney terrace house. As she got closer to the centre of town, every third, then second house was brick, then she clunked over a railway crossing, noted the sign indicating the police station was one left and one right turn away, drove past a takeaway chicken shop and a Salvation Army store and was abruptly in the town centre.

It was like the centre of every Australian country town she'd ever visited. An immaculate park with drought-defying green grass and seasonally impossible purple and yellow pansies peeking from the edges of the winding cobblestone path leading to a war memorial cenotaph in the centre. Across the road a TAB, a small pub advertising 'Counter Meals, KENO and Historic Murals', a Chinese restaurant, a ye olde tea shop attached to the Strathdee Local History Museum, a bakery and a newsagency. There was no one on the footpath except a water-delivery man in tight shorts and sweat-soaked t-shirt backing into an unmarked shopfront and a teenage girl pushing a double stroller past the TAB.

Although she had a green light, she stopped briefly at the intersection. There were no other vehicles in sight, only the spires of three churches, a Woolworths sign with an arrow pointing left, a sign directing travellers to the Happy Stay Inn (the motel too expensive for May's tight-arse employer) and, already, the sign pointing the way to the exit onto the road to Melbourne.

After a few minutes on the highway heading south, a flash of unnaturally bright colours to the left caught her eye. She pulled to the side, checked for traffic behind her and reversed back to the bursts of pink and yellow. Surprising that there was no other media there, given the police press conference wasn't until one. Possible that no one outside of the region was bothering with anything other than phoners. That's all she'd be doing if her unprecedented disaster of a love-life hadn't prompted her to insist on driving down to this fly-shit-speck of a town to report first-hand on the story. The fact her own hastily written, phone-researched piece on the body's discovery had been the site's most-shared that day made it an easy sell.

But that meant, of course, that the competition's stories on the body were probably just as popular and that they, too, had sent their best crime reporters/most-desperate-to-get-out-of-town fuck-ups to get on-the-ground colour. In which case, the lack of media at the body-dump site meant that they'd been and gone and were now back in town talking to, and alienating for all future reporters, the dead woman's family and friends, in which case, shit.

May slung her camera over her neck, grabbed her notebook and strode out towards the shrine she'd seen from the road.

A secluded field, she wrote. No. It was neither a field, nor particularly secluded. Cars zipped by at the rate of ten to twelve a minute. There was no fence, just a gappy line of ghost gums close to the road and then patchy grass and the odd spindly tree for seventy metres or so, before another line of gums battled against being absorbed by fair-dinkum, deep and dark outback bushland. She made a note to ask why the killer hadn't dragged the body that little bit further and dumped it in there, where it likely would've turned to compost undisturbed, rather than leave it out here in this *... low-key picnic spot for travellers on the road from –*

No, not a picnic spot, though a faded family-size KFC bucket and a Fanta can stomped into the grass suggested it was sometimes used as such. But no flaking wooden table or coin-operated barbecue plate or grimy toilet block. Not even a single blanket-sized patch of ground uncorrupted by weeds or rocky dirt or disconnected tree roots rising up like mummified knees.

A football-field sized expanse of grass and dirt, not so much hidden from the road as revealed in snatches. Snatches? Christ. *. . . revealed in strips.* That was worse. She was so off her game. Fucking fuck fuck fuck fucking Craig. Fuck.

May shoved the notebook into her bag and raised her camera. At the spot where, as far as she could work out from police reports, the body had been found, she took care to take shots from every possible angle and distance, stopping every minute or so to wipe the sweat off her face and camera lens. The sun was relentless, the air unmoving. The grass – the exact type of which she'd have to look up later (Craig would know what kind, the nerdy fucker) – brushed her ankles and deposited straw-coloured seeds on the uncovered tops of her feet. Her mouth felt gritty with dirt.

The shrine that had caught her attention from the road had been erected not at the place the body was found, but a few metres away against one of the anorexic, anaemic trees between the road line and the bush. Flowers – five bouquets of the type bought from a roadside stall, two flash-looking florist arrangements in ribboned boxes, fourteen scattered single blooms which may recently have been bound by the pink ribbon flipping its way towards the road. A pot plant, wilting. A smiley-face helium balloon on a stick, lodged in a child's pale green sippy cup. A larger balloon, screaming *I MISS YOU!!!* tied around the trunk. *RIP BELLA* on pink card in a foggy plastic sleeve. Five candles, two of them never lit, one of them with *BELLA* carved crudely into its white wax. Two small teddy bears, a plush bunny, a sequinned butterfly pinned to a ribbon tied to a branch. *BELLA MICHAELS 1990–2015 GOODBYE ANGEL* etched into the tree, shallow enough that the tree would slough it off before long. *YOU WILL BURN IN HELL MURDEROUS FUCKERS WHO DID THIS TO*

AN ANGEL ON EARTH written on the trunk in what appeared to be liquid paper. Beneath it, in green paint: *unless i find you first then youll burn rite here scum*. It'd been twelve hours since police had reopened the site to the public.

She should've been here last night, instead of flopping around on her bed sobbing like a heartbroken teenager. Might've got pics of some kind of impromptu vigil and interviews with local mourners instead of a snot-streaked pillow and tissue-chafed nose. Fuck.

The hotel bed – a double but smaller than any she'd slept in since childhood – flashed in her mind. The thought of spending another night weeping, this time in that grim little room with the bar fridge clicking on and off and the air-con thrumming and the cheap pillowcase scratching her already chafed nose caused a flutter of panic in her chest. She could drop into the medical centre she'd noticed on her way through town, get a script for some sleeping pills like the ones her mother had depended on during that terrible year when May's father left and her grandmother died and the house was sold from under them. May couldn't remember the name of those pills but she had never forgotten the way her mum went from being there to not fifteen minutes after taking them. No gentle drifting off, eyes fluttering, pauses between words growing longer and longer. It was a split-second, impossible to see coming. Awake, then gone. It had infuriated May to have her mother check out so purposefully and completely. *What if I need to ask you something? What if something goes wrong?* she would say whenever she caught her mother slipping the pill down her throat. *It can wait. You'll cope,* her mum would say then tuck herself in bed and wait for oblivion.

It had terrified May. How could you want that – that total absence? How could you want to be unreachable, to remain unknowing all night long? It was less like sleep – which May knew to be filled with interruptions caused by mosquito bites, brothers' snores and farts, suddenly too-heavy blankets or too-loud wind –

and more like death. But now that sleep had become the too-rare, too-brief interruption to her pain, she understood. She yearned.

Back out through the trees May photographed the verge where the car must have stopped. There had to have been a car, because there was no other way to get here, unless the killer or killers had somehow persuaded Bella to walk the five kilometres from where she was taken. And it would have to have been persuaded rather than forced because most of the way would have been in full view of passing traffic and at least some of the time in daylight. That's if she'd been brought here directly. May made a note to ask about the timeline at the press conference and headed back to her car.

Leaving the door open in hope of a breeze, she pulled out the tourist map the woman at the hotel reception desk had given her and studied the layout of the town. The road running off the highway exit ramp, John Street, bisected the town from north to south. Her motel was at the northernmost end, the more expensive place right before the Melbourne exit. Most of the west-east running streets cut across John and the parallel Elizabeth Street, forming a neat grid. A few stumpy streets, lanes and cul-de-sacs interrupted the pattern here and there. Wherever you stood in town there was a pub within four blocks. The nursing home where Bella worked was on King Close, a cul-de-sac off Elizabeth Street, close to the southern edge of town. This place, the place where Bella ended up, was just off the edge of the map, somewhere around the Pizza Genius and Imperial Hotel ads.

With luck, Bella Michaels was unconscious from the beginning and never knew what a drab, uninspiring journey her last one had been, nor what an ugly patch of nothingness she bled out onto. With luck, she went from there to not in an instant and was absent for all that followed.

■ ■ ■

My phone rang early. The cops wanted me to come down for another interview before the press conference at one. They offered to send a car but I didn't need that. I had Nate.

A few steps into the police station I stopped and looked around, confused. I knew I'd been there two days before but I recognised nothing. There was a poster advertising Neighbourhood Watch, another explaining about translation and interpretation services. A bench seat covered in navy vinyl, scratched blue and beige floor tiles, a wood-veneer counter with thick, clear plastic reaching up to the ceiling. I could've sworn I'd never seen any of it in my life.

Nate touched my shoulder and asked if I was OK. I nodded and stepped towards the counter, but before I could tell young Matt what I was there for he smiled at me and pressed a buzzer and said, 'Chris. Hello again. Detective Brandis'll be right out.'

A vaguely familiar skinny middle-aged man with thinning brown hair and a too-tight grey suit appeared from behind a door I hadn't noticed.

'Thanks for coming in,' he said, barely glancing at me, his gaze falling hard on Nate. 'Brandis,' he said, holding out a hand which Nate shook while giving his own name. 'You're the ex-husband?'

'Bella's brother-in-law,' I said, though it seemed no one was listening.

'You'll have to wait out here, mate. Or you can take off, if you like. We can get someone to drop Chris home later.'

'I'll wait.' Nate stepped back to the bench without taking his eyes off Brandis. I was overcome with a sense of protectiveness. It's always been that way. The more he acts like a goddamn macho bikie sergeant the more I worry about him being smashed up and broken.

'Good-o,' Brandis said. 'We'll try not to keep her too long.' He led the way back through the door, pushing it shut as soon as I was in the dim hallway. An invisible lock clicked loudly and I flinched in recognition. The smell back there was familiar too: wet dog and mildew underneath a sharp chemical scent like floral toilet cleaner. We turned a corner into a windowless room cluttered with wood-veneer desks and swivel chairs occupied by expressionless men or draped with jackets. A whiteboard on the far wall was mostly covered with a red felt cloth. *HROAT* scrawled in green marker peeped out from the bottom left corner.

'Chris! Thanks for coming down.' A young bloke with blond hair, thick blond eyebrows and a scaly pink nose rushed at me, placed a meaty hand on my upper back and propelled me towards a door to the right of the whiteboard. We stepped through into a small office which I recognised, but like it was something from a movie I'd seen once rather than a real-world place where I'd sat and talked and cried. The table, chairs, tissue box, blue plastic rubbish bin, black plastic laptop with attached oversized microphone all familiar but seeming to have nothing to do with reality.

'So how you doing, Chris?' the young one asked when I was seated. His face was all creased up, like he'd been practising concern in front of his mirror all morning.

'I'm OK. How are you doing? You got someone yet?'

'Chris, I gotta tell you, we've got nothing.' Brandis opened his hands up as though I might not have understood what 'nothing' meant otherwise. 'Jack. Bloody. Shit. No leads. No sightings. No theories. Nothing.'

'OK. But this thing this arvo, the press thing, that'll help, right?'

'It will, it will. Get the public mobilised. Hopefully someone saw something, heard something. But we can't rely on tips from strangers to solve this for us. We need the people who knew Bella to dig deep as well. Hard as that is for you, it's what we need to do.'

The young fella sighed, his own personal heartbreak, it was. 'Is there anything else you can think of that we should know about? Might seem something real small, not even worth mentioning. 'Cause, you know, sometimes it's stuff like that which busts things open. Small stuff.'

'I could tell you small stuff about Bella all day and all night. All month, probably. I can tell you how she did at school. What she got for her last birthday. I mean . . .' I heard my own voice going all shrill, the way it usually went only when I was fighting with Nate. I wished they'd let him come through, but then he'd get riled up by their questions and my voice and it'd all be much worse. I took a breath. 'I'm serious. I don't know what you're asking me. You want to know about how clean she kept her car? Where she bought her undies? What?'

'Nah, nah. I guess, Chris, we just want more of an idea about who Bella was outside of work. Like, what did she get up to on a Saturday night, say?'

I told them about her friends that I knew, said they should talk to them about what exactly went down at the movies or bowling alley or bloody karaoke on a Saturday night. They were barely listening, I could tell. There was something they wanted me to say that I wasn't saying and I had no clue what it was.

'One thing we were wondering,' the younger one said, after I'd run through the name of every person I'd ever known Bella to speak to. 'Is it possible that Bella might've been moonlighting?'

My mind hooked on to the word and all I could think was how pretty it sounded. I imagined Bella climbing a ladder and flicking a switch, bathing the world with gentle white light.

'Like yourself, I mean,' he added.

Moonlighting. Bella wasn't one for moonlight. She was a morning person if there ever was one. She must've been so tired on Friday night, on top of everything else.

'C'mon, Chris,' Brandis said. 'We don't want to bust your chops over it, but everyone knows you –'

'No.'

'Listen, you're not in any trouble, we just need to –'

'Not her. There's no way.'

The detectives exchanged another one of those looks and my hand went hot with wanting to slap their faces.

'You know it's a high-risk profession,' Brandis said.

'What is? Cleaning up old people's shit?'

'Chris,' Brandis said, and the younger one smiled. He fucking smiled.

We have to deal with this, I suppose.

The first time, three and a bit years ago, was an accident. It was a slow night at work and I got to talking with a long-distance truckie who'd stopped into the pub for a feed. At the end of my shift, when he said he'd be sleeping in his truck that night, I invited him back to mine. I'd been doing that a bit lately, asking blokes back. It hadn't been long since Nate left and I wanted nothing to do with love, you know, but the other business, well, I've always found it a good boost, to be honest.

Look, I'm no great beauty but I'm handy with makeup and keep myself fit and, harsh as it sounds, the same can't be said of most of the women my age around here. I'm not having a go, just stating a fact: being single and childless gives you more time to spend on making yourself look nice. In this town, most women my age haven't been single and childless since they were young enough that they didn't need to make any effort, so, in that – if nothing else – I have an advantage.

Point being, I've never had much trouble attracting blokes and in the years since I've been divorced it's only been easier. This probably sounds sad to you, but sometimes it's what's kept me going. Like, there've been times I've felt so low, so down on myself and my life, and then some fella in the pub would start hanging around, finding excuses to talk to me. I'd catch him looking at me when he thought I couldn't see. And it always gave me such a lift, no matter who he was. And if I liked him back, then even better. I tell you, it was a relief to learn as a divorced thirty-four-year-old that I could still feel that thrill, that bubbly, giddy, giggly excitement I had thought belonged to being sixteen and getting felt up in the movies for the first time.

I'm not talking about love. I'm resigned to the fact that Nate's my one and only when it comes to that. And I don't think it's even lust, although I can and do get swamped by that now and again, my god. But no, I'm talking about something less dramatic but much sweeter. A crush, I suppose is the word. A crush that might only last a few hours and might end up in awkward sloppy kisses or might end up with mind-blowing sex or might never end up at all, just float away with the summer wind but that, while it lasts, makes you feel fresh and pretty and like your whole life is ahead of you.

Anyway, one night, I invite this bloke back to mine. It's like a hundr– well, not that many, but like a bunch of times before. We have a drink or two and then a nice roll around under the covers and then in the morning he's gone. But this time was different because this time after the bloke left there was a stack of twenties on the bedside table, folded up with a note saying: *Had an early start. See ya next time I'm in town, gorgeous.*

I went to the supermarket and stocked up and went home again and stood for a while looking at the shelves of my cupboard, at the brand-name packets of biscuits and muesli, the bags of Italian pasta and tins of Campbell's tomato soup. I made myself a sandwich with the pricey, soft yellow cheese that comes in a wedge instead of thin slices between plastic and drank Moccona made with fresh milk. It wasn't until I was in bed that night that the word *prostitute* jumped into my mind. It was a shock, but not a big one. A fleeing mouse when you turn the kitchen light on kind of shock. *Ooh!* And then, *damn*, and then, *ah well*. I slept soundly that night, and although I've had plenty of sleepless nights since, not one of them has been over the help some blokes give me with my groceries. Not one.

Not that I go boasting about it or anything. A couple of days after that first time Bella came over and saw all the goodies I had in the kitchen. She hoed right into the choccy bickies and asked whether I'd won the lotto. I'd already thought hard about whether to tell her. I wanted to believe she would see it the way I did, but I remembered all the times we'd sniggered at the whores who haunted the off-ramp service station and the time she dumped a bloke because he admitted losing his V-card to a prozzy way back when he was a kid. 'Coulda picked up anything from the dirty bitch,' she'd said. I think I'd agreed with her. Why wouldn't I?

When she asked I said, yeah, actually I had won the lotto. She knew I'd never place a bet on anything, on account of the troubles our mum had with the pokies, so I said some bloke at the pub had celebrated the birth of his kid by putting a bet on for the bar staff and that my share of the winnings had been enough to restock my cupboards. 'Awesome,' she said. She didn't hesitate. I felt so rotten then, watching her hands, rough and red from all the cleaning chemicals she used at the nursing home, dip into the biscuit packet. She told me a story about slipping in some old man's piss and she laughed while she said it but all I could think was how much lower that was than picking up a hundred for letting a sweet, lonely truckie share your bed.

That first bloke stayed over again next time he was passing through and that time he asked if maybe I'd be up for keeping some of his mates company when they came through as well. I said they were welcome to come into the pub and if I happened to be free on

44

the night, then I might let them overnight in my house instead of in their trucks.

It's worked out alright, really. Once or twice a week a bloke will buy a counter meal and a beer and ask me what I'm up to after work. Depending on my mood and my bank balance and whether I like the look of him, I'll either say I'm busy or I'll say I'm planning a night in and tell him what time I knock off. Either way it's no skin off anyone's nose.

I never tell them a price, never ask for payment. They know they're expected to leave a little something on the table before they leave. A couple of blokes have taken advantage, leaving just a tenner or two. One bastard left me a six-pack of the beer he was carrying in his truck. It's OK. I'm always busy when the tight-arses next come through town. Word gets around. Blokes who want a chance at sticking their wick in before crashing out in my comfy queen know to leave at least seventy the first time. If they leave more then I'll remember and when I see them again, I show my appreciation.

I never spent the truckie cash after that first supermarket spree. It all goes into the pewter jewellery box my mum left me. When the box is full I take the bus out to the bank in Wagga (can you imagine the gossip if I turned up in the town branch with a couple of thousand cash?). At first I thought I'd just save enough to take Bella on a nice holiday up the Gold Coast, but I realised pretty quickly that if I kept it up I'd have enough for a deposit on a little house in a couple of years. I'd get a place with a spare room and Bella could stay there for nothing and save up her own deposit. Imagine that – the barmaid and the nurse's aide, daughters of a drunken welfare queen and a couple of no-good womanisers, both of us homeowners.

So that dream, that dream that I was well on the way to making reality, that's another thing those fuckers took from me.

Don't think I'm not keeping track.

I didn't tell the detectives all that, of course. They would've loved it, but. They dug and dug at me, asking me stuff that couldn't possibly have a bearing on the investigation. Stuff that couldn't have a bearing on anything except my dignity.

'This is obviously something you don't like talking about, but for Bella's sake, you need to give us a list of your clients.'

'Clients? You mean the drinkers at the pub? Geez, you'd have to ask Old Grey.'

'You know what we mean, Chris. The ones you take home from the pub.'

'Blokes I take home aren't clients. They're just blokes I take home. No one's business, is it?'

'Shitty thing about a murder investigation,' Brandis said, 'is that we have to make everything about the victim's life our business.'

'You're not talking about her life, though. You're talking about mine.'

The young one sighed again. God, I would've liked to slap him. 'Your life was intertwined with hers. It's possible some of your cli –' He broke off with a goddamn smirk. Held his hands up. 'Sorry. Your boyfriends. It's possible one of them might've taken an interest in your sister.'

'No, it isn't.'

'Why not? You've got pictures of her in your place, don't you? Bloke might've taken a liking, decided to look her up. Not unthinkable, is it?'

'You think whoever did that to her *liked* her? Jesus.'

'Alright, alright. Not a liking. Something else. Point is, it might've been the place of introduction so to speak. He sees her pic, he decides to –'

'No,' I said. 'No man I've ever met could do that.'

'You'd be surprised,' Brandis said, so soft I wondered if he meant me to hear him.

'Thing is, Chris, we have to operate with the assumption it could be anyone, and since anyone is a hell of a lot of people, we have to start close to home. Bella's workmates and friends, her neighbours and relatives. Her relatives' friends. So, you know, if you could give us your boyfriends' names . . .'

'Yeah, well, I would, but I don't know them.'

He fucking smiled, that little shit. 'You don't know the names of the men you take home?'

'Yeah, that's right. I'm a big old slut. Not a crime, is it?'

'Chris. Calm down. We're not trying to upset you. Like I said, it's a dangerous kind of . . . *lifestyle* you've got. It's not a safe thing, bringing men you don't know back to your place like that. Fucked-up men looking for women to do nasty shit to, well, a lot of the time they figure a whore is a good target. No one's going to worry too much, you know?'

'How can you say these things to me?' I turned to Brandis, brooding away in the corner. 'Is he allowed to talk to me like this?'

Brandis blinked a few times like he was just waking up. I tell you, I felt like I understood a little then about how someone could commit murder. For real, I did.

'Easy, Mikey,' he said.

Mikey raised his hands again. 'Listen, I'm not judging. I don't care about anything except finding whoever did this to Bella. If that's what you care about, and I know you do, Chris, then I'd ask you to spend the afternoon having a good long think. See if you can't dredge up some of those names from your memory bank, eh?'

Brandis stood up. 'Press conference isn't for a few hours yet. If you'd like to stay back here, gather your thoughts, I can organise someone to bring you a cuppa and a sandwich or something?'

'Nah, I'll go home now, I think.'

'Up to you. Important that we have you back here before one, though. I'll send a car to get you at twenty to, alright?'

Nate was in the waiting area, playing around with his damn phone. Reading the news or texting his woman. I didn't know which would've been worse, so instead of asking him I just believed both and shook away the hand he offered me as we walked out to the car.

'What did they want to talk to you about?'

'Just more bullshit about who she might have been seeing. Can't get it through their fucking heads that she isn't like that.'

Nate started the engine, looked over to check that I was strapped in. He did that every time and every time it softened my heart towards him for the moment. I reached across and patted his leg.

'Thanks for being here, babe.'

Nate nodded and released the handbrake. 'Long as you need me, only . . .' He drove out of the car park, heading for my place. 'I hav'ta head back up to Sydney later today. After the press thing, I'll –'

'I thought you said you had time off.'

'Yeah, yeah. There's just a coupla things I need to do.'

'Things.'

'Babe, come on. Be fair.'

'I never asked you to come in the first place.'

His giant hands slammed palm first into the top of the steering wheel. 'She was like my sister.'

'Yeah, I know the feeling.'

He sucked in his breath, drummed his hands, gently now, on the wheel. He was taking the long way, avoiding the street where Bella lived. These were the parts of Strathdee the tourists never saw, lined with red-brick and fibro rentals with squat steel fences out front. It was a few minutes before ten on a breezy, sunny Wednesday and most of the front yards we passed were occupied: I exchanged glances with a chain-smoking teenager half watching two toddlers beating each other with plastic tools, a pair of ancient Italian immigrants in wife-beaters and dress pants staring blankly at the road and a middle-aged woman in track pants and thongs watering weeds. A town's worth of dogs howled and barked, but I couldn't see any of them.

'You can just drop me off and go on your way now,' I said when we turned into my street.

'What about the press thing?' Nate pulled on the handbrake but left the engine running.

'Brandis said he'd send a car to get me.'

'It's a big thing to handle alone.'

'I'll ask Lisa to come.'

He looked at me in that way of his. Jesus, that man.

'I want to be here, you know that, but she was expecting me yesterday and I didn't show up. Didn't call until ... She understands and all, but she's ... I just need to go and calm her down, let her know it's all OK between us. Her and me. I'll be back tomorrow first thing. We'll need to ... Funeral and all that.'

'It'll be days, a week maybe. They need to ... Because it's a criminal investigation, it takes longer for them to release the body.'

He closed his eyes, drummed the wheel again. She was like his sister. He loved her. He was hurting, badly. It made me hurt for him and it made me worry.

'Does she, your woman –'

'Renee.'

'Does Renee know about you, your drinking?'

Fists squeezed shut, opened, shut. 'It's how we met. At a meeting.'

'Oh. OK. Good. That's good.'

'Yeah.'

'Alright. You go on now, drive safe. I'll see you later.'

'Tomorrow,' he said, still looking out the window.

I leant over, pecked him on the cheek, felt all the hurt in his clenched jaw. I couldn't get out of that truck fast enough.

■　■　■

As she approached Strathdee police station, May could see her competition out front. She'd been dreading a horde, but this wasn't too bad. A small knot of photographers weighing their cameras, looking at the sky. There was a reporter each from the *Telegraph* and the *Herald*, plus two others May recognised but couldn't place. The 7, 9 and 10 vans were there, but not ABC or Sky.

She parked around the corner, had a smoke and touched-up her make-up. She timed her walk to the station perfectly, arriving just as a uniform was welcoming them all to Strathdee. Behind him stood two men in suits, two other uniformed officers and a dark-haired woman in a light blue tracksuit – the tight, velour kind that was hip ten years ago – white high-top sneakers and pink pastel lipstick. Her head vibrated. She blinked in rapid bursts. The poor woman seemed genuinely surprised to find herself being gently pushed forward towards the cluster of reporters. May doubted that the woman would be able to get through a single sentence let alone a press conference. She cringed at the unkindness of it all and then elbowed her way to the front so she could get some good pictures of the collapse when it happened.

Back in the car, May played back the recording and made brief notes on the few actual details the cops had released. She scribbled out a list of story angles before she called Andrew to convince him to let her stay a few days despite there being no news apart from 'woman dead, sister sad, police know nothing'.

Reactions/recollections of:

Family (esp. sister)

Boyfriend

Friends

Neighbours

Colleagues

Implications for town – women's safety, tourism, nightlife (is there any?)

Similar crimes (murders in this town or recent rape/murders elsewhere)

'Yeah, good,' Andrew said while she was still on her first idea. 'Look, the piece we have up is still going nuts, being shared all over, so we need to build on that. Give me a straight-up report first, focus on the sister, use whatever scraps the police gave. Then I want an atmospheric overview of the place; give a sense of what it's like where she was killed, what the vibe is around the town. Jim reckons there was a famous massacre there back in settler days. See if you can work that in, too.

'I want to get the first up this arvo, get it shared around before the others have a chance to even file, and then have the second ready to go early tomorrow. So, an hour for the report and before six for the other, OK? Cheers. Talk in the morning.' He hung up.

Cross-legged on the hotel bed, having just sent off the second of her stories five minutes before deadline, May sent a quick email to her neighbour, Jack, asking him to keep an eye on her place until she returned. Jack was actually three doors down, but he was the only person in the terrace row she ever spoke to. The woman on her direct left was a whiny bitch who complained about mail sitting in the box more than one day, a bin left out overnight, music played just loud enough to be heard by someone with their ear to the speaker. On the other side of May was an elderly man visited by home-care every midday and taken away by ambulance at least once a month.

Sitting in this odourless, brown and beige box, May was stabbed with longing for the little rental on Devonshire Street. Her pale green walls and retro-printed green and purple curtains, white barred windows open to the night, the scent of Malay spices from the restaurant on the corner, the sound of trucks, bicycle bells, laughing and fighting and the occasional bottle smashing outside the pub one street back. And May seeing, hearing, smelling all that, lying on her too-squishy but so gorgeous vintage iron-framed bed and especially, yes, God, Craig's head between her legs, his tongue –

'Fuck.' She closed her laptop, yanked her runners out of her unpacked suitcase and pushed her bare feet into them. She pocketed the room key and strode out into the Strathdee dusk, thinking, if he turned up here I'd be on my back in seconds. I have no dignity, I have no pride. If I called would he come just for a night, just for old times? He can't be satisfied with her, pregnant and angry, and I'm here so ready and full of wanting.

May struck out in the direction she'd driven that morning. Six or seven lone men smoking on the verandah of the pub ignored her while a cluster of three made a point of stopping their conversation to watch her pass. The car rental agency next door was in darkness, the service station empty except for the teenage attendant casually fagging away ignition distance from the pumps.

Foreseeing a main road lined with staring smoke-machines, May turned left at the preschool and breathed easy down a quiet street lined with neat fibro cottages. She chose turns at random, keeping mental track of her route, focusing on her breathing and the feel of the road beneath her pounding feet, driving out the thought of Craig and his licking, lying goddamn tongue for as much as thirty seconds at a time.

'Hello!' a child called from behind a wire fence four or five houses ahead on her left.

'Hi.'

'Do you need a hiding place? We have a shed.'

May slowed. 'No. I'm just doing some exercise.'

'Oh. I thought those men might be chasing you.'

'What men?' She stopped, bouncing on her toes, looked into the little face. A girl of maybe five or six with a home bowl cut, dressed in grey track pants and a faded Superman t-shirt.

'The ones what kilded that lady. Did you know? A lady got kilded.'

'Yeah, I know.'

'My mum says the police will get 'em but not yet, so if you see them you should hide and if they find you, you have to shout really really really really loud.'

'Good advice. Bye now.'

'Bye. Have a nice exercise time.'

Craig's middle child would be around that age. May rarely thought about them, those blameless kids. She knew no children, had only ever been able to visualise Craig's as better-dressed and fed versions of herself and her brothers. The girl, wan and frightened-looking, features too big and old for her squished-up face. The older boy, fine-boned and long-lashed, mistaken for a girl so often that he stopped correcting people, threw up his pretty hands and said 'whatever' in a way that made Mum giggle and Dad squeeze his face closed. The youngest boy, his father's pride, stocky and gruff, able to tackle his older brother to the ground by the age of three.

She could've loved them. Even if they turned out to be nothing like her and Max and Jason, she could've found enough of Craig in each of them to love. He'd never given her the chance. He'd never intended to, she knew now. The fourth child, forthcoming, was proof of that. The family going from strength to strength while the mistress waits herself to oblivion.

'Hey. What you running for, sweet girl?'

May's pace didn't alter, her head remained high, her gaze trained six feet ahead. She was used to running in the inner city, where dickheads calling from cars were background noise.

'Aww, just a question. Why you running? Sweet arse like that, don't wanna go running it away.'

She kept moving, taking the next left, focusing her mind on retracing her route, determining whether to loop back at the next corner or go another few blocks. She realised only two or three cars had passed since she'd left the main road, tried to picture the town map, figure out a more direct route back to her hotel.

A car turned from the opposite corner, came towards her, headlights on high beam, then no headlights at all. May's vision flickered and swam. She noticed how dark it was, how few houses there were on this street, how much yard and driveway in front of each one. She ran harder, but only slightly, kept her pace steady as the lightless car reached the other end of the street and executed a screeching U-turn.

'C'mon, girl. Stop for a second. Just a second.'

The car was right behind her, engine revving, keeping pace. Up ahead, end of the street, maybe a minute away, was a lit-up house. She struck out hard.

'Aww, why you keep running like that? Jus' gimme a second, gimme a second.' The patter kept up, friendly, almost gentle, like she was a wild dog being coaxed into the back of the pound van.

The concrete driveway metres away was too far. She made a sharp turn onto the lawn, ran hard towards the brightly lit porch. The car sped away, tyres screeching as May knocked on the door.

A man answered, late thirties, striped pyjama pants and a white singlet. He raised his eyebrows, didn't speak. Behind him, the theme music to *Friends* blasted and children's whines rose and fell.

'I'm really sorry,' May said. 'I was out for a run and someone started following me. I just . . . Your lights were on and so I . . .'

The man peered behind her. 'Gone now, looks like.'

There was something familiar about him. For a mad second she thought he was the man in the car and her heart stopped before sanity kicked it back to life again. 'Yeah, um. I wonder if . . . I didn't bring my phone with me and –'

'That wasn't real smart, was it?'

'No. I didn't think I'd – Can I use your phone really quickly? Call a taxi?'

'A taxi? Where ya going to?'

'Strathdee Inn. It's just –'

'Yeah. Look, give us a sec and I'll drive you.'

'Oh, no, I didn't want to –'

'One sec.' He disappeared down the hallway. May heard a woman's voice, the kids piping up, a child's giggle. More muttered conversation and then he reappeared dressed in footy shorts and a navy blue t-shirt, keys and phone in hand. 'Come on then.'

His face and voice clicked into place. 'You're, um, you were at the press conference today? Constable Riley, isn't it?'

'Senior Constable Riley,' he said, then smiled very slightly. 'Tom, if you like.'

'I'm May Norman. I'm –'

'A reporter, yeah, I know.' He walked past her towards a grey station wagon, held the passenger door open while she climbed in.

'This bloke who followed you,' he said once they were out of the driveway. 'He in a shit-brown Ford? Number plate ROX111?'

'Um, brown car, yeah. But I didn't – I didn't notice the make or plates.'

'Nah? Thought that's what you lot did? Notice stuff – details and that.'

May bit back the apology. 'I thought it best to ignore him. Keep my eyes straight ahead. Usually works to get rid of pests like that.'

'Yeah. Thing is, fella you're dealing with here, Dean Rockford – Rox – he's all piss and wind. If it happens again, tell him to bugger off, give him the finger, something like that and he'll go on his way.'

'Does this a lot, does he?'

'When he has the chance. He's harmless, though. Take it from me, if you'd so much as looked him in the face he'd've sped off like nobody's business.'

They pulled into the hotel car park. May's heart rate was back to normal, but her chest ached and she couldn't seem to stop swallowing. 'Look,' she said. 'What if it wasn't this bloke, or if . . . I mean, whoever killed –'

'Wasn't Rox.'

'But how can –'

'Can't say more, you know that. But trust me that it wasn't him. Like I said, he's harmless.'

'OK, but . . .' He was looking at her as though she were a child refusing to believe in the absence of the werewolf in the wardrobe. 'What if it wasn't this Rox guy? Just now, I mean. I didn't get a good look at the car. It could have been . . .'

He sighed, grabbed his phone off the dash, dialled, smiled at her as he spoke. 'Rox, Riley here. Yeah, yeah, shut up for a sec and listen. You been out making a nuisance of yerself? You know what I mean. Hollering and kerb-crawling? Scaring girls.'

May sat still, hot all over. The tinny braying from the other end of the phone scratched at her spine.

Riley guffawed, shook his head. 'You're a right grub, mate. Need to cut that shit out, yeah? I mean it. If I catch you creeping around like that I'll – You better believe it . . . I'll . . . Yeah, yeah. Just keep your dirty thoughts to yourself from now on.' He slid the phone into his pocket. 'OK?'

'What?' May said.

'Definitely Rox. And he's nothing to worry about.'

'If you say so.' She opened the door, put her feet on the ground.

'But hey, just 'cause he's harmless doesn't mean it's safe for you to be running alone like that. Especially at night. Good-looking girl, no phone, no nothing. Not real smart given the current circumstances.'

'OK. Sorry.'

'I'm not having a go. You do what you like, free country and all that. Just that we don't want another Bella Michaels on our hands, do we?'

'No.' She got out of the car. 'Thanks for the lift,' she said, thinking *inside inside inside inside*.

'Not a problem. You stay safe now.'

May closed the door and then jumped and fell back against it when she saw the body wrapped in plastic poking out from underneath the bonnet of the four-wheel drive next to where she stood.

'You right?' Riley called from inside his car and she blinked and saw it was only a lazily dumped bag of garbage. She felt his eyes on her back and more eyes digging into her from inside the hotel reception. She couldn't bear to walk all the way across the car park to get to the path to her room. She cut across the metre-wide strip of pebbles and native plants, shuddered as fronds tickled her ankles like soft strands of hair.

■　■　■

SISTER PLEADS FOR HELP IN FINDING BELLA'S KILLER

May Norman
8 April, 2015

The grief-stricken sister of murdered Strathdee woman Bella Michaels has pleaded for public help to bring the 25-year-old's killer or killers to justice.

Standing between homicide detectives outside Strathdee police station, Chris Rogers' voice broke as she responded to a journalist's question about how she felt on identifying her sister's body. 'You seem to be a human being. Try imagining what it would feel like for you. Then understand that this feeling will never go away. That moment when I saw her, it's forever. It's part of me now.' She then began to sob and appeared to lose her balance and stumble towards the microphone stand before a female police officer steadied her and led her back inside the station.

After Ms Rogers departed, Detective Sergeant John Brandis continued the conference by briefing the assembled media on the facts of the case. Police believe Ms Michaels was murdered late on Friday night or in the early hours of Saturday morning after being abducted outside the nursing home where she worked. Her body was found near a highway exit on Monday morning.

Det. Brandis confirmed that Ms Michaels was sexually assaulted multiple times in the hours before her death and said that it is possible more than one person was involved in those assaults.

Responding to questions, Det. Brandis said police had interviewed 'a number of people' in relation to the crime, including several local residents with records of physical or sexual assault, but that they had yet to identify any suspects.

Before she gave the answer that resulted in her breaking down, Ms Rogers had read from a prepared statement. 'All who knew Bella are shattered by her death,' the statement said. 'Words can't come close to describing the hell we're experiencing, knowing that her last moments were likely full of suffering.

'Bella was a gentle, sweet soul who worked hard, cared deeply for her patients and was adored by her family and friends.

'We will miss her every minute of every day.

'Nothing can ever heal the hurt we're feeling, but we desperately hope that the person or people responsible for taking her from us can be found, both so that justice is done for Bella and so that no one else has to go through this unending pain.

'It's of utmost importance that anyone with information about the events of that night contact the police immediately. Anyone with information is urged to call Crime Stoppers or the Strathdee police.'

■ ■ ■

I'd taken the first two nights off work. I could've taken more – Old Grey at the Royal is a softie at heart and God knows I've put enough years in there to have earned some downtime – but why would I want to spend any more time than I have to alone in my bloody house thinking about my poor bloody sister?

Anyway, the pub is more home to me than anywhere else, really. I've worked there, geez, thirteen years? About that, anyway. I started in the kitchen and then moved to the bar once I got my alcohol service card. I know every last in-and-out of the place, could run it, easy, but I've got no desire to. I like my job as is and could happily do it until my legs give out from under me.

A while back the manager at the Imperial tried to get me to come work for him. Cheeky bugger he was, coming in and ordering a beer and then giving me the hard sell right under Grey's nose. He offered me more money and a full weekend off a month and for a day or so I considered it, but in the end I figured why fix what's not broken, you know? Besides, the Imperial is right in the centre of town so they get all the after-five office and shop trade. We're closer to the truck stop, caravan park and motel near the Sydney off-ramp, which means we get most of the stopover traffic. It's not like it was before the bypass, but we still get a good number of truckies and travellers and I do love having a chat with someone from a place I've never been. Even better, a place I've never heard of. You can learn a lot that way.

And, yeah, no denying it at this point: I do have a bit of a thing for truckies, the long-haul variety especially. I mean, physically, most of them could be in better shape, but there's something about thick, sun-wrecked arms and bristly cheeks. Plus the kind of patience it takes to stay on the road ten, twelve, fourteen hours a day, and the skill needed to manoeuvre those monster things in and out of all kinds of nooks and crannies, well, let's just say patience and manoeuvrability in the truck tend to translate quite bloody nicely to the bedroom.

Anyway, turns out tragedy is good for business. I've never seen the place as full as it was that Wednesday night of the week they found Bella. The usual scattering of folks passing through and then half the goddamn town. Honestly, more people than we've had on a weeknight in a decade.

Nobody said anything more than 'How you holding up, love?' but when I answered that I was OK, I could see the disappointment in their faces. They wanted tears or rage. They wanted details. I could see that, too. I could see that every one of them had read the papers and put real effort into imagining her. Everybody was respectful and sombre when they approached the bar to order, but as soon as they got back to their tables they dropped the act. It was like, 'How you doing love?' in almost a whisper, but then ten seconds later yahooing with their mates over fuck knows what.

It did hurt a bit, if I'm being honest. I'd known many of them all my life. Janie, who'd been my best mate all through primary but then went off to the Catholic school in Year 7. Her husband Mick, who wet his pants in kindergarten and was a swimming champion in his teens and who almost died of meningitis a few years back. Patrick, who was my kind-of-boyfriend when I was fifteen and who later married wall-eyed, stuttering Jenny, who we all tried hard to like in high school because she was the only person we knew with a pool. Mr and Mrs Creighton, who lived next door to us when we were kids and who I'd never in all these years seen inside the Royal.

At one point this woman I didn't recognise came up and rubbed my arm and started talking like she was my dearest friend. It took me until almost the end of the conversation (though it wasn't long – just her asking how I was holding up and me saying fine and then asking how she was) for it to click that it was Fiona Willard, who told everyone at the Year 6 dance that I was wearing a dress her older sister had donated to the Salvos the previous week.

Very late in the night one of the regulars, Lynn, said my name and looked into my eyes, properly into my eyes. I almost started bawling right then, because I didn't realise until that second that nobody had done that all shift.

'Listen, love,' she said. She was seventy-three, a widow, came in every night looking like the Queen, drank her body weight in gin and left looking like an unmade bed. 'Listen. You shouldn't be here.'

'It's fine,' I said, trying to brush her off, because, seriously, I was going to bawl.

'No. Listen. The papers said they don't have a clue who done it. So it could be anyone. It could be any of 'em.'

My belly filled with ice water. It could be any of them. The men I'd been serving drinks to, taking roast dinner orders from, telling I'm holding up OK. I don't know why I hadn't thought of it myself. I don't know what I was thinking or why in those days. Jesus. It could be any of them.

I'd not kept whiskey in the house since the awful night a couple of weeks after Nate left when I drank a whole bottle and Bella found me the next morning sleeping in my own spew. That was the lowest moment of my life and I promised Bella I would go easy from then on, only drink beer when I was home alone. She would have preferred I didn't drink at all, but she was realistic and understood about harm minimisation. We made a deal about spirits in the house and I'd kept to it ever since.

That third night that I knew Bella was dead I brought home a six-pack of beer and a bottle of Jim Beam. I drank one beer, one slug of bourbon, one beer, one slug of bourbon until there was only bourbon and then I kept drinking straight from the bottle.

I needed noise and distraction, but was scared of news breaks coming on the telly or radio, so I put on an old JJJ Hottest 100 CD. I pulled out my photo albums and looked through them all. I cried a lot. When I got to the wedding album and saw Bella, just a kid still really, but looking like a goddamn model in her pale pink satin mini, and me in my white slinky cocktail dress and there was Nate, one big hand on each of our shoulders, I nearly choked with the sobbing. I tried to call him but got his voicemail. Fuck knows what I said, but I said a lot. I think it was mostly about Bella, but it was possible I mentioned how sick I thought it was that he was up there fucking some other bird when his wife was down here grieving for her baby sister. It's very possible.

I woke in the middle of the night, still sprawled on the floor in front of the open wedding album, my guts heaving. I made it to the toilet just in time. While I was chucking I noticed how sore my neck and back and hips were. I used to drink until I crashed on the floor all the time when I was younger; it never hurt this much. Bella had a sore back most of the time even though she was young and fit. It was her work, all that bending and scrubbing and reaching and lifting. They were meant to use a swinging trolley thing to move the patients but there was only one of those in the whole place and she couldn't stand to leave some poor old bugger lying in their own mess for a minute longer than necessary, so she'd often just do the lifting herself. Most of them weighed less than a case of beer she reckoned. But I worried about her. Once your back goes it's fucked for good, they say.

Her back. *Jesus god help me jesus fuck her* back *oh god what she withstood what they did to her back Jesus god fuck.*

I cleaned myself up and staggered through to bed. My head was spinning and so I used the trick I remembered from my heaviest drinking days, kept my eyes open and focused on a single spot on the wall. I trusted I'd fall asleep and out of my misery as long as I didn't force my own eyes shut. I stared and stared at the dark spot on the wall and then felt the ice in my guts again as I realised I'd never seen that spot before. My walls are white and I keep them clean, wiping away any scuffs and greasy hand marks as soon as they appear. I would've noticed this before, this dark patch, a dappled, airless football. I hadn't closed the curtains and so the wall was lit by the full moon outside. A clear, light space marred by this terrible bruise.

I couldn't move with terror. I can't explain why. It was only a dark space on my wall but at that moment it felt like my life was about to end.

And then it was gone. Just like that, my wall was clean again. I pushed myself out of bed and touched the wall where the spot had been. It was like touching a hotplate you had no idea was turned on. It took me a second to understand my hand was being burnt and then I pulled back, dropped to my knees. I touched the wall near the floor and it felt like a wall. I reached up and with just my middle finger this time touched the spot that had burnt me. Nothing. I ran my hands up and down that wall and couldn't find the hot spot, the dark spot again. The palm of my left hand still stung with the heat.

I needed to vomit, charged through the doorway, past the kitchen into the bathroom. I didn't quite make it. Messed up the floor and the front of my nightie. I sat in front of the toilet until my heart stopped hammering and my stomach felt calm. Then I cleaned the floor, put my nightie in the wash, had a shower, took some Panadol with a big glass of water. I walked around the house, turned on all the lights, checked all the walls. Silly old drunk, I said to myself, but when I finally got back to bed and closed my eyes I knew with certainty that if I opened them again I would see it there, that impossible bruise.

■　■　■

AustraliaToday.com

A HAUNTED PLACE

May Norman
8 April 2015

Five minutes out of Strathdee, heading south on the Hume Highway, a series of unnatural colour bursts draw the motorist's eye past the line of eucalypts to the ordinarily drab green and brown grass strip beyond. Pulling onto the asphalt verge it becomes immediately clear that the garish pinks and yellows spotted from the road belong to a makeshift memorial shrine surrounding a lean ghost gum. Twenty or so steps to the left of the tree is the patch of dirt where the naked, violated body of popular, twenty-five-year-old aged-care worker Bella Michaels was found on Monday morning, partially wrapped in a blue tarpaulin.

The area was immediately sealed off by local police, then in came the detectives, the crime scene investigators and then the battalions of police, including trainees from the police academy at Goulburn, enlisted to search the surrounding area centimetre by centimetre. By 10pm Tuesday the vans and floodlights and army of searchers were gone. All that remained of them was a series of indentations and skid marks in the asphalt and mud dividing the grass from the road.

Strathdee, population 3,000, situated 450 kilometres south-west of Sydney and almost the same distance north-east of Melbourne, used to be the number-one stopping place for travellers on the road between the two cities. But thanks to the highway bypass completed five years ago, the thousands of cars, trucks and coaches that would once have stopped here for a stretch, bite to eat or overnight break now pass right on by.

Several hotels and restaurants as well as a major service station complex have closed and a few hundred locals have moved, many of them to the comparatively thriving rural hub of Wagga Wagga, 50 kilometres west.

Still, Strathdee is no ghost town. Its retailers and small businesses serve the surrounding cattle and sheep farmers and on any given night its four pubs, two hotels and large, sprawling caravan park are kept busy by a mixture of locals, long-distance truck drivers on their compulsory driving break and tourists taking it slow, stopping off to enjoy the quintessential Aussie country towns that lie between Australia's biggest cities.

On Wednesday, one such traveller, Glenys Morton of Cairns, was horrified to hear of the recent murder. 'It's such a lovely, calm little town,' said Mrs Morton who, with her husband, is spending six months caravanning down the east coast of Australia. 'It's the last place you'd expect to hear about that kind of violence.'

Arthur Tomesberry of the Strathdee Historical Society, however, has a different view. 'The town has been safe as houses long as I've known it, and that's coming up on seventy years, but the history of this area is a dark one. I've always felt, whenever I head out into the bush around here, that it's somewhat haunted.'

The 'dark' history Mr Tomesberry is referring to includes an alleged massacre of the Indigenous inhabitants in the early 1800s. 'Bunch of newly arrived Scotsmen came through looking to set up farms. They cleared the locals off the land like they were vermin. There's no documentation on it, but the stories have been passed down orally and every old family in the area knows something of what went on.' Mr Tomesberry also points to the 'reign of terror' conducted by the bushranger known as Mad Dog Morgan in the 1860s as a contributor to the 'eeriness' of the area surrounding the quiet, tidy town.

For the first-time visitor it's impossible to say whether the stretch of sparse, bristly grass by the highway five minutes from town has always felt as desolate and crushing as it does today or if the atmosphere of despair set in the moment Bella Michaels drew her last, no doubt terrified breath.

Thursday
9
April

May woke to her phone ringing, saw it was her brother Max and hit ignore. She made some coffee, slapped on some mascara and lippie, dressed in tight tan pants and a fitted, brown-and-white-checked shirt. Packing in Sydney she'd thought this outfit looked appropriately country, but now she was in the actual country she saw that it looked like a city stripper's idea of a jillaroo. As if she didn't already stand out here in the whitest bloody town in Australia. She swapped the tan pants for jeans. Now she looked like she was going to round up some senior citizens for a barn dance. Fuck. Tan pants, black t-shirt, black blazer. Not at all country but also not looking like she was trying to be. OK.

Her phone rang again as she was leaving the hotel. She leant against the car but it was already too hot for comfort. In April, for God's sake. She unlocked the door and slid into the stifling interior before answering.

'Hey, Max, I'm on my way to an interview so I don't have long.

What's up?'

'Why does your by-line suggest that you wrote your last two articles from a place called Strathdee?'

'Huh, weird. I'll have to talk to the sub desk about that.'

'Yeah, well, thanks for letting your family know.'

May picked up the map from the dashboard and fanned her face. 'I'm just covering a story. I haven't moved here.'

'Still could've let us know. It's school holidays. I would've loved a road trip.'

'Max, you would hate it here so much. It's, like, ten degrees hotter than anywhere else on earth. No breeze at all. Plus, no *banh mi*, no craft beer, no skinny jeans.'

'Sounds like Blacktown.'

'Please, Blacktown had *banh mi* twenty years before your gold-hipster-plated hood did.' May had never hated the suburb they grew up in the way Max did. But, then, she hadn't been a smaller-than-average, fine-boned boy with soft curls and a tendency to forget himself in public and sing out loud. Not that she wasn't bullied, but her tormentors were only at school whereas Max copped it everywhere outside their home. God, imagine how he'd fare here, where even preschoolers looked like Clint Eastwood.

'Whatever. When are you coming home?'

'Don't know.'

'Ugh. I'm bored.'

'You sound twelve.'

'I might as well be. Nothing to do all day, no money, no car, no sex.'

'I can't help you with any of that. And I really have to go.'

'Selfish bitch.'

'Yeah, love you, too.'

At the police station she had a chat with the sweet young guy on the front desk who, it turned out, was not only one of the first response officers when the body was called in but also knew Bella personally. May asked if she could buy him lunch and he blushed and told her he could meet her at Frederica's – 'it's in the mall, but really nice, not in the food court or anything' – at twelve, and then she hotfooted it out of there before someone with guile or experience came along to ruin things.

She drove over to the nursing home, but turned around when she saw the Channel 7 van out front. Next was the sister's house, where the door was answered by a bearded giant who told her that Chris wasn't doing interviews. When May persisted, asking him if he might like to say a few words about the deceased, he told her that she should be ashamed of herself for harassing the grieving.

May almost told him that harassing the grieving was the least of what she was ashamed of, but her remaining morsel of dignity asserted itself in time. She thanked him and, after he closed the door in her face, slid her card underneath it. She dragged her shameful self up and down the street, knocking on doors, collecting a handful of tidbits that would do if they had to, then headed to the mall to meet the young cop.

She still had fifteen minutes before he was due, so she spent the time talking to smokers leaning against the grey, rippled concrete walls, grabbing a few more quotes, each a variation on the same theme. *It could've been me. Could've been my daughter. Could've happened to any of us.*

Constable Matt Drey was five minutes early, grinning from oversized ear to ear. He took her elbow as they entered Frederica's and pulled out her chair to seat her.

'What's good here?'

His grin, impossibly, got bigger. 'Oh, everything. I'm a bit biased, but. It's me aunty's place.'

'Your aunty is Frederica?'

'Nah, nah. Her name's Jo, but you can't call a restaurant that, can you?'

No, May thought, but then this isn't really a restaurant, is it? She asked him to order for them both, which seemed to be the best thing that had happened to him for a long while. The waitress was a girl he obviously knew well, though not, from what May could tell, a relative or girlfriend. May was a bit concerned the girl didn't take in anything Matt said, so busy was she looking at May from under her heavily augmented eyelashes. If Matt noticed, it only added to his air of extreme contentment. May wondered if she should ask him if their engagement would be official once they'd finished the meal.

'So, um, I hope you don't mind, but I looked you up. Like, on the internet not on the database or anything. Ha ha ha ha.'

'Hey, nothing to hide here.'

'Nah, I never thought that. It's just the name of the newspaper on your card, I hadn't heard of it, so I thought I should check it out and that.' He knocked back half a glass of water in one go, then added reassuringly, 'It looks like a really good publication. You should talk to Mr Chin at the newsagency about stocking it here.'

'Oh, no, it's digital only.'

'Like just a website?'

'We call it a newspaper because that's the format, But it's not printed on actual paper, no. Our subscribers get a full edition sent to their iPads or whatever each morning and the website updates all day and night.'

'And you make money from that?'

'Well, I get paid a salary. The owners will make money at some point, I guess, but it's a new venture. Only been operating a couple of months, so, ah, not exactly a cash cow at this point.'

'Huh.' He sat back, nodded. 'And, um, your profile thingy on the site said you grew up in Sydney but, like, hope you don't mind me saying but you don't look like you – I mean, like, are your parents from …'

May kept her pleasant, neutral reporter face in place. Let the silence hang.

He swallowed nothing. '… from overseas somewhere?'

'Nope, both born and raised in the western suburbs of Sydney.'

'Yeah? Huh. Alright! Here comes the pumpkin soup. Aunty Jo makes it herself and never skimps on the cream. So what's it like being a crime reporter up in Sydney? Bet you've seen some exciting stuff.'

'Oh, please, you're a cop. You wouldn't bat an eyelid at anything I've seen.'

'I dunno. Sydney's a whole different kettle of fish, I'd reckon. Round here, don't see much worse than pub brawls and domestics. Up till now, anyhow.' He scooped a dripping spoon of soup into his gob. 'Yeah, I'd be pretty happy to go the rest of my life without seeing anything like that again.'

May itched for her notebook. 'Pretty bad, huh?'

'You ever seen anything like that?'

'Like …?'

He glanced towards the counter then leant forward. 'A murder. Body all messed up.'

'Not like that, no.' May hoped her tone suggested the viewing of countless other kinds of bodies messed up in different but no less traumatising ways rather than the embarrassing truth, which was that she'd never even been to the scene of a murder before this morning, let alone caught a look at a body. Six weeks ago she was still the senior reporter at the tiny community paper she'd been hired at as a cadet. The *Australia Today* job wasn't any better paid, but it was an opportunity to do the kind of work she'd wanted to since uni. It had taken her so long to get to it partly because journalism jobs were few and getting fewer all the time, and crime reporter positions in particular were held by old-timers who gave the impression they wouldn't hesitate to use some of the underworld tactics they'd learnt on the job if some upstart tried to push in on their beat.

But even so, she probably could've done more to advance her career. Some time in her mid-twenties she'd stopped nagging her editor to let her write longer-form pieces, stopped subscribing to any industry e-news because it made her feel bad to see people she'd been at uni with getting city and national jobs or being nominated for Walkleys. She stopped boring her friends with rants about advocacy journalism and how when she finally had a high-profile position she was going to . . . What was it she'd been going to do? End sexism, racism, homophobia and poverty? Bring about world peace? She couldn't remember exactly. What she did remember was drinking cask wine on the floor of her share-flat and realising mid-rant that her friends were swapping cringes and side-eying the fuck out of her. She'd gone to the bathroom and in the mirror she saw a puffy, transparent, needy loser. Pathetic to reflect on it, but she'd felt that way ever since. Until Craig . . . No, fuck him. Focus.

'Seeing her in particular – someone you knew – it must have been really distressing.'

'I'll tell you something, Miss Norman –'

'May.'

'I'll tell you, May, there are some things a person is better off not ever knowing and what a body left wrapped in a tarp in the rain for two days smells like is one of them.'

'So when you got there she was . . .'

'C'mon now, let's leave all that. Eat your soup before it gets cold or Aunty Jo'll be wild.'

After soup and garlic toast and chicken schnitzel with pasta salad, accompanied by questions about where she lived in the city, whether she'd ever been robbed, what kind of security she had on her place and what car she drove, May managed to slide in another question about Bella Michaels. The food must've sharpened him up though, because he said he couldn't really tell her anything and definitely nothing on the record. She suspected he actually didn't know much about the investigation anyway, but that was OK. The stuff he shared when she encouraged him to talk more about the town was detailed enough that she at least had a good idea now of who she needed to hunt down.

He wouldn't let her pay for the enormous meal, asked her if they could do it again sometime. 'That'd be lovely,' she said. 'But I don't know how long I'll be in town. It all depends on –'

'Us doing our jobs and getting you more stuff to report.'

'Exactly.'

'Speaking of, I better get back to the station.' He lurched forward as if for a kiss. May caught his arm and slid her hand down to force an awkward shake. 'Ah, righto. Um, see ya.'

He ambled off towards the street. May found the public toilets and did her best to get rid of the lunch, though it had taken so long to eat that half of it was too far gone to get back now.

Walking to her car, she switched her phone off silent and saw she had a message. She dialled in, stopped short in the middle of the car park at the sound of his voice.

'May, it's me.'

Fuck. A car beeped politely, she waved and continued walking, the phone pressed hard to her ear.

'Listen, I'm sorry about that message. I had to, but . . . I need to see you. I know I said . . . Jesus, I miss you. I can't get away for long, but maybe, I don't know, we'll figure something out. Um, don't call me back, because – well, you know. I'll, ah, try again when I can.'

May made it to her car and collapsed into the seat. Her finger hovered over his name. But he said don't. If she did and his wife was there it would get him into trouble and then he'd be mad at her and then . . . Fuck. She put the phone in her pocket. He'd call back. He would.

May spent the afternoon with a man who'd lived next to Bella Michaels' mother until her death. He had some good colour for her, but it was so embedded in endless, interconnected stories about each and every person who'd ever lived in the street and their relatives and their jobs and what they'd done in the bloody war (which one, May had no idea and could not risk asking), that two minutes' worth of information took almost three hours to extract. May touched the phone in her pocket so often that if the man hadn't been almost blind he might've thought she spent the whole time masturbating.

At four o'clock she dropped the car back to the hotel then walked across the road to the pub where the fragile, tracksuit-wearing sister worked. The deep red carpet was streaked with sunlight from the glass panels set high on the front wall. There were four small clusters of drinkers spaced through the room and three loners sagging over the bar. A big-screen TV silently broadcast a game show. She bought a beer from an old man with a silver tooth then took a table near the back wall.

To her left and slightly in front were four men in high-vis shirts and King Gees. Two of them were younger than her – a pinch-faced redhead and a far too good-looking sandy-haired surfer type. The third man was in his late thirties and unusually tall; his shirt, pants and face lacked the grey dust speckled over the others. The fourth man had his back to her, but judging from his slumped posture and white hair he was older than all of them.

'Yeah, you gotta do it. Least if you want them to do it back to ya,' the young redhead said.

'That's the thing, hey,' his sandy-haired mate agreed. 'If it's just a one-nighter then fuck it, but if it's your girl, like long-term, and you ever wanna get your knob polished, then you've gotta get down there now and then.'

'Fucking faggots,' the oldest one said.

'Faggots don't eat pussy, you moron.'

'I dunno what to call youse. I just know you won't ever find me eating something that can get up and walk away.'

'So dead chicks and cripples only, eh. Knew it, you sick bastard.'

'Oi.' The tall man said it softly, but the young blokes flinched as if he'd bellowed and exchanged a look, like kindergarteners busted painting their faces instead of the paper. 'Have a bit of fucking respect.' His head jerked towards the bar. 'What if Chris'd heard that?'

'Shit. Didn't think, hey.'

'She's not even here, you soft cunt,' the old man said.

'Maybe she's out the back. Maybe she's walking in any minute. Maybe that bird listening to every word we say is her friend, gonna run off and tell it all.' Fast, he looked up, met May's eyes. 'Or maybe she's a cop. Sussing out who's saying what. That it, love?'

May held his gaze for as long as she could bear – two seconds, three – then raised an eyebrow, shrugged and picked up her phone. She scrolled through her emails, picked one at random, began to read it word by word.

'Oi. Asked you a question.'

She didn't look up. 'You did? I'm sorry. What was it again?'

Several beats and then a sinewy, blond-furred forearm on her table, right by her hand. 'You a copper?'

May clicked her phone screen off, smiled up into the tall man's sun-burnt face. 'No.'

'You know Chris?'

'Never met her.'

He narrowed his eyes. 'You work for a paper?'

'Sort of.'

The man tapped his fingers on the table. 'What's that mean? "Sort of"?'

'I'm a reporter for *Australia Today*, it's a digital news site. That's –'

'I know what it is. What d'ya want with Chris?'

'I didn't say I wanted anything with her.'

'Yeah, well, I'm not an idiot and you stick out like dog's balls, you know that?'

She tried another smile. 'Are you always this aggressive with strangers?'

'Yes.' His face didn't crack.

'Wow. Um, OK. Best not be a stranger then.' May pushed her hair behind her shoulder, held out her hand. 'I'm May Norman and I'd love to buy you a drink.'

He stiffened, snatched a look back over his shoulder where his mates were smirking into their beers. 'Nice name, that,' he said, taking her hand, squeezing for a second, releasing. 'I'm Chas.' He smiled, bright and kind. 'And I'm buying.'

He turned on his heel and stalked towards the bar, stopping to murmur into the air between his mates on the way. The redhead cackled loudly and the old bloke slapped him on the back. May fiddled with her phone, reminding herself she was good at this and in control and that getting the story was more important than feminist principles – or no, not even that, it was that feminist principles demanded she tell the truth about this heinous act of violence against a woman and the blokey, misogynist community in which it happened, and if that required flirting with one or more of said blokey, misogynist community members then that was for the greater good.

■   ■   ■

I woke just after nine. Early for me. Straight away I knew Bella was dead and that I had drunk too much and that Nate had gone. I knew everything right away. I lay in bed and lived with it as long as I could and then I got up and went out to the kitchen. My legs and back ached and when I held the kettle under the tap to fill it, I noticed my hands trembling. I felt weak and empty and shaky, but the thought of food made my stomach clench. I had done damage to myself in the night – the drinking and weeping and passing out on the floor – but this was something else. I felt like something had been ripped out of me. Something important. A lung or kidney. Maybe a few ribs. Not my heart. That kept bloody pounding.

I imagined Bella coming in and fussing over me, feeling my forehead, insisting I go back to bed. Instantly, I saw that I had become one of them, the people she cared for, hunched over the table, my hair lank, my dressing gown pilled and faded, my body racked with mysterious pains, my mind not yet gone enough that I didn't understand I was losing it. This is what it's like to be old, I thought.

The kettle clicked off and I shuffled over to the bench to make some coffee. A movement caught my eye and I looked through the window and there she was in her nursing home uniform, looking right at me, hair scraped back so I could see every bit of her unmarked face. Unmarked except for the vertical line between her brows. She was frowning something wicked, must've known I'd been boozing up and carrying on like a kid.

My body understood before my mind. I was still thinking what to say to her to make her stop being angry, when my legs went out from under me. I grabbed at the edge of the sink and slowed my fall but my ankle turned as I hit the ground and I wasted seconds rubbing it. When I pulled myself up, she was gone.

I actually believed for a few seconds that she must be coming around to the front door. I watched the space, waiting for her to fill it and then it wasn't like anything changed, I just knew that she wasn't and wouldn't and hadn't been.

'I'm in shock,' I said out loud, and it must've been true because I heard her voice then, saying, *You're shocking, that's for sure.*

I was making the coffee when my phone rang. Unknown number, but I answered it anyway. I'd never do that now, but this was early days. I didn't get that a bunch of strangers saw themselves as lead characters in a thrilling story which began with the discovery of a pretty dead girl, who happened to have been played by my sister.

Feel free to take that personally, by the way.

Anyway, that morning I answered the phone and a woman said, 'Chris? It's Monica Gordon,' in a tone that made me think I knew her.

'Oh. Hello,' I said, my brain scrambling to place her.

'Oh, Chris, I'm so very sorry for your loss. It's the most terrible thing. I've been beside myself since I heard. How're you holding up?'

'Oh, you know,' I said. I was stumped. She sounded young, but like someone used to being listened to. Someone from the nursing home head office? One of Bella's school friends who'd moved to Sydney for uni?

'I can't imagine. I just can't.' She sighed. 'Look, I hope you don't mind me calling you directly like this, but the police liaison wanted me to go through this whole rigmarole and when I realised you were listed in the phone book I decided it was better if I just looked you up and –'

'Wait, sorry. I'm a bit dazed at the moment. I've lost the thread here. Who are you?'

'Monica Gordon. I'm with Femolition. We're a feminist activist coalition. I'm sure you've seen the interventions we've been making into the public discourse around Bella's death and –'

'The public . . .?'

'Yes. I mean, in the papers and on talkback radio and such?' She sounded less sure now, and younger still. 'You know, there's been all this victim-blaming rhetoric and it's been very important to us at Femolition that we counteract that message. So we've been, you know, stating that case.'

'I'm sorry. I actually have no idea what you're talking about. I haven't been reading the papers or listening to radio. This is the first I've – What do you mean "victim blaming"? Are you with the police?'

A long pause, then her voice back in control. 'Chris, wow, I'm so sorry. It didn't occur to me you wouldn't have been keeping up with public discussion, but of course it should have. I've gone about this the wrong way. I should've said at the outset: I'm on your side, on Bella's side.' A sigh. 'The thing is, some people have been talking about the ways in which Bella may have invited, or contributed to, what happened and we think that's, that's, you know, it's bullshit.' She spat out the word like she meant it. Like I would've said it. 'What we'd like to do, Chris, is honour Bella's memory by holding a march against victim-blaming and violence against women. We want it to be a public demonstration that despite the loudmouths questioning what Bella might have done to put herself in danger, there are many, many more of us who believe all the blame lies with the perpetrators.'

I don't know if I said anything then. I was reeling. I might have said *hmmm*.

'So, we've got it tentatively scheduled for next Wednesday evening – to be confirmed once we hear back about the council permits for the road closures etcetera. And, of course, pending your availability. We were thinking from Belmore Park to Town Hall, ending with some speeches and a candlelight vigil. Of course we'd be honoured if you'd march in the front line, maybe holding a banner or a favourite photograph of Bella, and, if you feel able, to say a few words when we reach Town Hall?'

'Town Hall? Like in Sydney?'

Another pause. 'Perhaps I could come and see you to talk this over? It might be easier in person. I could be there in, I don't know, how long's the drive? Four hours? Five?'

'No, thank you.'

'Um, OK. So, is Wednesday . . .?'

'No. No to all of –' My vision blurred and I had to steady myself with a hand on the sink. 'Just please stop this. It's not . . . Just, please. No.' I hung up. The phone rang almost immediately and I answered and told her to leave me alone and then I turned the damn thing off.

Around 3pm I was in bed staring at the wall when there was a violent thumping on the front door. The thumping stopped and was replaced by Nate hollering my name, so I pulled my bones together and went to let him in.

He stomped in, knocking the front door with one shoulder and me with the other, and then slammed his phone onto the table. 'What kind of a fucking message was that?'

'I'm sorry. I got pissed.'

'Yeah, no shit.'

'I'm sorry.'

He glanced at me, then up over my head, then back at my face. 'Did you sleep at all?'

'Not much.'

He sat down, mumbled something I was glad not to understand. I sat across from him and we were silent like that for a while.

'Listen, I had a big talk with Renee and she –'

'Spare me.'

'Please, babe, listen.' He had my hands again. 'Listen, she

understands. She knows I need to be here with you for now. She's so cut-up about what happened. She *wants* me to be here for you.'

'Saint, isn't she?'

'But listen, she's not comfortable about me staying here. And I think she's right, you know. It's too easy for us – for you and me – to slide back into living like husband and wife. We're both real vulnerable at the moment. It'd be easy to fall into old ways.'

'Are those her words or yours?'

He was cringing inside, I knew, but his face stayed calm. 'Hers, yeah, but I agree.'

'Right.'

'Chris, I love her. You know? And she trusts me. I don't wanna fuck it up.'

'You're a saint too, now.' I pulled away and went to the sink, rinsed his heat from my hands, then scooped cold water from the tap to my mouth, which was like the bottom of cocky's cage. I splashed my face, dried it on a tea towel that smelt like old eggs.

'I'm trying to do the right thing,' he said when I was facing him again.

'Can I remind you I never asked you to come in the first place? And I never asked you to stay over when you did. I never asked you to come back today. So don't look at me like I'm some whiny little homewrecker. I didn't ask you for anything.'

'You didn't have to, babe. You know I –'

'Stay, don't stay, I don't care, but don't tell me about you and Renee and don't act like I owe you anything and don't – please, Jesus, please – don't fucking fight with me. OK?'

He came to me and wrapped me up and that was fine. It was always fine when he did that.

At five o'clock Nate dropped me at work on his way to his mate Melvin's place, where he usually stayed when in town with a tour group. He offered to pick me up when I finished but I told him I'd get a lift.

'Don't you walk,' he said.

'I said I'd get a lift.' I went to open the door but he'd child-locked it. I glared, waited.

'Who you getting a lift with?'

'Someone who cleans their car once in a while,' I said, picking a chip packet out of the garbage pile beneath my feet and tossing it in his lap. He brushed it off without looking, shrugged. I tossed the chip packet back on to his lap, added an empty Coke can and a crumpled McDonald's bag.

'All you're doing is making me hungry. So tell me how you're getting home and I'll let you out and go get myself a feed.'

'I'll get a lift with Suze or Grey. OK?'

'I can come and get you. No trouble.' His hand hovered over the lock on his door.

'Appreciate that, but it's not necessary. You get an early night.'

'Alright. But you call me if you need.' The lock clicked up. I opened the door and I climbed out. 'I'm serious,' he called as I walked away. 'Don't you walk home.'

I waved without looking back. Bella used to rouse on me for walking home, too. But it was ten minutes, fifteen tops. Best way in the world to wind down after a shift. I'd never been threatened, never frightened.

But Nate was right. Those things hadn't just happened to Bella; someone had done them. Someones. Someones who were still walking, driving around free and easy as could be.

But they'd been driving around free and easy every other night I'd walked home. Tonight was no different except now I knew they existed, had seen with my own poor eyes what they could do.

It was a good night behind the bar. We had a busload of footy players from interstate and not a one of them had any idea who I was or what had happened. I still had the odd regular giving me the *poor old thing but what's the goss* look, but mostly I got to talk and laugh and bend for tips like nothing in the world could be wrong.

The busload left for their hotel around midnight leaving only a pack of local boys around the telly up the back and a few long-distance truckies and coach drivers holding up the bar. One of them, Tyler, was a semi-regular sleepover friend of mine. He was one of the younger fellas I'd taken home, only twenty-eight, but with a good decade of life on the road under his belt. Not married, no girlfriend last I knew. Lived with his mum in the outer suburbs of Melbourne. Shy in the bedroom. Shy and grateful. Now that the crowds of footy players were gone I saw he was watching me from his perch near the smoke machine.

'Hey, Chris,' he said when I came close.

'Haven't seen you in here a while. Cut back on the long-hauls, hey?'

'Nah. Been on holidays. Took me mum to Thailand.'

'Good on you! Thailand, hey? Come to mention it, you do have a bit of extra colour in your cheeks.'

He didn't until I said that. He blushed like a bloody virgin.

'Yeah. Just got home yesterday. Straight back on the road today.'

'No rest for the wicked, hey.'

'You'd be one to know.'

'Cheeky bugger,' I said, and swatted him with my towel.

'So, ah, you got a big night planned?'

'Oh,' I said. 'You know . . .' I stopped myself. He obviously didn't know or he wouldn't have asked me. I could tell him and have him be sorry and ashamed and slightly thrilled like the rest of them, or I could let it go, tell him I was tired. Or I could do as I promised

Nate and get a damn lift home and while I was at it avoid being in my goddamn house alone all night.

'Nah, it's cool, I just thought –'

'Actually, my feet are killing me. I'd love a lift home if you don't mind hanging around until close?'

Like I said, he was a shy one when it came down to it. I set him up with a beer while I had a shower, put on my low-cut red nightie and changed the sheets on the bed. Then I called him in and took off his clothes. He was scrawny with a pinched, ferrety face but he had this lovely thick, golden, wavy hair. Such a waste on a bloke, I always thought.

I lay him down and straddled him, hanging my tits in his face, letting him nuzzle and knead me while I reached over to the drawer where I kept my supplies. While he could see nothing but tit I scooped out a bit of lube and stuck it up myself, then unwrapped a condom.

(You're the one wanted to know how I could jump back in the sack so soon. This is how. Don't ask if you don't want to bloody know.)

I readied myself then sat up straight. I rolled the condom on him as he continued kneading my breasts. He let go for a second when I stuck his dick in but then grabbed hold again. Normally I'd've played with him a little, tried to give good value, but I was so damn tired and sad I couldn't bear to draw it out any longer. I held his hands down and lay almost flat so my boobs would slap his face with each thrust. Slap slap slap slap and – boom – he bucked up and moaned, sank back down, sighed.

I kissed his forehead, carefully removed the condom and went to the bathroom to chuck it out and clean myself up. When I got back he'd snuggled deep under the covers. I switched out the light and climbed in next to him, happy to feel his weight and warmth next to me after the lonely, drunken horror of last night.

'That was awesome,' he said, resting a hand on my chest. 'Like, so much better than any of the Thai girls.'

'Yeah? I've heard they're pretty good over there.'

'They're alright. They try hard, but they don't have these, do they?' He honked my left breast and giggled. 'Some of them have big ones, but they're fake. No movement, you know? It's like, come *on*, give me some jiggle.'

I imagined some tight-bodied eighteen-year-old Thai girl bouncing up and down while he lay underneath slapping her hard, expensive tits. If I could've turned my flesh to stone I would've right then.

'And when it's over, it's over, you know. It's in-out, in-out and then get dressed and piss off. I'd be like, "Where's the fire, love?" No wind-down, no cuddles.' He squeezed again.

'Hmm. Most blokes would want that, I reckon. I think you're the only one I know who gets chatty after.'

'Yeah, well, I'm just glad you let me come over, that's all. I really appreciate it, Chris.'

'OK, you big sweetie. Let's get some sleep, hey?'

'Alright. I just wanted you to know that I appreciate you doing this. Especially with what happened to your sister and everything.'

If I could turn to stone or ice or ash . . . If I could become fire . . . I lay and stared and stared at the wall until the bruise came and I listened to him snore and wished ugly death on him and me and the whole world and the bruise seemed to promise I would have it, have all the ugly death I have ever wished for and then some.

I must have dropped off to sleep because when I woke he was gone and there were two hundred-dollar notes on my bedside table.

■ ■ ■

AustraliaToday.com

LOCALS UNITED IN DISBELIEF OVER 'POOR BELLA'

May Norman
9 April 2015

People all over Australia are talking about the murder of 25-year-old Bella Michaels, but here in her home town the 'm' word is never used. It's 'the tragedy', 'this terrible thing' or, simply, 'poor Bella'.

'Poor Bella . . . It beggars belief,' says 76-year-old retired carpenter John Highsmith. 'I've lived here my entire life and never in my worst nightmares would I have thought something like this was possible.'

The message is echoed by Highsmith's 45-year-old daughter Melanie. 'It's like a thing that happens on TV or in movies. Not here. I haven't slept properly since I heard. I keep checking the doors and windows. Before last week I never even bothered to lock them.'

While all the locals express shock at 'this terrible thing', those who knew Bella personally are battling grief along with their disbelief. A popular aged-care worker and community volunteer, Bella Michaels was born in the Strathdee hospital, attended the local public primary and high schools and, except for eighteen months in Sydney in her early twenties, lived and worked in the centre of town her entire adult life.

'I've known her since she was a baby,' said a neighbour of Bella's late mother, who asked that his name not be published. 'The family had its troubles, but Bella was such a good girl, just an absolute ray of sunshine.'

The 'troubles' the resident referred to include a mother who struggled with alcoholism and gambling from her teens until her death from cancer five years ago. Bella's father left when she was barely two and, according to the neighbour, her mother was involved with a succession of men, at least one of whom was physically abusive.

Bella's half-sister, Chris Rogers, 37, has refused to speak to the media since breaking down at a press conference yesterday. Her ex-husband, Nate Cartwright of Sydney, has reportedly returned to Strathdee and is staying with Ms Rogers in her home a ten-minute drive from where her sister's body was discovered.

Richard Grey, owner and manager of the Royal Hotel, where Ms Rogers has worked for the past decade, said the relationship between the two women was 'watertight. Young Bella was the only person in the world who Chris'd listen to. You'd laugh if you saw it. Chris can stare down a 200-pound drunken truckie without blinking, but if little Bella went crook at her she'd be a puddle.'

'They always looked after each other,' the former neighbour says. 'Sometimes it was Chris being the big sister and sometimes it was Bella, because though she was young, she was such a nurturer, you know. They really were the world to each other. I worry terribly about Chris now.'

The police are revealing very little information to the public at this stage, confirming only that the cause of death was blood loss and that sexual assault took place prior to death. Meanwhile, local gossip and speculation are spreading like the wildfire that took out 8,000 hectares just east of here two summers ago. There are rumours of torture and mutilation. Some of the descriptions seem to have been taken from the most extreme of Hollywood horror films. A drinker at the Royal, when asked what he thought had happened to Bella Michaels, matter-of-factly painted a nightmarish scenario involving dozens of separate, individually described acts of brutality.

'It's terrible, the talk you hear,' Mr Grey said from behind the bar where much of it is taking place. 'Truth is, we don't know what happened exactly. We know it was bloody terrible, but. We know she suffered. Yeah. There's no dodging that.'

Anyone with information is asked to call Crime Stoppers or the Strathdee police.

Friday
10
April

Three messages from Monica Gordon when I turned my phone on in the morning after Tyler left. I tried to find the card Sally Perkins had given me on that first day but couldn't. I called the station instead and they put me through to Brandis, who sounded like my call was the best thing that had ever happened to him.

'Chris, Chris, good to hear from you, mate. What's up?'

'Some woman called me about a march in Sydney. For Bella?'

'Yeah. Heard something about that. So you're not involved with it, hey?'

'You need to stop it.'

'Not up to us to stop. It's a Sydney thing. If they've got permission –'

'They don't. I haven't given permission for anything.'

'Permission from the city, I meant. To hold a public demonstration. They don't need permission from you.'

'I'm the next of kin.'

'Chris, mate, this is a thing that happens around high-profile cases. All kinds of people – lobbyists, crazies, nasties, well-meaning idiots – they try and get involved, make it about them, about their cause. Best to stay out of it, leave them to it. Go about mourning Bella in private.'

'Leave them to it.'

'Best thing. And you should think about changing your number, getting an unlisted. Don't make it so easy for them to get to you. If they start getting too obnoxious, coming around to your place or work or whatever, then give us a call and we'll send a uniform to shoo 'em away.'

'You think people will come to my work?'

'Not people: reporters. Speaking of, leave the TV off for the next little while, hey? Don't read the papers or the internet. All that shit out there, it's got nothing to do with anything. Real breakthroughs, real developments, you'll hear from me, yeah?'

'So are there any? Developments?'

'Like I said, you'll hear from me when there are.'

'Right. So I'm meant to shut myself off from the world, sit here waiting for you to call?'

'We're doing everything we can, Chris. Now, I gotta go, but you make sure you call us with your new number, yeah?'

'OK'

'OK. Take care now.'

I went straight across to Lisa's and asked if I could use her computer. I'd done this plenty of times in the past, but now she said, 'Oh, I don't think that's a great idea, hon.'

I played the victim card, I don't mind admitting, told her I needed to email some long-distance relations whose phone numbers I didn't have and that I needed to do some online banking because I couldn't cope with going into town. Both of these things were true, I realised as I said them. I also realised I could just buy a computer of my own with some of the money I'd put away for me and Bella. But that would come later. Now, I needed to know why Brandis was so keen for me to stay away from the news.

Lisa left me alone with the computer while she made the apparently legally-required-for-grieving-relatives cup of tea. I started typing Bella's name into the search bar and before I could finish the auto-fill function suggested:

Bella Michaels murder
Bella Michaels photos
Bella Michaels raped

I clicked on the first search result, a newspaper opinion piece. Bella was a reminder, the first paragraph declared, that none of us were safe. I returned to the search results, opened a Facebook page called RIP BELLA MICHAELS. There I saw my own grinning mug, pressed against Bella's flushed, giggling one. Bella's eighteenth. Her boyfriend at the time, a shy, goofy plumber's apprentice whose name I've forgotten, was on the other side of her, whispering something into her ear. On my left was Mum, smiling in that closed-mouth way that made everybody think she was annoyed or anxious when really she was just embarrassed of her crooked front teeth, and beside her, my cousin Kim, who I hadn't seen since the night the pic was taken.

Bella Michaels my darling cousin and one of my closest friends was taken from this world by the actions of an unknown monster. This page is a tribute to this beautiful soul who is now an angel in heaven. Please 'like' to show you care and share to help get the word out about this senseless tragedy.
This message, written by Kim, had been 'liked' three thousand and

ninety-seven times. The page itself was being followed by seven thousand and forty-five people. I scanned down:

I never met Bella but feel as though I've lost a sister. RIP angel

Bella you were too beautiful for this world.

RIP Bella your death won't be in vain it will always be a lesson to young girls out alone

YOUR KILLER WILL PAY FOR WHAT WAS DONE TO YOU. HOWEVER LONG IT TAKES WE WILL NEVER FORGET

Underneath that last one, was a long comments thread:

Violence begets violence

If I get my hands on the fucking animal who did this then he will know what violence is

Ive been reading all the reports and does anyone else think its a bit sus that there were no signs of struggle near her car??? Like maybe she willingly went? I won't say who told me but someone who knows says that she had a reputation for being 'easy' so maybe the police should consider that she wasn't abducted from the car park??? Of course what happened to her later is still a terrible crime and whoever did it should be punished but worth asking if this was a 'crime of passion' rather than random abduction.

Fuck you and your fucking victim-blaming

Not victim-blaming, just putting it out there as its important to get facts right in such cases. Lots of females are scared of being grabbed but maybe scared for no reason as long as they don't go climbing into cars???

You are talking shit mate and anyway Bella was not easy ask anyone who actually knew her she was a VERY MORAL PERSON

'Oh, honey,' Lisa clattered a mug down on a side table and hugged my shoulders. 'This is what I was worried about. You can't be reading this stuff. It's ridiculous, clueless nonsense. These people are –'

'Family,' I said. 'One of them, anyway. Goddamn cousin who hardly even ever saw her.'

Lisa reached past me and clicked the window closed. 'Family or not, they're idiots and what they have to say is irrelevant. Meaningless.'

I felt I should open the window back up and type some furious replies but all the air, all the fight had gone out of me. I took the tea Lisa slid into my hand and sipped. It tasted like parsley steeped in dishwater.

'It's a special blend I made for you. Soothing. I was going to bring a tin of it over this arvo.'

I couldn't even say thanks, I just kept sipping the foul stuff so she'd know I appreciated her.

After a few minutes she said, 'Listen, there was a reporter here yesterday. Apparently she'd tried her luck at your place and Nate told her where to go in no uncertain terms. Little miss came straight across here, as if I'd have any sympathy! I sent her packing, too, but you should know that she went on door-knocking right along the street. I watched best I could from my window but I had a big cook going and so kept losing sight of her. I think she got inside at Carrie's, maybe at old Frank's place, too. I'm sure they didn't say

95

anything you need to worry about, but just thought you should be aware, you know, aware that these people are out here desperate for any little bit of info.'

'What . . .' I cleared herbal moss from my throat and Lisa rubbed the top of my back. 'What could anyone tell her anyway? Bella hasn't even lived here for years.'

'I suspect that's all it'd be, honey. Reminiscing about what a sweetie she was. How she used to sing so loud when she was gardening out the front that you could hear her from the top of the street if you had your car window down and the radio off. How she'd offer to walk everyone's dogs and leave out little treats for all the cats because you, you mean old cow, wouldn't let her have a pet.' She hugged my shoulders again. 'There's only nice stuff to remember about Bella. How many people can you say that about, eh?'

'Some woman rang,' I told her. 'Said she's planning a parade or something. For Bella. I didn't know what to say. It seems so . . . mental.'

'People feel very bad. They don't know what to do.'

'That must be hard for them.'

'Oh, honey. Listen, is Nate at home – at your place, I mean?'

'No. He's staying at Mel's. He said he'd come over late morning. What is it now?'

'Just after ten. How's about I give him a call, hey? Tell him to get his lovely bum in gear?'

'No,' I told her, getting up to leave. 'Can't have him thinking I can't go a couple of hours without him.'

'You're too independent for your own good, Chris. It's OK to lean on people during hard times.'

'I've leant all over you just now, haven't I?'

'Any time, honey. I mean it.'

I knew she did. I felt her eyes on me as I crossed the street and unlocked my front door. God bless sweet neighbours, hey? Though the know-better bitch went ahead and called Nate as soon as I left. He came roaring up twenty minutes later, full of concern and guilt. Fuller than usual. Overfull.

'Lisa said you were distraught. Why didn't you call me?'

'Lisa's a drama queen. I wasn't distraught. I was annoyed.' I told him about the phone call and the Facebook page. He nodded along like he knew it all already. Said he'd been keeping an eye on all that, that I didn't have to worry.

'Now, tell me honestly, how are you? How did you sleep last night?'

'Fine,' I told him, thinking of Tyler and the black hate of the wall bruise. 'I had company, actually, so I was good.'

I've never enjoyed hurting him, yet it was one of the few things I was great at and so I was rarely able to stop myself when the opportunity arose.

After he left there were these weird convulsions in my throat. Made me want to choke myself. I wandered around the house coughing and swallowing for a while then picked up a book one of the neighbours had dropped off the day after Bella was found. *An Unnatural Loss*. It was for parents who'd lost a child. I didn't try to read it, just hugged it to me, tried to feel the warmth I'd got from this woman, Edie, when she dropped it by, held my hands, told me she knew Bella wasn't my daughter but that she thought of her that way. Every time she saw Bella coming and going she thought, There's Chris's girl. Anyway, she said, she knew I'd grieve hard, as hard as any mother who'd lost her child. I liked it that she said that, this woman, mother and grandmother herself, thinking of me – of us – that way. But I don't know if she's right. I'm not a mum, can't know what that feels like. They say it feels like nothing else, don't they? That you can't understand love until you've held your own baby in your arms. I don't know, I don't know, I can't. And anyway, Bella was more parent to me than I ever was to her. Practically speaking. But I loved her fiercely, you know? It sounds dumb to say. We loved each other fiercely. If there's a love greater than what I had for her then I'm happy I never had a baby of my own because I couldn't take it. Oh, the love I could take, who couldn't? The love is easy. But this is the flipside, isn't it? Bigger than this I couldn't take. Don't even know if I can take this, to be honest. The loss of her is already too much and then there's the other thing – the end of being loved in the way only my sister could love me. What I feel for her survives and that hurts like battery acid every minute, but worse is that what she felt for me died with her. I will never be loved like that again.

Anyway, I was standing in the living room sort of hugging the book, thinking all this, when everything went black. I dropped the book, froze, trying to figure out what had happened. Even with the lights off and the curtains closed that room gets a good bit of light on a sunny afternoon like this one. I held my hand in front of my face and couldn't see it.

Something moved behind me. The rasp of a shoe against carpet. I spun to face it, felt hot breath on my face, sprung backwards, slamming into the wall. I lashed out with both arms, but there was nothing there. I looked and looked, straining my eyes as though darkness could be overcome by effort.

I blinked and it was light again and everything just as it had been, except my pulse was going like the clappers and the back of my head hurt where I'd hit the wall. I wanted so badly to call Nate to come sit with me awhile. Instead I called Melvin and asked him if he could come and have a look at my wiring some time soon. I could hear Nate in the background asking if I was alright and so I waited until the very last moment to leave for work, more than half expecting that Nate'd come round, or at least call to check on me, but he never did.

■ ■ ■

The good thing about a town like Strathdee was that the phone directory was slim, very few people were unlisted, and in the rare case you couldn't find the person you were after you could bet you'd only need to ask two or three not-quite random people – a taxi driver, a supermarket manager and a retired school teacher, in this case – and you had the address plus a fairly detailed life history of the person you were looking for.

Melvin and Julie Atkins, the friends Nate Cartwright sometimes stayed with in town, lived in a neat brick three-bedroom behind the hospital. May knew from her informants that Melvin would likely be at work – he was one of only two electricians left in town and so was always busy – but that Julie, who worked nights at the TAB, would probably be home.

Julie answered the door before the bell had finished its electronic jingle. She was a solid block of a woman, a foot taller and at least twice the weight of May, with a smooth, wide face and close-cropped, bleached hair.

'Good morning. My name is May Norman. I'm –'

'A newspaper writer from Sydney, I know. I've just had Cheryl Sands on the phone blabbering apologies about having given out my address.'

'I hope you don't mind, I –'

'Nah, it's fine. Come in, come in. I've just made a cuppa, d'ya want one?'

'No, thanks.'

Julie's living room reminded May of her grandmother's place in Blacktown. Spotless peach carpet, grey fake-leather sofa, glass coffee table bearing a weekly gossip magazine and a romance novel, mantelpiece holding a series of photos in matching gold-coloured frames and a cross-stitch of the serenity prayer. Julie drank her tea from a mug saying SAVE A FUSE, BLOW AN ELECTRICIAN.

'I should tell you that I didn't know Bella very well. We'd say hi if we saw each other at the shops but other than that . . .' She shrugged, smiled apologetically.

'I was hoping you could tell me about Nate Cartwright, actually.'

Julie's smile slackened a little, but her tone remained light. 'Not much to know about Nate. What you see is what you get.'

'Was he close to Bella?'

She sighed, put her mug down on the table. 'He was once. She lived with him and Chris for a while. But since he moved up to Sydney, he hasn't been great at keeping in touch. I mean, we see him when he passes through but don't hear much in between.'

'Why did he leave town? Was it a bad breakup?'

'Look, I hope this doesn't sound rude, but I don't think that's really anyone's business.' She turned her mug around in her hand.

'I get that, it's just . . . The news has been full of stories about Bella's death, and that's fair enough, I mean, it was terrible and people want to know the details, want to understand, but I feel that what's been lost in all this is the story of her *life*. Who she was before she was turned into news.' May noticed Julie's eyes tearing up; she leant forward, spoke softly. 'And who she was, I think, was a woman who cared about her family and friends very much. And from what I can tell she counted Nate in that group, but I also understand it was complicated because of his relationship with Chris. So, I'm trying to get a picture – a true, full picture – of who she loved, who loved her and –'

'OK, yeah, yeah, look, I can tell you some stuff, but I'm not going to, you know, invade his privacy or anything.'

'Julie, it's no secret that he and Chris have a continuing

relationship. I mean, he's hardly left her side since they found Bella, but he refuses to speak to the media – which I respect, I understand – but rightly or wrongly, it does give the impression that he's got something to hide, you know?'

Julie shook her head, smiling with a kind of desperation that made May want to tell her to stop being so fucking accommodating. People-pleasers made May's job so easy and her spirit so tired.

'It's not a matter of hiding anything. It's a very, very hard time. None of us can take it in, what happened. Me, as soon as I even start to really think about it my mind kind of shoots off in another direction, because it's just too much. And if I feel like that, then imagine what Chris is going through. And you know, if Chris is suffering then Nate will be ...' Her smile dropped, then came back smaller, less pleading. 'You're right about him and Chris, you know, it's so complicated. I mean, the way those two were together, geez, nearly ruined my marriage. Like, you know all that stuff you believe about love when you're eighteen and then by the time you're twenty-five you realise it's total crap? Like, you accept that real love – long term and that – well, it's not going to be a thrill a minute, it's not going to be constant bliss. Not that I don't love Melvin, but he's not exactly Christian Grey, if you get what I mean. I accepted that, thought, well, this is what real love is. Not a thrill a minute but nice all the same.' She shrugged. 'But then those two hooked up and suddenly it seemed I was wrong about what was possible. I felt ripped off. Like I'd settled. I mean, seriously, you never saw a couple so perfect together. Hands all over the place like teenagers, but in between that you'd see them talking or listening to the other one talk to someone else and you could just see how much they liked each other. I was happy for 'em – I mean, I love Nate like a brother – but geez I was jealous, I tell you what.'

'So what went wrong?'

Julie shook her head. 'Private stuff. Stuff that's none of my business let alone yours. I can say, though, it made me appreciate what me and Mel have. Calm, no drama.' She looked up at the mantelpiece, seemed to remember something, turned back to May. 'Bloody hell, I can go on with some rubbish! Look, none of what I've said has anything to do with anything. What's important – I mean, if you're going to write about any of this – what's important is that Nate and Chris are very good friends, always have been from day one. Things didn't work out with the marriage and that's their business, but there's no way that Nate wouldn't support Chris through this. Not being able to stay married doesn't mean the bond between them is gone. I can't imagine him not being there for her right now. And, yeah, he loved Bella. He really did.'

The interview with Julie had given May some useful colour and phone numbers for several of Nate's local mates. It had also poked at her pain so acutely that she had to waste an hour buying, cooking and eating five packets of two-minute noodles smothered in processed cheese slices and then emptying her guts into the hotel toilet. It was, like smoking, a disgusting habit that she thought she'd ditched when she finished uni but which had reasserted itself in the past week. So there was another thing to hate Craig for: her regression into a pathetic nineteen-year-old stinking of vomit and fags.

She brushed her teeth then sat on the bed and listened back to the interview. *That stuff you believe about love when you're eighteen and then by the time you're twenty-five you realise it's total crap?* Such grief and shame at those words. Such fury. Thirty years old and she'd imagined herself cynical and street-smart yet had believed entirely in the idea that Craig was her everything and she was his and that nothing could part them.

They'd met at a funeral of all places. She'd just completed a profile piece about the old poet who'd passed; Craig was a mate of the poet's grandson. Like in a cheesy romance novel their eyes met across the room and it was all May could do to stay in her seat for the rest of the service. She searched for him in the milling crowd outside the chapel, had a second to take all of him in – young, lean, snake-hipped, expensive grey pants worn too low – before he saw her looking, closed the space between them. Within an hour of old Charlie's body being lowered into the ground they were fucking in May's entry hall.

They swapped scraps of their lives between breaths between kisses between violent bucking between sated naps. He worked at the council, in records, which wasn't what he cared about but was the best job he could get around here with his degree, which was in history, plus it was undemanding and so gave him lots of time and access to do what he was really interested in which was research his family – Oh! Family history interested her, too; in fact, she'd considered studying history but had decided on journalism because it seemed to offer better prospects but ten years later here she is still doing – Ten years? So she was . . .? Huh, same age as him, almost to the day, born in the same hospital, even. If his family hadn't moved north when he was three they might well have gone to kindergarten and primary and high school together. They might have been lifelong friends by now, childhood sweethearts married young, a houseful of kids together before they turned twenty-five. But as it happened he'd lived in Cairns all those years and only returned here five years ago because his wife got a job working at – Yeah, a wife. And kids, three of them if she could believe it, which she could, because of all the things that had happened to her this day the existence of three children was the least remarkable of all. But she was worried, because she just assumed – No, no, it's his fault, he should've said something but the energy between them was so – I know, I know, it's just I thought – He kissed her lips, her forehead, her lips again.

It's OK it's OK, it's OK. What had happened was a once-in-a-lifetime, and even then only if you're lucky, kind of thing. Love at first sight! They laughed; such a silly phrase but it's what it was. If he'd known today was coming – that she was coming – he wouldn't have ever married, but how could he know? And now, she said, now we'll just have to deal with it the best we can, with as little hurt as possible, and he nodded, kissed her until she couldn't breathe, and she thought how it would have seemed to her, mere hours ago, a ridiculously, embarrassingly, presumptuous thing to assume that a man whose surname she didn't know would leave his marriage and children for her, and yet as it happened it was completely and utterly obvious. Of course he would. Of course the two of them, May and Craig, were together and it was serious. It didn't need to be said.

May glared at her un-ringing phone. What a fucking idiot child she had been.

She made a cup of tea to help soothe her raw throat and began to phone the contacts Julie had given her. On call number three she hit pay dirt.

■ ■ ■

BELLA'S BROTHER-IN-LAW A 'CRIMINALLY VIOLENT MAN'

May Norman
10 April 2015

As Strathdee police continue to search for answers on who might have abducted, raped and murdered 25-year-old aged-care worker Bella Michaels, it has emerged that the deceased's brother-in-law, Nate Cartwright, 40, has a history of violence towards women.

In 2001 Cartwright was sentenced to twelve months in prison following a cowardly attack on his then girlfriend Liza Townsend. Court records show that Cartwright punched the woman, who was half his height and weighed a mere 50 kilograms, breaking her nose and causing a concussion which required hospitalisation.

Cartwright's defence claimed that Townsend had attacked first, slashing his chest with a broken bottle. The court accepted this as a mitigating factor and Cartwright was only required to serve one month of his sentence in prison, with the rest served as home detention.

Julie Atkins, a close friend of Cartwright, spoke yesterday about the continued relationship between her friend and Ms Michaels' sister, Chris Rogers. 'Not being able to stay married doesn't mean the bond between them is gone. I can't imagine him not being there for her right now,' she said, though she refused to comment on just why the two were 'unable to stay married'.

Meanwhile, two different sources close to Bella Michaels' family have alleged that Cartwright assaulted Ms Rogers on at least one occasion. *AustraliaToday* has been unable to confirm these allegations.

According to Monica Gordon of the women's rights activist group Femolition, 'most women who are murdered die at the hands of someone they know well and most of those killers have a history of violence. Of course Mr Cartwright has the presumption of innocence in the case of Bella, but that doesn't change the fact that he is, by definition, a criminally violent man. One hopes the Strathdee police are taking the potential threat this man may pose to Chris Rogers and to other women in the community very seriously.'

Strathdee police confirmed that they have interviewed Cartwright in relation to his former sister-in-law's death, but said that he is not considered a suspect. Cartwright and Rogers were contacted by *Australia Today*, but declined to comment.

Saturday
11
April

'Babe, listen.'

'What I usually do when I pick up the phone.'

'Yeah, serious though. You at home?'

'It's six in the morning.'

A breath. 'So thing on the radio just now. They've found a body.'

'A body.'

'A woman's body. They're not saying if –'

'Like Bella, you mean?'

'They're not saying. Could be nothing to do with –'

'Oh, fuck. Nate. Fuck.'

'– Bella. I just thought . . . You haven't heard from the cops?'

'I haven't heard anything. Jesus, Nate. They've done it again, haven't they? The fucking cops have been pissing around asking about bloody bullshit nothing shit and meanwhile these things have been out there and they've –'

'Babe, please. Take a breath. We don't know. We don't know

anything. Just . . . Listen, I had to drive up to Sydney late last night, I'm still here, but I'll be back in Strathdee by this arvo. Can you maybe head over to Lisa's or something until then? Wait for the police to call. If it's anything to do with Bel they'll call, otherwise, try not to worry about it.'

I stared at the wall, wishing for the dark spot. I don't know why. I stared and then squeezed my eyes closed, popped them open. Nothing nothing nothing.

'Chris? You right, babe? Come on, you right?'

'Yep.'

'You sure now?'

'Right as rain. See you later, hey?'

My phone rang again as soon as I hung up. Unknown number. I ignored it, dialled Detective Brandis. Went through to voicemail. I showered, stood naked in front of my wardrobe for so long that when I snapped out of it I was dry. I dressed in my gym gear and sneakers and headed out. Lisa was at her window; she did a double take and then waved. I waved back, kept walking, all brisk and focused like. I imagined her feeling pleased I was getting some exercise.

The walk to the cop shop was just under half an hour. I kept expecting to be stopped along the way, but either no one noticed me or they saw the look on my face, which I reckon must've been as grim a picture as anyone'd ever seen, and let me be. I walked fast, had to admit it felt good. Better than curling myself around my pillow and staring at the wall. Better than bouncing on top of that Tyler shithead. Almost as good as bourbon. Almost as good as pressing my back against Nate's chest and feeling him mould himself around me.

Out front of the station the reporter from the Wagga TV news and a couple of newspaper types were clustered together smoking and drinking coffee. They all seemed to spot me at the same time, dropped their smokes and cups, slung cameras and recorders out of nowhere as they jogged towards me.

'No.' I kept walking, bumping elbows and hips and feet with the fuckers. 'No,' I said again and pushed through the station doors, letting them swing shut behind me. Inside, I leant against the wall and tried to catch my breath. Sally Perkins spotted me and called out to someone behind her. It took seconds before Brandis's sidekick was closing his cold dry hand on my sweaty forearm, leading me through to the room with the whiteboards and chairs and pot plants.

'Chris, mate, what's happening? You look a little – Alrighty, let's get you sat down, eh? That's the way. Now, tell me what's this about? Did you think of something –'

'They've done it again, haven't they?'

'Sorry, mate. Not sure what you're –'

'Another woman, killed like Bella.'

He screwed up his brow, scratched his head. Every fucking move the man made was straight out of the picture book my cousin used to teach her autistic son how to identify emotions. 'Chris, if you know something about –'

'She's talking about Miller.'

The dickhead turned towards the woman who'd spoken. 'What's that got to do –'

'Fucking Roddro talking about it on his show this morning. Implying it's related.'

'Why the fuck would he do that?'

The woman put down the coffee pot she'd been rinsing, dragged a chair from behind a nearby desk and sat with her knees almost touching mine. She was in her late forties, dressed in a grey pants suit that looked as if it'd feel like clouds. Best thing about her was that she was almost blocking the dickhead cop from my view entirely.

'Miss Rogers, I'm Detective Sergeant Belinda Mancini. I'm over from Wagga on a matter unrelated to your sister's case, but I have been following it and I want to tell you how sorry I am for your loss.'

'Thank you.'

'What's happened is that we have unfortunately had a murder overnight, but there's no connection whatsoever with your sister. We know this for certain, but we can't release any of the info to the public yet and so idiots like Roddro on 2SB are filling in the gaps for themselves and stirring up all this fear and panic and, for you –' she touched my hand '– real distress. I'm so sorry about that.'

'How do you know for certain? I mean, another woman murdered this close to –'

'We can't tell you that for the same reason we can't release to the public.' The boofhead scooted forward in his chair, his big legs crowding into the space between Belinda and me. 'You've just gotta trust us on this one. It's nothing to do with your sister.'

'OK, so, have you . . . Is there anything, have you found anything about –'

'You know we're working hard on it, Chris.'

'You need to work harder! Someone else could be –'

'Chris, mate, I gotta go. Brandis is waiting for me. We'll be in touch when there's something to be in touch about, alright? Belinda, get her a cuppa or something and make sure she's got a way to get out of here without those maggots out the front grabbing her?'

'I don't want a cuppa,' I told Belinda. 'I just want to know how you can be sure that this girl wasn't – by the same – because they're still out there, they're still –'

'Miss Rogers.' She squeezed my hand and leant in very close. 'Between us, right? We know who killed this woman last night. We know this but haven't finished gathering the evidence we need to arrest him so we can't say anything.'

'But what if it was – was she –'

'Nothing like Bella. This was . . .' She closed her eyes, looked back into mine with a look of such deep sorrow I felt my chest split open.

'Fast,' I finished for her.

She nodded. 'I'm sorry.'

'I know. Thank you.'

Young Matt offered to drive me home and I accepted but soon as I got in the car with him I started shaking like I did on that first day, so I told him I felt like walking. He drove until we were clear of the media mob and then let me out.

I'd only been going a couple of minutes when an Avis rental car pulled up beside me.

'Ms Rogers, Joel Frankle from –'

'No,' I said and kept walking.

The bastard parked right there in the bus lane, came after me on foot. 'Ms Rogers, can I talk to you for a moment about your relationship with Nate Cartwright?'

I kept walking.

He trotted alongside me, smelling like sweat and tomato sauce. His recorder hovered near my chin. 'Given his history of violence, aren't you concerned that –'

'I'm not giving interviews.'

'Did Nate Cartwright have something to do with Bella's death?'

Like a punch in the stomach, it was, but I didn't stumble or gasp or even look at the grub.

'Are you covering for him, Ms Rogers?'

'Fuck off,' I managed to say.

'I'm only trying to –'

'Fuck off or I'll call the cops, charge you with goddamn harassment.'

He let out a little laugh, said something about not being my enemy, but he turned and headed away from me.

I went straight to Lisa, asked her if she knew what the dickhead had been on about. She ducked and dodged a bit but then gave in and showed me the *Australia Today* article about Nate.

Look, yes, two years before I met him, Nate spent a month in jail for breaking his girlfriend's nose. He would have spent longer, but the fact she'd first slashed his chest with a broken bottle meant the judge went easier on him. Nate got sober right after it happened and stayed that way for almost six years. He fell off the wagon on my thirtieth birthday when I begged him to have a glass of champers to celebrate with me. He said no a few times and I nagged and sulked and then he took a sip and then knocked back the glass. He whooped and kissed me and we finished that bottle and then bought another and then started on the bourbon. We had a blinder of a night. Drinking and laughing and fucking and then drinking some more. Next day I was so hungover I could barely open my eyes, but when I did I saw in his face that he would never forgive me and he never really has.

That we lasted as long as we did after that is testament to what a wonderful bloody man he is. He's hurt me like I never thought possible, but he's the best of men, best of people, he really is. He tried hard to forgive me for getting him on the booze again. Tried hard to take responsibility for himself even as I continued encouraging him to drink with me each night. And when he decided to get sober again he spent months trying to talk me into doing it with him. He tried so hard. And I tried just as hard to keep him drunk. I don't know why. I suppose I was scared of losing him, but I had no reason to think that's what would happen if he sobered up again. He'd fallen for and married me while straight, after all.

In the end, he got into a fight outside the pub after Grey kicked him out for bothering me when I was working. When I finished up and came out he punched me in the face, and when a bloke passing by told him to lay off, Nate knocked him over and then kicked him in the guts a few times before I managed to get him to stop. The bloke didn't press charges, thank Christ, although the police wanted him to. Wanted me to as well, but I couldn't. I'd asked for it, really. Not the punch, but the man who'd thrown it. I'd egged him on for years.

We had a bad few days after that. Screaming and hating at each other. I told him if he hit me again I'd send him back to jail. He believed me, even though I'm not sure myself I would've done it. But he believed I would and that was enough. He told me he needed to get sober again no matter what. I told him he was pathetic, that most men didn't use booze as an excuse for belting women. I accused him of being weak, compared him to the winos who got maggoted every night down at the footy oval. Broken, cowardly, weak losers who'd been barred from all the pubs 'cause they couldn't enjoy a couple of drinks without turning into whiny, self-pitying thugs.

Nate listened to all that and then he told me he loved me and packed his stuff and left.

■   ■   ■

LOCAL WOMAN VICTIM OF DOMESTIC DISPUTE

May Norman
11 April 2015

Police have this afternoon confirmed that the husband of Tegan Miller, 22, who was found dead in a Strathdee shopping centre dumpster, has confessed to her murder.

Mrs Miller had been shot in the back of the head before being placed in the dumpster outside StrathTown on Elizabeth Street, where a security guard found her late Friday night.

The local rumour mill churned with speculation that the killer or killers of Bella Michaels may have struck again, but all such talk stopped with the arrest of 24-year-old Bradley Miller.

The Millers had been married for three years and, according to a source close to Mrs Miller, had a 'tempestuous' relationship. 'They were always fighting, making up, fighting again. But arguing, not physical fighting, far as I knew. I never would have thought him capable of this. He loved her so much,' said the friend, who asked not to be named.

Strathdee police have confirmed that Mr Miller was suffering from self-inflicted knife wounds when arrested. He is under police guard at Strathdee Hospital until he is well enough to be transferred to Wagga Wagga for a court hearing.

Sunday
12
April

I woke at dawn the next morning, feeling desperate to get out of the house. Me, who only ever sees the sunrise from the other side if I can help it. I felt energised but not in a healthy, just-had-a-solid-eight-hours-then-juice-and-cornflakes way. I was nervy, speedy. I wondered if it was some weird wearing-off effect of Nate's tablets since I'd not taken them the night before. Whatever it was, I couldn't stay in bed. That's not a figure of speech, understand; I literally could not stay there. My legs – no, that's not right – my innards were coursing with electricity.

I swear, it was like in this movie I watched with Carrie's kids one night where this evil future government uses mind control to turn all the incredibly hot teenagers into soldiers. I was like those young babes, except I dressed in a tracksuit instead of combat gear and grabbed my wallet instead of a weapon. And off I went, striding out into the morning, seeing my street, my neighbourhood in a light I'd only ever seen drunk out of my mind at the tail end of a big night.

Telling you now, it's like telling a dream. I wasn't in my right mind. I noticed everything. The tips of the grass were wet. Birds cawed and sang. I counted three trucks going by on the highway, four cars moving in nearby streets. One street over from mine, a dog barked and barked, and as I got closer I heard the rooster it was barking at.

I walked to the newsagency on John Street and bought a copy of the local rag. The face of the girl from the bakery on Elizabeth Street took up nearly the whole front page. Mrs Chin held my hand for a long while when she gave me my change and her eyes filled with tears. Normally that might've made me tear up too, but, like I said, I wasn't myself.

At home I spread the paper out and started to read, but the words faded off the page faster than I could get to them so by the time I was at the third paragraph there was nothing but pale grey smudges in neat little lines.

I see that look you're giving me, but I'm just saying it like it happened.

I closed my eyes and opened them again. Closed the paper and opened it again. I turned the page and read about Thursday's council meeting and a break-in at the Catholic school just fine. I turned back to the front page and watched as the girl's face lost its vibrant colour and then any colour and then its shape. I watched her fade until I felt so drowsy I couldn't any more. I stripped off and climbed into bed and slept soundly until Nate showed up around eleven.

He told me off for buying the paper, said it could do nothing but upset me right now. I asked if he'd read it and he had.

'Yeah, that poor girl. Bad shit, babe. Bad, bad shit. But you don't need to read it, OK?'

Nate had already chucked it in the outside bin but when he left to get some fish and chips for lunch I went and pulled it out. There was nothing to read until page three, I swear to you. Nothing but a masthead and a large, very pale grey smudge where her face used to be.

You know that the woman who was murdered, Tegan, was even younger than Bella? Just twenty-two. I wonder when she knew, if she knew. It'd been fast, so maybe not.

But Bella had to have known. The question is how much and how soon. When she closed the nursing home door behind her and strode out into the street with her keys in her hand (did she have a key protruding between each finger of her closed fist the way our mother taught us?), did she feel it, a shiver of fear, a tiny premonition that something bad was going to happen? Did she – for even an instant – think about going back inside and asking one of the orderlies to walk her to her car and then shush her own mind, still her own heart as she imagined saying the words, actually admitting that she was afraid to walk less than a hundred metres? How stupid she would feel asking for an escort for such a short distance, in such a clear space, in daylight, based on nothing but a tingle at the place her ponytail met her scalp. So she walked on alone and what? When did she know something, if not everything?

When a man approached her and asked for directions, to use her phone, for a date, for the time? And she, being polite, being kind, being unwilling to assume the worst, turns, smiles, answers and even when she sees the knife or gun or feels his hand on her throat she doesn't scream she just says something kind and quiet, trying to disarm, to calm, like she does when a dementia patient goes ballistic, like she did when her older sister and her boyfriend came home drunk and rowdy and started smashing glasses in the kitchen.

Or was it when a car pulled up beside her and she heard a voice say – what – what might they have said? When she was sprawled or sat primly on the back seat of a strange car or coming to on the floor of that car, old dirt or reeking cigarette butts under her cheek? Or finding herself, waking maybe, beside the highway, a man looming over her, her skin screaming, and she remembers the shiver when leaving work, remembers and remembers and remembers and rehearses in her head how she would advise other women, advise her sister, to always pay attention to that shiver, because look because look because look.

And maybe this other girl, Tegan, maybe she had been following the news about Bella. She would've felt sad for her – because every human with a heart must – and she would've got stricter about personal safety – because every woman with a brain did. Wouldn't have walked around or parked her car in deserted areas even in broad daylight. Would've walked with her keys between her knuckles, her phone in the other hand, looked twice at slow-cruising cars, trying to memorise the numberplate just in case. She wouldn't have gone out after dark alone. Would've been glad to have her husband at her back.

■   ■   ■

May spent the morning at the primary school's Sunday produce market, interviewing anyone who'd agree to talk to her. In the four days she'd been in town, she'd filed six stories and taken enough notes for a month of weekend features, so collecting more anecdotes about Bella's kindness to old people and dogs was not at all necessary, but anything to keep busy. Such a cliché, she knew, but then it had been the most horrifying cliché of all – a romance with a married man – that had smashed her heart and life into a thousand tiny shards in the first place, so the thirty-year-old-woman-throwing-herself-into-work-so-as-not-to-face-up-to-the-holocaust-that-was-her-private-life cliché seemed appropriate.

And it was her entire private life that he had shattered, because she was now a stranger to her family and friends, who had no idea about the whole revolting mess. Nobody had even known she was in love. She had planned to tell them after Craig left his wife and moved in with her, which he was going to do as soon as the car was paid off the promotion came through his mother-in-law recovered the youngest child started school the baby was born. The what now? Ha. Ha ha ha ha ha. Ha.

That wasn't the end, him telling her his wife was pregnant. If she had any self-respect it would've been, she knew, but if there was one thing Craig had taught her about herself it was that she didn't. If there was a second thing he'd taught her it was that she could sleep fine knowing she was keeping a father from his children and a husband from his wife as long as said father/husband made her come so hard the cow next door banged on the wall screaming at her to shut up.

The end came three weeks after May found out Craig's wife was pregnant. It came via a phone call. From the wife. Carmel. She told May that she knew everything, that Craig was sitting beside her and that they were together on this. She said that Craig would not be going anywhere near May again and that May would not be going anywhere near Craig. Then she hung up.

Craig called a few hours later. May's phone was off. He left a message telling her he'd meant everything he ever said to her. But he needed to do the right thing and recommit to his family. He wished her well.

That was the day before Bella Michaels' body was found, so at least the timing was good. Finally a big, national story with which to prove herself. There was some kind of irony in the fact that she wouldn't even have the crime reporting gig if it wasn't for Craig. He'd got her talking about why she went into journalism and when she tried to sarcasm her way through the conversation, he pinned her to the wall with his eyes, demanded she take herself as seriously as he took her. 'We're still young,' he said, and May heard a promise about their future together that made her determined to be worthy of a man like him.

Crime reporting, she admitted, that was the dream ever since she was a ten-year-old reading pilfered copies of her mum's true-crime books under her quilt by torchlight. Specifically, she said, when Craig pushed her, she wanted to write about murder. But there weren't enough of them for that to be a full-time job anywhere in this country and so she'd take crime in all its forms to be in a position to report on the murders when they happened.

'And once again you blow my mind,' Craig had said. They were in her bed, as usual, post-, and May hoped also pre-, coital. 'I never would've picked it. Thought you were going to say politics or social justice. Murder. Should I be scared?'

'Well, yeah, I'm terrifying. Had you not noticed?'

'Seriously, why murder?'

'Seriously? It *is* a social justice thing, I think. I mean, writing about murder victims is a way to make sure their deaths aren't forgotten and to help authorities identify the killers. And given how many of those victims were occupying the lowest rung on society's ladder when they were killed, that makes it even more important.'

'OK, but wouldn't writing about the social and political conditions that put those people on the bottom rung be a better use of your energy? Help them while they're still around to benefit? Maybe even get them up a rung so they're not so vulnerable?'

'I guess so.' May pretended she was stretching so she could check the time. Clock-watching irritated Craig but she couldn't help herself. She needed to know how many minutes she had left with him so she could ensure not one of them was wasted. One hundred and four minutes. So, a little more talk and then she'd stop his questions by climbing onto his face. 'But it's not either/or. Most murder victims are killed by someone they know. Gangsters killed by other gangsters. Kids killed by parents. Wives killed by husbands. Occasionally the reverse. And in every case there's a history, a backstory that, once you know it, you think, Well, yeah, this was always going to end badly.'

'Sounds dangerously close to saying the victims were asking for it.'

'No, no, not at all. I'm saying that if we paid more attention, a lot of those bad endings could be prevented. Like, if everyone who knew him saw that this dude was eventually going to go too far with his beatings and kill his wife, then why did no one step in? If looking back we can see that every young man from a poverty-stricken migrant family who dies in a western-suburbs knifing or shoot-out has followed a similar trajectory, then what are we going to do about intervening at that first point along the well-worn path?'

'Mmmm. Might it also be that creating narratives around murder allows a measure of comfort? Murder in the abstract is terrifying; in the details, you realise it has nothing to do with you.'

'It might have something very much to do with you if you keep Socratising instead of fucking me.'

And so that was that, but after he'd gone home to his family she ran the conversation through her head and realised what it was he was poking at and she was protecting. The squishy, reeking black truth of it was that reading about murder thrilled her in the exact same way, she supposed, that it thrilled the masses who snapped up true-crime books in the millions and watched cheesy crime re-enactment shows and moody, gritty cable dramas. It was just so *intimate*.

Not only the act itself, though obviously that was, but the way that everything gets dug up and laid out in the aftermath. Homicide investigations – police ones and, sometimes even more so, media ones – open up private lives in an unprecedented way. Someone dies of natural causes, everyone's all about respecting privacy. Someone gets murdered and it's considered OK – helpful and responsible, even – to delve into every email and text message, to lay out her underwear and porn collection, to note body-hair removal habits, how often the sheets were changed, whether she preferred tampons to pads, condoms to an IUD. And not just of the victim, either. The victim's current and ex-partners, siblings, parents, kids, workmates, friends. All their nasty habits and dirty secrets laid out in the name of truth and justice. It was as terrible as it was irresistible.

Every so often, after having read a particularly juicy account of a murder investigation, May would be gripped with a horror of evidence and tear through her bags throwing away receipts, deleting messages and photos from her phone and the history log from her laptop. She worried, too, about the vibrator and dirty fiction in her bedside drawer and the various creams and pills in the medicine cabinet, but decided the embarrassment of living as a horny, rashy, hyperventilating mess was a worse prospect than a hypothetical homicide detective's sniggers and raised eyebrows. Anyway, she probably had it coming. Live by the breathless murder site inventory, be humiliated after death by the . . .

Bella Michaels, murder victim, had so far refused to supply the expected nasty, dirty thrills. No drugs or alcohol in her system and by all accounts that would've been true even if she'd been killed on New Year's Eve. The woman didn't even drink coffee, for god's sake. There were rumours of a secret boyfriend, but nobody was able to offer a name. The sister had a rough reputation and there was the business of her violent ex, but Bella herself was pristine.

And yet, well into her third hour of interrupting people buying their weekly fruit and veg to ask for their thoughts on the murder,

May realised that there was a salaciousness to the way some people spoke about Bella – but only post-mortem. *Sweetest girl you could meet. Always ready to lend a hand. Too good for this world.* And then... *What those mongrels did to her,* followed by a visible shiver, like the speaker had taken too much icy gelato into their mouth at once. *When I think about what happened to her – I mean, really think about it* – rapid blinking, tongue darting out to wet lips – *I mean, it's hard not to imagine, once you know.*

'How do you know all that?' May asked an artisanal goat's cheese seller who'd been describing – in hot, sour-smelling whispers – the condition of Bella's body when it was found.

The cheese monger stood back, gave a crooked smile. 'Come on, like you haven't looked at the photos.'

May felt the flush spreading up her neck. Only rookie reporters feel embarrassed at not knowing more than their sources, she reminded herself. 'Are you saying you've seen photos of Bella Michaels's body?'

The man blinked. 'Yeah, I assumed...' He leant in close again. 'I thought it was common knowledge that they'd been leaked. I guess not, though if the journos aren't onto it yet. Look, I don't want to get anyone into trouble. Is it too late to say off the record? Ha, ha, ha.' He stepped back, looked around hopefully for customers, then began rubbing a yellow cloth over his glass cheese case.

'I won't publish the photo stuff, of course. Can you tell me where you saw them?'

He leant close to her again, whispered a five-word phrase, pulled away abruptly and continued wiping the spotless glass. 'Anyway, better get back to work,' he said.

May wove through the crowd, bumping against straw baskets and hessian bags, elbows and sweaty forearms until she reached the exit. She stood against the school fence waiting for her pulse to slow. The accessibility of the photos was irrelevant. She couldn't describe them in her reporting. Even mentioning they'd been leaked would be legally questionable and ethically foul.

There was no reason for her to look. So she wouldn't.

Back at the hotel she took a cold shower, flinched at the sting of water against her freshly sunburnt neck. Still too hot for comfort, she sat naked on the bed and began going through the morning's notes, entering any potentially publishable snatches into her computer for later use and noting anything that called for further investigation. There was very little of either.

She opened the web browser, started to type the cheese man's phrase, closed the window and then the laptop.

If she were killed tonight, here in Strathdee, the police would go through her browser history, her computer files, her notebook. The hypothesis that she'd been murdered because she got too close to the truth about Bella Michaels would be laughed out of consideration.

They'd listen to her voicemail, hear Craig's saved messages – one telling her never again, the other taking it back – and he would then be the chief suspect. That thought made her feel as she did after a binge and purge, sick and satisfied at the same time.

But he'd have an alibi, the shithead. His smug bitch of a wife would say he was with her all night and, even worse, it would be true. The police would have to dig deeper, find any other men May was involved with. The way people in this town talked it wouldn't take them long at all to turn to that fella from her first day in town. Chas. He'd turned out to be such a good interview, full of local lore and tips. They'd talked the afternoon away and then he'd walked her back to the hotel. It might have looked, to anyone passing by, that he'd been angling for an invitation and that she had hesitated a bit too long so that the eventual firm goodnight seemed harsher and more of a figurative as well as literal door-closing than it might've if she'd cheerily waved goodbye from the pub.

May slid the laptop under the bedside table then flipped through her notes to find Chas's number. She'd done loads of interviewing and research since she'd spoken to him last. There were plenty of new questions she was sure he could help her with.

■   ■   ■

Nate was still out at the fish-and-chip shop and I was sitting around thinking about Bella and Tegan when there was a knock on the door. I had the curtains closed because I was still in my nightie and so I hadn't seen anyone coming up the drive. I pulled on this big old rain jacket of Nate's that was hanging near the front door and stood for a minute and tried to feel a bit of Nate in me – oh, not like that, you dirty bugger. His way of talking to people, I mean. Polite but absolutely bloody unmoving.

I opened the door to a man of about my age with the saddest eyes I'd ever seen on a human. Dog eyes, you know? Broken, beaten, minutes-from-euthanasia shelter-dog eyes. He was wearing beige cargo pants and a stripy polo shirt and wasn't holding a notebook or camera or recorder that I could see.

'Chris. Hello. My name is Glen Goodes. You don't know me, but I knew your sister very well and I hoped I could –'

'You knew Bella?'

'Very well, yes. I hoped we could talk?'

I let him in and left him at the kitchen table while I put some proper clothes on. When I came back out he was gone. 'Hello?' I called, my heart racing because that's what it likes to do nowadays at anything more surprising than toast popping up three minutes after I've put it down.

He stepped in from the living room, his sad eyes streaming. He was holding the framed photo of Bella at my thirtieth party. 'Sorry, I just . . . I hadn't seen this one.'

I took it from him. 'Why would you have?'

'Chris, I – Can we sit?' He gestured to the kitchen table and I nodded and sat across from him. I kept the picture against my chest.

'Me and Bella . . .' he started and then gazed off out the window.

'You and Bella?'

'We were in love.' He held his open hands out to me and I looked but there was nothing in them to help explain. They were pale and smooth, no sunspots or calluses. No nicks or scars. Little boy hands, except for the gold wedding ring.

'I know it's a shock. She was adamant about not telling you, not until . . . There were complications and she felt . . .'

'I don't understand what you're saying to me. You were in love with her?'

'We were in love with each other.'

I didn't say anything. What could I say? He might as well have told me Bella was an astronaut or Russian spy. He kept talking as though he was speaking sense.

'It's been very difficult, because, well . . . my wife is sick. Cancer. It's not likely she'll . . . Anyway, I couldn't leave her. She's a good person and she doesn't deserve . . . Bella agreed, of course. She was . . .' He grimaced. 'Conflicted. She broke up with me several times, tried very hard to stay away, but we just kept . . . We worked together, saw each other every day. I'm a geriatrician at the . . . She talked about quitting, but it's not like there are jobs up for grabs around here. But seeing each other all the time, it was just . . . She was ashamed. Didn't want anyone to know. You in particular. She told me you were her Jiminy Cricket and that if she told you it'd have to be over between us forever.'

'Stop,' I said. Jiminy Cricket, for God's sake! Bella used to beg me to watch her stupid fucking *Pinocchio* DVD with her and sometimes I did but barely ever with as much attention as she hoped. Fifty times per viewing she'd glance sideways at me and I'd be painting my nails or reading a magazine or maybe even napping a little and she'd nudge me with her chubby little fists and say, 'Chris, you're missing it.' Me, her Jiminy bloody Cricket! God, she was a character.

'I'm sorry. I know this must be very hard for you, but I've been going out of my mind. I've lost the person I loved most in the world and I've had to act like I'm mildly distressed over losing a colleague. My wife's been following the case so closely, the TV is constantly on and so I keep seeing Bel, hearing what –' A huge sob ripped through him and the room went cold.

'You need to go to the police.'

'What? No! Oh God, Chris, you can't think I had anything to do with what –' He sobbed again, tears running freely now. 'My wife … It can't get out. I just needed you to know. Because you loved her as much as I did.'

Freezing air. My skin stung with it. I wanted to ask him if he felt it too, but my tongue was ice. If I spoke it would shatter.

He kept pleading with me not to tell anyone, babbling about how he'd been away at a conference in Canberra when it happened and I could check for myself, he'd give me the number.

Key in the lock, the door swung open and the outside air rushed in and thawed me instantly. Or maybe it was Nate who did that.

'G'day,' he said, calm as anything in front of this babbling, wet-faced liar. 'Nate.'

'Glen.' The man swiped a hand across his nose and mouth. 'Sorry, you've caught me at a bad –'

'Chris?' Nate looked to me. 'You OK here?'

I swallowed the vestiges of ice water and nodded. 'I am, but I need you to call Brandis for me. Tell him there's a bloke here claiming he was in love with Bella.'

'Mate, please.' Glen stood up as if that was going to help. He came up to Nate's nipples. 'I made a mistake. I'm going to leave now and I hope, look, I'm sorry I upset her so much, I should've realised she'd be too grief-stricken to . . . Anyway, I hope you can calm her down, that she'll be OK.'

'She seems calm to me.' Nate hadn't taken his eyes off Glen. 'Chris, you calm, babe?'

'Completely. Call Brandis, hey?'

'Please.' The man looked directly at me and those eyes, those eyes – I almost split open with the sadness.

'You have an alibi. Nothing to worry about,' I said.

'My wife . . .'

Nate snorted. 'Yeah, I think you leaving is a good idea.' He didn't touch him, but the man moved as if pushed. 'Chris, you know his name and all that?' I said I did. Nate followed the man out the door and locked it behind him. I heard him sobbing out there and the ice came over me again, but then Nate put the fish and chips on the table, knelt beside me and took my head in both hands and kissed my forehead and I was so warm.

Brandis got to my place so fast I wondered if he'd been sitting in his car at the end of the street when I called. He tore into my driveway, parked crooked, arrived at my door with his face dripping sweat. Soon as he was sitting at my kitchen table with a glass of cold water he turned all professional and cool, pretending like he wasn't excited as fuck about what I'd told him.

'We interviewed Dr Goodes along with all the staff at the home. Obviously we'll interview him again. Ask why he lied to us about his relationship with Bella.'

'Maybe he didn't. Maybe he's lying now,' I said.

'He looked fair-dinkum shattered,' Nate said.

'Could be he's delusional. Thinks him and Bella had something more than they did. It happens. If he says no one knew, it'll be hard to confirm either way.'

Nate squeezed my hand, leant towards Brandis. 'There have been whispers about something like this though.'

'A lot of rumours going around, Mr Cartwright. Not a good idea to put too much stock in any of them.'

'I'm just saying, they must come from somewhere. Whoever's been saying that . . . Might be that someone did know about this bloke and Bel.'

'Maybe. First thing is for us to speak to Goodes again. I'll head round there now.'

'Don't go to his house.'

Nate and Brandis looked at me.

'I mean, can you call him and get him to come to you or something? His wife has cancer. No point upsetting her if it turns out to be nothing.'

Brandis nodded and shook our hands. 'I'll be in touch.'

When he was gone, Nate came up behind me and rubbed my shoulders in that way he knew I loved. 'You're the softest-hearted little thing in the world, aren't ya?'

'Bella didn't want her to suffer any more than she already is.'

'Yeah, both of you. A couple of softies.'

'He said Bel called me her Jiminy Cricket.'

'Her what?'

'Her conscience. As if, right?'

'Nah, you always gave her good advice. I remember hearing you giving her a talking-to, think it was after she'd come back from Sydney that time.' He stopped rubbing, let his hands rest heavy on me. 'I can't remember what you said even, but I remember thinking that I wished you'd take your own advice. That we'd both be better off if we lived the way you expected Bella to.'

'I don't remember that. I don't remember ever giving her advice. The odd ear-bashing, sure, but more often it was the other way around.'

'Not how I recall it. Obviously not how she did either.'

'Do you think it's true? Could her and that buggerlugs have been. . .?'

He gave my shoulders a squeeze and said lunch was getting cold. So I guess that was a yes.

■   ■   ■

AustraliaToday.com

WOMAN ATTACKED IN STRATHDEE NEAR SITE OF BELLA MICHAELS ABDUCTION

May Norman
12 April 2015

A woman was assaulted in Strathdee on Friday night in the vicinity where Bella Michaels was abducted before being raped and murdered earlier this month.

The 32-year-old local woman was walking past a small park on the street behind Strathdee Haven nursing home when she was grabbed from behind by an unknown attacker.

Police have confirmed that the man attempted to drag the woman towards a parked car but was disturbed by a passing motorist who stopped on seeing the struggle.

The offender fled the scene in a white Toyota Camry which was later found abandoned outside the Strathdee bus station. Police confirm the vehicle was stolen.

The woman sustained no injuries but was treated for shock at Strathdee Hospital.

The offender is described as Caucasian, aged in his 30s, and of a slight build. He was wearing a dark-coloured hoodie with black jeans.

Police refused to comment on whether this attack might be linked to Bella Michaels' murder, but locals are taking no chances. On a clear, warm Saturday afternoon the streets, parks and walking tracks of this small, tight-knit community were all but deserted.

Anyone with information about this assault or the abduction and murder of Bella Michaels should contact Strathdee police or Crime Stoppers.

■　■　■

May was about to meet with Chas when the cowardly, married, beloved bastard finally called.

She leant against the outside wall of the Royal, closed her eyes. 'Craig?'

'May. Thank God. It's so good to hear your voice. How are you?'

'I'm OK.'

'I miss you so much.'

'Why haven't you called? I've been –'

'I know, I know. Carmel made me take leave so we can work full-time on saving our marriage and it's just been impossible for me to get away for even a second. She's watching me like a hawk. This afternoon's her mummy-to-be yoga class though, so . . . God, when can I see you? We need to figure something out, soon.'

'Are you serious?'

'Of course.'

'Craig, you can't just –'

'I know you're hurt, but . . .'

'I can't do this right now. I'm about to meet a source. It's important. I can't be all fucking teary.'

'Sorry, sorry.' He took a long, deep breath. 'What are you working on?'

'Obviously you don't read my work then.'

'I can't read it with Carmel around, can I? You've got no idea what it's been like here . . . Look, tell me about what you're working on. I want to know.'

'Woman murdered in Strathdee. It's this godforsaken truck stop of a town. I'm hanging around straining to come up with new angles on week-old news hoping there'll be a breakthrough and I'll be the last reporter left standing.'

'Shit. Yeah. I heard about that poor girl. Awful you have to stay there. Is it safe?'

'Sure. I don't know. I think so.' May saw Chas climbing out of a gleaming, dark green ute. 'I'm going to have to go. When can I –'

'No, come on, don't go yet. Carmel's not due back for an hour and I don't know when I'll have the chance to call again. Christ, May, I miss you. We need to find a way to make this work. Right? Right?'

May swallowed a sob. 'I have to go.'

She hung up, flicked the phone to silent, stepped through the door Chas was holding open for her. The pub was half full. May scanned for Chris Rogers but could see only a scrawny blonde and the ancient owner behind the bar. Her phone vibrated in her pocket and it was all she could do not to reach for it.

'You right?' Chas asked. 'Your face is all pink.'

'Bad day.'

He led her to a table up the back, pulled out her chair. 'Something stronger than beer then. You a gin, vodka or whisky girl?'

'I shouldn't.'

'Why?'

'I'm working.'

'You can't work pissed? Geez, call yourself a journo.'

She laughed. 'I'll have a beer.'

'One whisky double coming right up.'

'You're not a great listener, are you?'

He leant in close, both forearms on the table. 'I'm more of face-reader. And your face is telling me you need –'

'I'm not going to get drunk and have sex with you.'

He moved closer. She could smell his smoky breath and count his pale eyelashes. 'That's cool. We can do it sober.'

Her phone vibrated again. She pulled it out, pressed ignore. The clock flashed up. Four hours until she had to file. 'What are we doing hanging around here, then?' she said.

He blinked, rocked back on his heels. Oh God, May thought, he was joking. He was joking and now I've made a complete and utter fool of my stupid slutty self.

A slow smile. 'Well, alright, alright.' He nodded towards the door.

As they left May thought she heard someone call out his name and something like 'good on ya' – or maybe it was 'get on her'? Chas didn't seem to hear it. He kept walking naturally, not touching her or even smiling until they were across the road and in her room with the door locked and the curtains closed against the stupidly bright autumn sun.

May waited several minutes longer than what she thought might be the appropriate amount of time and then gently nudged Chas's shoulder. 'Don't mean to be rude, but you need to go.'

He pulled himself up onto his elbows and looked into her face. Sweat dripped from between his eyebrows onto her lips. 'You Sydney girls, always in such a hurry.'

'I need to work. I've got a deadline.'

'It's OK. I won't bother you.' He rolled to the side, pulled a sheet up over his torso, feigned sleep.

'Don't you have a home to go to?'

'Can't hear you. Sleeping.'

May went to the bathroom, rinsed off under the shower and dressed in tracksuit bottoms and a t-shirt. She smiled at herself in the mirror and thought it looked real enough. When she returned to the room, Chas was up and dressed, flicking through her notebook.

She took it from him, swatted his arm with it. 'That's confidential.'

'Can't read your writing anyway. Like a bloody spider's web.' He went to the fridge, pulled out a can of beer and cracked it open. 'Looks like the last one. Share?'

She took the can, slugged some down, passed it back to him. She picked her pants up from the floor and dug her phone from the pocket. Four missed calls from the bastard. No new messages.

'So what's the latest on Bella? Is there a suspect?'

She shook her head. 'Police say they're following several lines of inquiry. Won't say what they are. Most people I've talked to around town seem to think it was an outsider. Someone passing through.'

'Makes sense.'

'Why?'

He handed her the beer. 'We all know each other here. Well, not personally, but we all know someone who knows someone who knows someone, if you get what I mean. Anyone here who could do that, we'd be aware before now. Word'd get round. It always does.'

'Always? So you've had things like this happen before?'

'Not like this. That's what I'm saying. I'll be the first to admit there're some shitheads in this place. Wife beaters, daughter rapers, cat poisoners . . .'

'Cat poisoners? Plural?'

'Yep. But we know who they are. Sometimes we know because they're in and out of jail and sometimes we know because we talk, but either way we know. Like little Tegan. We all knew her husband was a violent cunt. Soon as we heard she was dead we were like, yep, yep, saw that one coming.'

'Saw it coming. Christ.'

'What? You think we could've stopped it?'

'I don't know. Did you try?'

'Fair go. Didn't even know her except as that pinch-faced little mouse who worked in the shit bakery, the one you go to on Sundays only because the good one's shut then.'

'But you knew her husband was violent?'

'Yeah, because people talk. That's what I'm saying. There are a hundred girls working cash registers here – don't know one from the other unless there's a reason to. Like, people say, "Did ya see poor Tegan at the bakery? Back from her honeymoon a week and already sporting a shiner," and you'll go, "Which one's Tegan? The blonde with the tits or the brunette with the legs?" And they'll go, "Nah, nah, the quiet little thing at Morello's," and then you know who Tegan is and you know her old man belts her and so each time you need to get bread on a Sunday you see her and sometimes she's normal and sometimes she looks like she's never slept and once or twice she's bruised and you say, "Alright?" and she goes, "Can't complain," and you get your bread and walk away and if you bump into someone you know on the way home you tell 'em, "Dickhead's laid into her again, looks like."'

'Fucking hell, this place.'

'Point is, you hear about something – bashing, car theft, cat poisoning and go, "Oh, yeah, I bet so-and-so is behind that," but what happened to Bella . . . Can't think of a man'd do that. No one here can.'

'What about Nate Cartwright?'

'Nah. Barking up the wrong tree there. He's alright, Nate.'

'People can hide themselves pretty well, you know.'

'You can't hide being that fucked up.'

'Maybe the more fucked up you are, the better you are at hiding.'

'By that reasoning it could be anyone.'

'Yeah.'

'Could be me.'

'Yeah.'

'Do you really think that?'

'I guess. I mean, I obviously don't think it's likely or I wouldn't be here, but, you know, whoever it was is with someone right now – a wife, a girlfriend, a mate – and that person is thinking the same thing.'

'That's fucked up.'

'Tell me about it.'

■ ■ ■

I was in the storeroom behind the pool table at the back of the pub when I heard these four blokes talking. Blokes I knew. Regulars. Two I'd fucked, one I wouldn't have minded before this.

'She had that smile, you know?'

'Yep. Like Chris, but, eh, y'know, fresher. Sunny.'

'Fuckin' shame.'

'You can 'magine it, though, eh? Smile like that, buncha blokes out on the piss, looking for trouble.'

'It was five o'clock in the fucking afternoon. They wouldna been on the piss.'

'Nah, wouldna been on the piss. Prob'ly Muzzies out from the city. You know how they drive around, the Lebs and that, fucking hoon around in their wog cars. See a girl like that.'

'That smile.'

'Not just that. The blonde hair. Nice, sweet white girl. Prob'ly wanted a virgin, y'know? Prob'ly out looking for someone they could really, like, fuckin' degrade. Fuckin' grubs.'

'She wasn't, but. Pete – plumber Pete, not bottle-o Pete – he used to go out with her. He's not saying much, pretty cut-up about it all, you know, but back when they were going out – look, I don't wanna speak ill of the – I'm just sayin' she wasn't no virgin.'

'Missing the fuckin' point, mate. I'm not saying she was or wasn't. I'm saying it's what those grubs woulda thought, lookin' at her. They woulda wanted someone who looked pure, you know?'

'Yeah. Yeah. Bloody hell. You know what they did to her? Like, not what's in the papers, but what I heard from me mate who knows one of the coppers who saw her? Sick shit. Some seriously sick shit.'

I hip-bumped the door open, my torso and face guarded by the double-stacked boxes of serviettes I carried. I felt, rather than heard, their silence. I kicked the door closed behind me.

'Chris! Shit, let me help you with that, hey?' It was Hock. Red bushy beard, biceps the size of my thighs. So much my type it's ridiculous. I pretended I didn't hear. Carried my burden across to the bar.

I was halfway through unpacking the boxes, sliding the little plastic-wrapped bundles of serviettes into the nooks behind the bar, when Hock came up and ordered another round.

'How you doing, Chris?' he said while I was pouring.

'Oh, you know. Good as can be expected.'

'Yeah, yeah. Surprised to see you here, to be honest.'

'Yeah, well, no point sitting around feeling sorry for myself, is there?' I put his beers on a tray and told him how much and he paid.

'Ah, you've always been a tough nut.' He picked up the drinks. 'Come have a drink with us after you finish, hey?'

'Working till close.'

'Well, if you feel like it then, I'll grab some takeaways, drive you home.'

'Thanks, mate, but not likely I'll feel like it, you know?'

He nodded. 'Yeah, 'course, 'course. Another time? When things are back to normal.'

And off he went. *You know what they did to her? When things are back to normal.* Honest to God. Like, seriously. Honest to fucking bastard God.

That night I woke up sudden, like someone had screamed in my ear. I sat up, listening, one hand on my phone ready to call 000, but there was nothing to hear. I was sweating all over. When my heart stopped racing, I stood up and turned on the light. My hand on the switch was streaked with blood.

I don't think I took it in at first. I kind of stood there looking at it. I looked at my other hand and it had a rusty streak on it too. I sat down hard, started thinking – oh, God, all kinds of crazy things, I can't even tell you what – and then I noticed the blood on the front of my nightie and on the inside of my thighs and, Jesus, I nearly hyperventilated. The things going through my mind. Well, they were the things always going through my mind but this time happening to me instead of her.

I called Nate. He answered straightaway, panic in his voice, and

I told him he had to come and hung up and sat still listening to the sounds of the house and the street, just looking at this nightmare mess.

Look, I know I'm mad and all but I swear I'm not as stupid as this story makes me sound. Thing is I hadn't had my period in yonks. After Nate and me had tried for a baby for a couple of years, I saw a doctor and found out I couldn't. So after that I went back on the pill to save myself the bastard cramps and breakouts that always came with my monthlies. I'd been on it ever since, skipping those little sugar pills and living without the useless blood-letting. 'Course, with all that had happened I'd forgotten to refill the prescription which I remembered now had run out the day the cop came to the door to tell me they'd found her. I'd had it in my bag, ready to go. It's probably still there, crumpled beneath all the detective and reporter business cards, the fresh and used tissues.

Once I realised, I ran to the bathroom and jumped in the shower, chucked my nightie underneath a bunch of other stuff in the basket in case Nate came in. He turned up just as I was getting out, came running through the house calling my name. I wrapped up in a towel and met him as he was about to barge into the bathroom.

'You OK? What's happened?'

'Yeah, sorry. I had a bad turn. Woke up in a big panic, thought that . . . I don't know what. I'm fine now.'

He took a few big breaths, looked over my head the way he always did when he was pissed off. 'I thought you were hurt. You sounded like you were being –'

'I know, like I said, I woke up in this state and I think I was still kind of out of it when I called you. Sorry.'

'Right.' He turned to leave.

'Look, it's four in the morning. You might as well stay. I can go on the sofa and –'

'This isn't OK, Chris.' He remained facing away from me. 'You can't call me in the middle of the night, come up to me nearly bloody naked and then –'

'That's not what –'

'I'll talk to you tomorrow.' He left without looking back.

I put the towel down on my bed, lay on it and stared at the blood streaks on my bedside table. Such a weird thing, isn't it? Leaking blood every month. I know we're meant to be all grown up about it, natural process, happens to half of humanity, why be embarrassed and all that, but honestly? Lying there waiting until it was late enough to go out and buy some damn tampons I almost couldn't cope with it. To have to walk around for days, bleeding. That we have to accept this as girls, accept that some of our time in this world will be spent cleaning up gore expelled from our own bodies, part of our income spent buying mass-produced bits of cotton wool to soak it up, part of our minds spent tracking, remembering, planning so that no one ever notices the fact that we are sometimes transformed into victims of satanic possession, blood gushing out of our uninjured bodies. Pointless loss of blood and pointless to rail against it, I know, but I tell you, lying there that morning I couldn't stop thinking about that joke, the one about not trusting something that bleeds for five days and doesn't die. Stuff of life smeared all over my sheets and bedroom furniture, washed down the drain in the shower. And it's fine! Wake up in the middle of a fucking crime scene, oh, it's fine. It's *normal*. Jesus. Look at yourself! No wonder men back away in fear, shrivel in disgust.

Monday
13
April

AustraliaToday.com

NO ANSWERS IN BRUTAL SLAYING

May Norman
13 April 2015

One week after the body of local woman Bella Michaels was discovered on a patch of dirt outside of Strathdee, police are struggling to come up with answers and, in their absence, theories and rumours are thriving among the close-knit community.

Outside Ms Michaels' apartment near the centre of town a single strand of blue and white crime-scene tape tied to a door frame flaps in the breeze. The doorstep is cluttered with floral arrangements and cards expressing grief and anger.

Ms Michaels had moved into the apartment five years ago after her return from a brief period in Sydney, said Barbara Stein, the building's owner. 'She was a dream tenant. Quiet, clean, reliable with her rent, always quick to lend a hand with a lost dog or heavy shopping bag.'

Many in town believe an outsider is responsible for the murder, one of the many travellers or long-haul truck drivers who stop here for a meal or a sleep on the road between Sydney and Melbourne. 'We all know each other here,' said a 37-year-old man who's lived in Strathdee, a town with barely 3000 residents, his whole life. 'Anyone here who could do that, someone'd be aware before now. Word'd get round. It always does.'

Suggestions that Ms Michaels had been seen hitchhiking close to the Melbourne exit have been dismissed as 'nonsense' by the police investigating the murder. But the idea that she willingly climbed into the vehicle assumed to have taken her to her death persists among town gossips.

Those who admit to the possibility of a local being responsible point to the fact that there appear to have been no signs of a struggle at the point of abduction as evidence that Ms Michaels' killer was known to her. Talk at each of the four pubs in Strathdee the evening before the funeral included the possibility of a recently dumped boyfriend, a married lover or an obsessed admirer. Police, meanwhile, have refused to comment on whether the popular, young, aged-care worker was in a relationship at the time of her death, but said that any men known to have been involved with her in the past have been interviewed and cleared as suspects.

'Still, the cops can't know everything, can they?' a 49-year-old woman shopping at the weekend farmer's market asks. 'Things happen between people, doesn't mean they post a notice at the community centre announcing it.'

'She used to come here sometimes with a group from the nursing home,' a barman at the Imperial Hotel recalls. 'I wouldn't call her a party girl, but she wasn't a shrinking violet either. She was very friendly, sociable. Bit of a looker, too. Always at least a few blokes hanging off her every word.'

Ms Michaels went missing between the nursing home where she worked and her car parked barely three minutes' walk away. Another small shrine has popped up on that street, joining those at Ms Michaels' workplace, apartment and the site where her body was found. This one consists of several small bunches of flowers and handwritten notes sticky-taped to a telegraph pole.

Caitlin Fischer, 23, and her friend Jody McDougall, 22, had brought a bouquet of dahlias that they'd picked and arranged themselves. They laid it at the base of the pole with a note which read RIP Bella. We'll never forget you. The women did not know Ms Michaels personally but say they've been deeply affected by her murder. 'She was just like us. Going about her life, not doing anything wrong or dangerous, and this has happened. You can't help thinking, "It could've been me,"' Ms Fischer said.

'Could have been me, my sister, my friends. It just feels so close,' Ms McDougall added.

Asked if they had any idea who might be responsible, the women shook their heads. 'Had to be a traveller, I reckon,' said Ms McDougall. 'Otherwise why now? If it's someone who's been here all along, why would he just start doing this now?'

'Probably a truckie or traveller, yeah,' her friend agreed, tucking her note more securely into the neck of the bouquet. 'But you don't know, do you? That's what's so scary. It could've been any of us killed and it could've been anyone who did it.'

■ ■ ■

The first time a man hit me I was fourteen. Mum's boyfriend Brett had been living with us for about a month. He told me to clean the kitchen and I told him to get stuffed and he swung his arm and smacked me in the side of the head. I ran and told Mum, who was putting Bella to bed. She asked me to stay with Bella and so I settled in next to her, my darling frizzy-haired little munchkin, snuggled right down under the covers with her. I remember she wrapped her arms around my neck and pressed her cheek against my face right where Brett had hit me and from the other room I could hear Mum and Brett angry-whispering and I tried so hard not to cry but the tears came anyway and Bel said, *No sad, Kiss*, which is what she called me then, and rubbed at my tears with her soft little two-year-old hands.

I slept in her bed that night and in the morning the kitchen was clean and Brett had made scrambled eggs and Mum had a split lip and puffy eyes.

I don't know how many times he hit me and Mum after that. It wasn't a lot. I mean, it was, but it wasn't constant. We could go months without being belted. Mum always stuck up for me and I always stuck up for her and I guess that's why usually we both got hit. If we were smart we would've agreed to take it in turns, halving the number of blows we each had to take. We weren't smart though; we were loyal and mouthy and, to tell the truth, if Mum had ever let him touch me without going at him herself my heart would've broken in two.

I don't know why I never asked her to kick him out or why it took her so long to think of it herself. I suppose it didn't seem that bad at the time. Mostly he was alright, Brett. He worked hard and was kind and easygoing, except when he wasn't.

Anyway, I didn't reach my limit with him until I was sixteen and Bella was four. Mum was out – it might've been when she worked at the servo – and I was on the phone and Brett was pacing around in front of me telling me to get off. I didn't though. Can't for the life of me remember who I was talking to or what about, but at the time it seemed more important than anything Brett could say or do to me.

This went on for maybe half an hour and then he cracked it. He didn't say anything, just knocked the phone out of my hand and yanked the cord from the wall. Then he picked the handset up off the floor and whacked me on the side of the head with it. My ear was burning and ringing and I'd just had enough. I grabbed the base of the phone – it was one of those old-fashioned heavy beige things with a dial – and I swung it hard and smashed it in his face. He let out a noise almost like a laugh. Like he couldn't believe it. He dropped the handset and covered his nose and mouth. I saw blood and my whole body started to shake.

I ran into Bella's room and grabbed her from her bed. She was asleep and started to panic when I picked her up but I just held on tight to her wriggly body and ran as fast as I could out the back door. I don't know what Brett was doing – cleaning up the blood or finding a murder weapon or sitting on the floor and crying like a baby – but at the time I was convinced he was going to come after me and break my neck.

I ran as fast as I could with Bella squirming and punching my face with her little fists. When I got to the end of our street I slowed to a walk and put Bella down, though held tight to her arm so she couldn't get away. God, she was furious at me! *Why you take me! Bad Chrissy! You don't take me. I don't want to walk!* She got tired quickly though and moved to just giving me an occasional hurt look accompanied by an exaggerated sob.

When we got to the primary school I lifted Bella over the low fence and carried her up to the little plastic playground. She perked up a bit then and happily climbed all over the equipment for a few minutes, which gave me time to sit and really freak out. I couldn't go back. I thought about friends I might go to but they all had the kind of sweet, involved parents who'd want to call the police or DOCS or something and I'd rather get whacked by Brett every day of my life than be put in a foster home.

Bella came and sat on the bench beside me, put her head on my chest and yawned. Her eyes were flickering closed. I carried her up into the little fort and we lay down together, her head on my arm. After a while she said, *I'm cold, Chrissy*. I sat up and took off my jacket and covered her with it. *I'm very, very cold*, she said a few times, and so I wrapped my goosebumped arms around her and held her tight against my body until she stopped shivering and fell asleep.

In the morning when we got home, Mum was in the front yard crying at a cop. She whooped loud enough to raise hell when she saw us. She kissed Bella all over her face and said, *Haven't you had a big adventure?* and Bella started to tell her about the playground and the fort and how she slept under my jacket and Mum looked at me hard, and for a minute I thought she hated me, but then she said, *I'm so sorry, darlin'. He's gone now. OK?*

And it was. Later that day we had a big D&M about it all and she apologised eight thousand times and promised it'd never happen again, asked me to promise I'd never let a man take me over like that.

'When I was your age,' she told me, 'my mum told me that blokes only want one thing and believing that's been half my trouble. The thing you need to understand, Chris, is that a fella who only wants one thing from a woman is a rare find. Most of them want a damn sight more and some of them –' she ran a hand over my red and swollen ear '– some of them want bloody everything.'

I hadn't thought about any of that for years and years. I don't know if I'd thought about it at all since it happened. But the morning of the funeral I was putting my make-up on in the bathroom and I heard Bella saying, *I'm cold, Chrissy. I'm very, very cold*. I don't mean I remembered it – that came afterwards, the remembering about that night in the fort. I mean I heard her. I heard her voice right in my ear telling me she was cold.

I was looking in the mirror and the only thing to see was me, but the voice was as real as mine is right now. *I'm cold, Chrissy. I'm very, very cold.*

The funeral was as terrible as you'd imagine. Nate and Lisa and a couple of Bella's mates had organised it, mostly. I think they went through it all with me the day before, but I honestly can't remember. I suppose I told them it was fine. What on earth difference would it make, you know?

Bella's dad turned up looking a hundred years old. He hugged me for the longest time and though we've never really got on I knew he was really hugging her and so I didn't mind that much. All Bella's workmates were there, including Glen, which was disappointing because it meant he wasn't locked up somewhere being interrogated or whatever. I caught him giving me this hangdog mournful look and part of me felt rotten for him but a bigger part of me wanted to go over and ask him if Bella had been popping up at his windows, talking into his ears. Yeah, didn't think so, mate.

Apparently there were a lot more people outside the church. The whole town, Nate said, but I read later there were a thousand, so that's only a third. Still, nice that they all came even though they weren't allowed inside. I heard that the whole bunch of them from the pub were there and some of the regular customers, too. Again, I thought how good it'd be for Bella to see all this, hear all the love. She was such a goddamn sweetie, you know? And all these people crying over her because of it.

And then there were the news people, hanging around the edges of the car park, a bunch of fucking blowflies around a rotting corpse. Nate's expression. He yelled it at them as we drove in. The bastards didn't even flinch. The funeral home knew it would happen, but. They were prepared, had private security organised to make sure no press got in. Thank God for them. I never would've thought to arrange all that. They did it for free, too. Or, no, the security firm did it for half-price and the funeral home paid that. I think that's what happened. I wasn't in the best state in the lead-up to it all, but people were very kind and generous and I let them be.

There was a closed coffin, obviously. Part of me wished it wasn't. Part of me wished that everyone there would be forced to see what I'd seen instead of being allowed to imagine that what lay inside that box resembled the photo placed on top of it. But, of course, that wouldn't be right. I'm her sister, her blood. It's right that I keep her secrets for her, let everyone talk about how beautiful she was and not ever let on that she wasn't in the end.

Old Grey had offered to hold the wake at the pub and I agreed because I couldn't imagine putting something like that on myself. It was only when I was sitting in Nate's car out front that I remembered how much Bella hated the place, would never come unless it was to pick me up and leave right away. I had cried so much all morning that I didn't know I had more in me, but turns out I did. I sat there bawling my eyes out and Nate sat there rubbing my back and handing me tissues.

'Stop it,' I said to him. 'Just go in and tell them it's cancelled. There's no wake.'

'I can't stop it now. People are already in there. Bella wouldn't mind, babe, I'm sure of it. She'd want you to do whatever was easiest on you. She'd be fine with it.'

'That's just a thing people say after someone's dead. "What she would've wanted." It's bullshit. You don't know.'

'On this, I know. I know she would've wanted the people who loved her to be able to sit around and be nice to each other. Doesn't matter where. That's all this is. People who loved her being nice to each other.'

He was right, of course. She would want that. I blew my nose and got my concealer and lippie out of my bag, leant in to the rear-vision mirror to fix myself up. Nate said, 'Good girl,' and kept rubbing my back.

I was finishing my lippie when something black filled my side vision and Nate's hand jerked off my back. 'Fuck,' he said. My heart banged hard in my chest. Nate was out of the car and running and my heart was bang-bang-bang and the air rushing in and people running, running from the front of the pub, running to where Nate was holding someone by the back of the shirt.

A photographer. Nate told me later that not snapping the bloke's pencil-neck took more willpower than not taking a drink. Next day he regretted it, said if he saw the fucker again he'd break his neck and worse.

You saw it I guess? Front page, clean shot of me puckering into the mirror, while Nate stroked my neck. They ran it next to a picture of Bella at her work Christmas party, her fuzzy hair decorated with green and red tinsel. Top corner of the page was another photo. A black sheet over a lumpy shape, a blue tarp by the side. If you looked hard you could see her big toe poking out. I'm sure it was her toe, that tiny pale smudge. I stared and stared at that picture and the longer I stared the more obvious it became. How did no one at the scene notice that her toe was sticking out like that?

Nate found me crying over the paper and took it away. He thought I was upset about the photo of me and him looking like sweethearts out on a date. As if I give a fuck. All that Bella had been through and not one of those busy-bees crawling all over the crime scene could bother to check that no bits of her were left hanging out in the cold, cold air.

At the wake, after the photographer had taken that shot, Nate downed a schooner of Coke like it was a shot of rum and I saw from the tendons in his neck and the cracking of his knuckles over and over that he was close to the edge. I nicked a couple of smokes off Old Grey and led Nate back through the kitchen to sit on the outside step.

Nate took a deep drag. His phone beeped. He glanced at it, took another drag, shook his head at me. 'I can't be here.'

'Here at the pub or . . .?'

He closed his eyes, leant back against the door frame. His phone beeped again. He whipped it out of his pocket, punched in a reply.

'That her?'

'Yeah.'

'Checking up on you?'

'Yeah.'

'You shoulda brought her down with you. For support.'

'Hard for her to get time off.'

'What's she do?'

'Social worker.'

'Just what you need, eh?'

He closed his eyes again. 'Chris.'

I noticed my smoke was finished. I dropped the butt and brushed some dirt over it. 'If I go back in there, I'm going to have to drink a lot.'

'I know.'

'And if I go home, I'm going to have to drink a lot, too.'

'Yeah.'

'Or what? What am I meant to do now? What is there to do? How do I just . . . What do I do now?'

'I dunno.'

'What would *she* say? Renee? What would she tell me to do?'

He took a breath, gave me that look of his, checking to see if I was being a smartarse. He must've seen that I was legit, because he picked up both my hands and held them in that way that made them still. Made me still. 'Want me to call and ask her?'

'Might have to, 'cause I'm fucking clueless here.'

'What would Bella say?'

'She'd tell me to go home, clean the house then get an early night, because everything's easier to deal with when things are tidy and you're well rested.'

He laughed. 'Sounds about right. You going to do that then?'

'No.'

'No.' He looked out over the boxy concrete lot like it was a green, green field stretching all the way to the horizon.

'Do you think they're in there?' I said.

'What?'

'The ones that did it. Are they in there now? Drinking to her memory?'

'Chris . . .'

'That's why the cops are hanging around, hey? They think the –'

'Stop.' He stood, dangled a giant hand for me to pull myself upright. 'Come on. Inside. Say your thanks and goodbyes and then we're leaving.'

I let him heave me up and lead me through the kitchen. I barely spoke as we did the rounds, kissing and being kissed. Everybody was sorry and wanted me to tell them if there was anything I needed. I needed so much, but none of them could give me any of it and so I clung to the one who could until we were in his car and then I put my head back and closed my eyes and told myself it didn't matter what happened next.

In my kitchen I went for the bourbon and he stopped my hand with his and then kissed me long and hard and then we fucked on the kitchen floor and for as long as it lasted I felt that everything was exactly as it should be.

And then it was over. I pushed him off me, stood, pulled my skirt back down over my hips, ignored the ooze down my thighs.

In bra and crumpled skirt I poured and drank a thumb of bourbon. Nate said my name like a warning and I poured and drank another slug. My name again, a lament. Another drink, easy easy easy on my throat now. He got dressed, grabbed his phone and went outside.

I stood near the window with the bottle and the glass and listened to him tell his girlfriend that the funeral was *brutal* and that I was a *trouper* and the news photographers were *scum* and that he couldn't stop thinking about whether any of the men at the funeral were the ones that did it and whether he maybe made small talk with the bloke who – or shook the hand that – or or or and he wanted a drink so much, so much much much but he wouldn't he wouldn't he wouldn't, baby, baby, baby, wouldn't, couldn't, because although things were worse than he ever thought they could be, things were also much better than he ever thought because there was her, Renee, there was her and there was the baby, soon, soon, their baby, their little fella, and he could get through anything, anything – get through it sober – because of them.

A soft weight on my head, pressing just hard enough, moving from my hairline to the top of my ponytail. I sank into the nearest chair, shaking. The sharp smell of anti-bacterial hand wash made my nose twitch. The pressure again, perfectly judged. I whispered her name, felt myself breathing more slowly, closed my eyes, let her stroke me the way she always had when I was worked up or sad or shaky. After a minute I reached up, as I always had, to trap her hand beneath mine, to let her know she could stop, I was fine.

There was nothing to trap, nothing to stop. I sat shivering, hand on my head, until Nate came back inside.

He looked as hangdog and shifty as I'd ever seen him. His eyes darted from my tits to the floor to the window. Before he could pour his bullshit guilt out on me I told him straight, 'I think Bella's still here.'

'What d'ya mean?'

'Her spirit or whatever.'

He sat at the table, glared at the bottle. 'Chris.'

'Yeah, I know. Sounds mad, but . . . A couple of things have made me . . . I dunno.'

He didn't say anything. He was embarrassed for me. Or for himself. Ashamed, scared. I don't know.

'Do you believe in stuff like that?'

'In ghosts?'

'Yeah, nah. Not like a *ghost* in a movie or anything, just like, that people who've died might be . . .'

He cracked his knuckles. 'After Dad died, Mum'd say she saw him. Just sitting at the dinner table or out on the verandah having a smoke. Said it wasn't scary, just like he was still there. Then after a while she didn't see him any more. She reckoned he'd hung about a bit to help her get used to the idea of him being gone.'

'Do you think that's true?'

'I think she saw what she needed to see to get through those first weeks.'

'Do you think that's what I'm doing?'

'I don't know, babe. If you are it's not working real well, is it?' He poked the bottle.

'I had three drinks.'

'So far. And you were so rotten the other night I'm surprised you remembered how to make a phone call. If Bella *is* hanging around she'll be disgusted.'

He was right, of course. That's why it hurt so much. I hoped so hard then that he was right about all of it. That Bella wasn't here, that I was comforting myself with delusions of her presence, 'cause otherwise she'd seen me spewing up and screwing that grub for money and then all this carry-on with Nate. I hoped so hard she hadn't seen any of it and then right away I was crying, thinking how that wasn't true, how I didn't care what she saw, what she knew about me, that I'd take all the shame and judgement and disappointment. I called her name, I think, or I thought it so intensely that Nate knew I was calling to her.

'Chris, babe. Jesus.' He rubbed my back, stroked my hair. If I'd stood and turned he would have kissed me and it'd be all on again, but the idea was sickening now. I shook him off and went to my room. He followed, apologising, but it was like he was made of smoke. I waved him away, cried into the pillow and wished wished wished for the sound of her voice, touch of her hand, hospital-grade-clean smell of her. There was nothing though. Wishing for her was no good at all.

Tuesday

14

April

AustraliaToday.com

'WE'LL SPEAK OF HER OFTEN, THINK OF HER ALWAYS'

May Norman
14 April 2015

Forty of Bella Michaels' closest friends and relatives said goodbye to her in a private ceremony at St John's Anglican Church in Strathdee yesterday while almost a thousand more gathered outside and wept for the woman whose brutal death has shocked a nation.

Bella's friend Vicky Moreland was the first to speak at the service. She told the assembled mourners that she had spoken to Bella every day for the past five years and that she would think of her every day until she died.

Bella's father Tony Michaels spoke next, describing his daughter as 'a bright light that I never imagined I'd see put out'. He said that although he didn't see Bella often, he always felt good knowing she was 'here in quiet little Strathdee, shining her light on everyone she crossed paths with'.

Bella's former brother-in-law Nate Cartwright spoke on behalf of his ex-wife, Chris Rogers, who sobbed inconsolably throughout the service. 'Bella and Chris had some tough times in their younger lives, but neither would've changed a thing because those tough times are what made them as close as they were. Anyone who knew either of them would've heard the other one's name mentioned within the first five minutes of conversation. I know that won't change for Chris. She'll keep speaking of Bella often and all of us who knew Bella will be glad about that. We'll all speak of her often, think of her always.'

Another of Bella's friends, Sarah Loome, then rose and said that Bella had never been one for poetry but that she loved the film *Four Weddings and a Funeral* and 'cried like a baby' during the funeral scene which featured the poem 'Funeral Blues' by WH Auden. Ms Loome then read the poem, drawing laughter from the mourners when she apologised to Bella for 'not sounding as sexy as John Hannah'.

The service finished with an address from the Reverend Peter Longley, who spoke of Bella's generous spirit and deep, patient kindness. He ended with a prayer for peace for Bella's loved ones.

Mourners inside the church left via a private door at the back of the building as Judy Garland's 'Somewhere Over the Rainbow', from another of Bella's favourite movies, *The Wizard of Oz*, played. Those gathered outside sang along, wept, prayed and swapped stories about their connection to Bella.

'She took such good care of my dad at the nursing home,' one woman said, wiping tears from her face. 'She was Dad's favourite. He wanted to be here today, but it's very difficult for him to get around and so I came in his place. I didn't expect to be as moved as I am. Just seeing how much she meant to so many people, it's such a tragedy.'

A spokesman for Parson Brothers Funerals confirmed that a private security firm had been hired for the event and provided with a list of approved mourners prepared by the deceased's family. 'Numbers had to be limited due to the size of the church building,' the spokesman said. 'However we understand that many not in Ms Michaels' immediate circle would wish to pay their respects, hence the placement of speakers outside to broadcast the service.'

Members of the media were restricted to standing at the back of the outside broadcast and asked to refrain from recording or photographing the event. In a statement written by a close friend of Ms Rogers and handed out at the gates by a Parson Brothers employee, members of the media were asked to respect the privacy of Bella Michaels' family, friends and colleagues.

'We wish to express our gratitude for the love, concern and support we have received from friends and strangers throughout this last, horrific week. While we appreciate that the media must report on crimes and their consequences, we respectfully point out that our pain is not breaking news nor does it constitute a development in the case. We therefore ask that you allow us to grieve our beloved Bella in privacy.'

Also in attendance both inside and outside the church were Strathdee police officers and detectives from the Wagga local area command, a reminder that this grief is not the result of an accident or disease, but of the deliberate and monstrous actions of a person or persons yet to be found.

■ ■ ■

'Why does the *Tele* have a front-page photo of the dead girl's sister getting cosy with her murder-suspect ex at the funeral?'

May sat up, rubbing her eyes open. 'Morning, Andrew. Sorry, what's your question?'

'My question is what the actual fuck, Norman? Where were you?'

'I was at the funeral getting quotes from mourners.'

'Instead of following the sister and the ex-crim?'

'The family asked for privacy.'

'Christ! Are you new here? *Tele* says the lug-head ex took a swing at a photographer. *Herald* says the two of them left the wake together after fifteen minutes and he didn't leave her place until late at night. But we reported that some random woman's father was sad, so that's good.'

'OK. I'm sorry. I fucked up.'

'I want you back up here tomorrow.

'I said I fucked up. I'll do better.'

'Story's run its course.'

'Andrew, believe me, it really hasn't. There are all kinds of rumours about –'

'I want you back up here to cover the big femmo march thing tomorrow night. If there's anything new to report down there you can head back, but there's just no need to hang around. It's dead, May. Right?'

May called Max and arranged to see him before the march the following night, then tooled around on Facebook, catching up on the latest career triumphs, awesome parties, cute babies and anniversary dinners of her friends, colleagues and distant acquaintances.

She went to the status box and typed

Adequate sex with a source + microwave noodles = best night yet in Strathdee.

Delete.

Indigestion, beard rash and mosquito-bitten ankles: another top night in Strathdee.

Delete.

Two days since phone call from married lover caused me to seek consolation-sex with local yobbo. Two minutes since I last thought about calling married lover and begging him to leave his wife. Two seconds since I wondered if it's wrong to search for leaked murder photos online.

Delete.

Fuck all you smug smiley arseholes. Fuck my married lover and fuck his pregnant wife. Fuck AustraliaToday and fuck the police in this shitty little hole who can't come up with a single murder suspect in a town full of rapists, wife beaters and animal poisoners.

Delete.

Fuck my life.

Delete.

Ever since Craig she'd been unable to share the best things about her life and now that he was gone there was nothing she wanted to share. She posted the links to her latest articles, more to remind people she existed than out of any great pride in the writing itself.

Must do better, she typed, then deleted, but repeated it to herself out loud. That's the truth, she thought. I really, really must.

May psyched herself up to approach Chris Rogers' door again by reminding herself of the advice Andrew had given when he sent her out on her first death-knock to interview the parents of a little boy killed in a hit-and-run. 'It feels like you're imposing, but often grieving relatives are grateful for the opportunity to talk about their loved one. You're actually doing them a kindness.'

She knocked, waited a minute or so, then knocked again. After another minute she called out, 'Chris? Sorry to bother you, but it's quite important I speak to you.'

She heard footsteps, smoothed her hair, got ready to smile sympathetically. Nothing.

'Chris? Are you there? My name is May Norman. I've been writing about this terrible crime for *Australia Today* and wanted to tell you personally how sorry I am.' She held her breath, heard faint rustling on the other side of the door. 'I feel I've come to know Bella a little bit, just by talking to those who knew and loved her. I know our readers feel the same way, too. But of course nobody knew and loved her the way you did. I wonder if, knowing how much Bella has come to mean to so many people, you might agree to share a little bit of what she meant to you?'

May could hear breathing, heavy, uneven. She felt certain someone was watching her from behind a lacy curtain across the road. 'Chris? If we could just talk for a –'

A roar sent her stumbling back, half falling down the porch steps. She stood stunned. Had that sound – so deep and bestial – come from Chris? There it was again. Loud enough to make May shudder even way back on the driveway. She resisted the urge to run, forcing her legs to move in what she hoped was a natural, unmortified way.

That first-ever death-knock had conformed to Andrew's best-case scenario. The parents had sat on either side of May on their lumpy orange sofa and talked her page by page through the photo albums they'd kept since the dead seven-year-old was born. It was an emotionally wrenching afternoon, but May never felt she was pushing the parents or taking advantage. They wanted the world to know about their little boy, how loved he was, how happy he made people. They *were* grateful to May for giving them that chance.

As it happened, May hadn't had to knock on the doors of any grieving relatives in the five weeks since then. She'd done a few quick interviews after press conferences or as bereaved loved ones were leaving court hearings but she'd been part of a pack and any angry words or looks seemed to be directed at the lot of them – at the whole world even – rather than her personally.

She sat in her car shaking so hard it took three attempts to light a cigarette. The woman had roared at her. Roared. What kind of person does that?

What kind of person causes someone to do that?

The rest of the day she played the moment back, tried to figure out if it was something specific that she'd said or just her persistence that had provoked the roar. Drifting off to sleep, she repeated to herself, It's fine, you're OK you're OK you're OK. Then the thought like a slap: it wasn't about you. When did you become such a shitty, self-absorbed human being? Think of what the woman has been through. As if your breathless little sales pitch could make a dent.

May sat up, grabbed her computer from the bedside table, typed in the phrase, clicked the link.

'Oh.' She closed the window, punched herself in the leg, reopened the page. 'Jesus fucking fuck.' The same expanse of dirt and dead and dying grass she'd photographed the day she arrived, taken from every angle and a range of distances, but here with the police tape and plastic numbered markers and what was left of Bella Michaels still in place.

May couldn't bring herself to save the photos to her hard drive, but she forced herself to take careful notes. When she was sure she'd recorded every detail she closed the browser, went to settings and deleted the history. She stuffed her notebook into the bottom of her bag. A cramp attacked her lower stomach, then another. She made it to the toilet just in time.

She double-checked the door and window locks and crawled into bed. A real crime reporter would look at those pictures and wish only that she'd got to the scene in time to take them herself, May thought. You must do better, May. You must you must you must.

Wednesday

15

April

AustraliaToday.com

THOUSANDS MARCH FOR BELLA

May Norman
15 April 2015

Between four and five thousand people marched through Sydney's CBD Wednesday evening to mourn murdered Strathdee woman Bella Michaels.

Police closed sections of George, King, Pitt and Market streets between 6 and 8pm to allow the mourners to pass freely through the city.

Many of those attending carried signs bearing feminist slogans and messages about violence against women. Others carried flowers, cards and other funereal mementos which organisers said would be collected and passed on to Ms Michaels' family.

Femolition's Monica Gordon led the way with a handmade sign declaring END VIOLENCE AGAINST WOMEN 4EVA, 4 BELLA. Ms Gordon said her group had been inspired to organise the march after seeing the 'overwhelming' social media response to Ms Michaels' murder. 'All of these people, from all kinds of backgrounds, were expressing such grief and shock and horror. There was such a sense of hopelessness. We decided to organise this event to bring together all of those grieving for Bella and all of those who feel overwhelmed by the extent of violence against women in the community.'

Kaylene Johnson, 47, who marched with her three teenage daughters, said it was the sense of hopelessness which brought her out. 'My girls and I have been weeping about Bella ever since we heard. We've been talking about what we could do. This doesn't change anything for poor Bella, of course, but it does give you hope to see how many people care enough to come out. It makes me feel a bit better for the sake of my girls, to see that people do care.'

No members of Ms Michaels' family were present at the march. According to Ms Gordon, 'They are grieving privately, which we respect.' Asked if it wouldn't have been more appropriate to have held the march in Strathdee, Ms Gordon argued that although the crime took place there, it is one that has had a national impact.

'I'd like to see marches like this all over the country. Anywhere that young women think twice before going out alone, anywhere parents fight the impulse to lock their adult daughters inside, anywhere that people have shed tears over Bella Michaels – we should be out on the streets uniting in our grief, our outrage and our determination to make a world in which women can move about freely without fear of violence.'

According to the Strathdee Council, no permissions have been sought to hold a march in the town where Bella Michaels lived. Walk down any of the six streets that make up downtown Strathdee, however, and you'll see the grief of the community in the prayers for Bella on the signs of the Anglican, Catholic and Uniting churches. It's there, too, on the handmade and professionally printed signs hanging on shopfronts and power poles, all bearing some version of the message 'RIP Bella'.

And at the nursing home where Ms Michaels worked, and was last seen alive, the Australian flag out the front is at half-mast, the windows of the front office hung with black organza. A makeshift shrine on the nursing home's verandah grows by the hour as local residents, passing holidaymakers and out-of-towners on a mission bring flowers, balloons, teddy bears and cards.

A similar shrine has appeared where Ms Michaels' body was found beside the highway a few minutes from town. This one, being out in the open and unprotected from wind, sun and rain, looks wrecked, abandoned, even as it, too, grows.

Ten days on from the discovery of Ms Michaels' body, police have yet to make an arrest. Sources close to the police department report that there are no suspects and few leads on the case, though an official spokesperson refused to confirm this, saying only that investigators are 'pursuing several lines of inquiry'.

■ ■ ■

You saw the march, I guess? Amazing, hey? I watched news clips of it on Lisa's computer and at first I almost felt bad about not getting involved. All those strangers holding up pictures, crying for Bella. But then I saw the close-ups of those ladies leading the thing, tears but no swollen eyes or red noses, their make-up not even streaky, and I felt so angry I couldn't breathe.

Look, for the record, I believe they were sad and scared. But that march was about them, for them. That's fine. Whatever gets you through this life. But they shouldn't've pretended it was for Bella. How could it have been? They had no memories of her to celebrate, no way of understanding just what it was the world lost when she died. And the coverage that damn thing got, well, it made people – all the goddamn compassionate, sad people out there – feel like something had been done, some kind of justice. It made a lot of those nice ladies and men marching through Sydney feel better about what had happened and that was the opposite of what was needed. We needed rage and heartbreak, we needed the whole country to be unable to sleep, to eat, to move on with their lives until the men who did this were found. Instead we got warm feelings about community and sweet quotes about paying tribute. They got peace and we – Bella and me – got jack-fucking-shit.

Sorry. The screws start popping when I talk about all that stuff. That's Nate's expression. When I start getting worked up he'll say, 'Calm down, babe, the screws are popping.' If I keep going – which, let's be honest, I usually do because who's ever been calmed by being told to calm down? – then he'll say, 'Yep, those hinges are busted all the way off, now.' He usually says it right before clearing the hell out of my way.

Anyway, in the days leading up to the march, Nate organised to have my number disconnected and a new one set up and called the people we wanted to have it, told them to keep it mum. He also arranged that Lisa and Carrie would take turns to pop around and clear the messages from it for me, so that I never had to answer a call from someone I didn't know or didn't want to talk to, but wouldn't have to worry about missing anything important. And, of course, he put that sign about trespassers and photographers out the front, too. For all the good it's done.

Anyway, after he'd taken care of all that, Nate told me it was time for him to go back to Sydney.

'I've used up all my leave, and Renee's –'

'About to pop.'

He started at that, dumb idiot.

'You got a voice like a thunderclap. So when's she due?'

The look he gave me then, geez, it had our whole young lives in it. Those years we'd tried before the doctors told me I wasn't fitted right. The slow slide when I understood the last reason not to get drunk and stay that way was gone.

'Still a few months to go.'

'You could've told me.'

'I would've. Just the circumstances, you know – felt like I'd be rubbing it in.'

'Yeah.'

'I'm really sorry, babe.'

'Don't be. It's a happy thing. Never be sorry about happy things.'

Oh, the smile he gave me then. Kidding myself to think I'll ever be over him.

'I've asked to be put back on the Melbourne run, so I'll be passing through here all the time, staying at Melvin's still. And even when I'm not, you only need to call and I can come. Seriously. Call me whenever, for anything, Chris, I mean it.'

'No you don't. Not for anything.'

Another smile. 'No, OK, not for that. But . . .'

'I know. Appreciate it. And you keep me updated, when the bub comes and all that.'

His goddamn eyes started leaking a little. It was just too much. I kissed his forehead and thanked him for everything and all but pushed him out the door. Fine, fine, tickety-fucking-boo-fine.

I had a fear of abandonment as a kid. That's what the school counsellor called it, anyway. I was sent to see her because of all the days I'd had off without a note. I didn't have notes because my mum was too pissed or else too sick to write them, and even if she hadn't been I wouldn't have asked her to write me notes because then she'd realise I was staying home and make me go and then I wouldn't be there if she slipped and hit her head or got in the car three sheets to the wind and drove it into the creek. So if she was out of it enough not to know it was a school day, then I had to stay home and keep an eye on her. The school counsellor didn't get that I wasn't scared of her abandoning me on purpose; I was scared she'd die.

Everything changed when she met Tony. Him and me never warmed to each other, not really, but Mum was much better when he was around. Hardly drank, hardly cried. She even quit smoking when she fell pregnant and then stayed off them for months after Bella was born. I wouldn't say she was happy, but she was better than I'd known her. If you ask me about my childhood, it's those couple of years I think of, even though I was already a little woman to look at by then. But inside I felt like a proper kid finally, never worrying about what was for dinner or whether the electricity bill'd been paid or if all that vomiting meant I needed to call a doctor or just wash the towels and mix up some Lucozade.

Things got hard again when Tony left and Brett came, but in a different way. Mum was still sober, but under the influence of a dickhead, which was worse. Then he left and the beltings stopped but the boozing and panic attacks started again. By then I was pretty much over it all. Sounds harsh, but I was a teenager.

Bella was always better than me. Responsible, forgiving, kind. You know, thinking on it, the more she helped Mum the harder I got. Don't know why. I was over it all, like I said, but it was more than that. I suppose I felt it was Bella's turn. Fucking idiot, I was. Every bit of resentment I had against Mum for being such a shit adult, well, I should've been feeling it for myself the way I let that poor munchkin do all the tough stuff. Before long the little darlin' was taking care of me, too.

When Mum was dying, we took care of her together. Afterwards, all my old issues came roaring back. Yeah, clichéd *Oprah* bullshit, I know. Adult woman feeling abandoned by her mummy. Whatever, Bella was my rock. And then Nate left me and of course I fell apart again, and of course, again, Bella put me back together. I remember saying to her, 'What would I do without you, Bel?' and she, cheeky thing, said, 'Probably choke on your microwave dinner and only be found a month later when the neighbours complained about the smell.'

She could joke about it because it would never happen. Not the choking on my dinner – the doing without her. I would've bet every last cent, bet my life, on her always being there for me. I mean it. I feared abandonment, big time. I clung to my mother, to my boyfriends, especially to Nate, like a polyester dress on cheap tights. But I never clung to Bella, never felt a need to. There was no scenario, no matter how catastrophic, in which she wasn't there. I could no more imagine life without her than I could imagine my own non-existence.

The cops called to say they were releasing Bella's car and would I like to come get it. I couldn't, and so they offered to bring it around to me. Funny, but I heard it coming up the street. I don't think I'd ever thought of how her car sounded – it's a ten-year-old hatchback, good nick, nothing special. But that afternoon I was in the kitchen and it was like – whoosh! Here she comes! Bella's car chuffing up the street, coming to a stop in the driveway. I leant forward so I could see out the corner of the window and there was its red hood sparkling away at me, filling me – against reason – with the pleasure of anticipation I always had when my little sis dropped around on a whim.

Once I'd signed all the papers and young Matt Drey had left in the police car that'd followed him, I took the keys and opened the driver's door, slid in and rested my hands on the wheel. It felt so comfortable, adjusted perfectly for my height. The cop's adjustment, I realised, not Bella's. She was shorter than me and always drove with the seat fully upright. Nate and me would bag the hell out of her, sitting up like a school bus driver, as serious and alert as a kid sitting her driving test.

What Bella always pointed out though, when I hassled her, was that at least she *could* drive. 'Got you there,' Nate would say, but he wouldn't carry on about it because I knew he didn't want me driving. Not as long as I was still drinking so much anyway.

It was comfortable, sitting with my hands on the wheel, my feet on the pedals. I could imagine easing the handbrake off, reversing back down the drive. It was ridiculous that I couldn't. Ridiculous and stupid and neglectful. When Bella went missing I could do nothing but make goddamn phone calls and hope for the best. Even if I'd got that message on the Friday night, there was nothing I could've done except call around and ask others to go looking. But if I'd been able to drive, had a car sitting out here waiting, I could've headed on out the second I heard and at the traffic lights I might've looked over and seen Bella in the back of a car full of men and I'd've leapt out and slammed on the hood until they let her out.

Even if I didn't catch them still in town I could've kept going, driven all the way out onto the highway, and when my headlights hit the gang of them dragging her from the car they would've bolted and I would've run to her, helped her up and she would've been shaken and hurt – maybe badly hurt – but fixable, here.

How late would've been too late? How late could I have found her? I know what they did to her. I don't know how long it took. How late might I have gone out and found her and given her CPR, which I'd learnt so I could get a small pay bump at work, and wrapped her in my jacket and driven her to the hospital?

I popped the glovebox. Nothing but the owner's manual and rego papers. The back seat was empty, the floor looked freshly vacuumed. Bella always kept the car clean, but the absence of even a stray hairband or piece of fluff, the lack of any *smell*, was too much. Of course it had been gone over with a fine-tooth comb, every hair and fibre and scrap of paper taken as potential evidence. They wouldn't have given it to me if there'd been any remnants of Bella inside.

I turned the key in the ignition and 'Love Her Madly' floated out of the radio. Bella and her classic hits, another thing we'd bag her about, her middle-aged taste in music. At least the police hadn't changed the station. I jerked the seat as far back as it would go, closed my eyes.

A knocking startled me and I slammed my elbow into the door.

Lisa peered in at me, an apologetic smile on her face.

I wound down the window.

'Sorry, honey, didn't mean to scare you, I just wanted to check you were OK.'

'Yep, fine.'

'Good, good, it's just . . .' She gave a weird little shrug. 'You've been out here quite a while and I worried that . . . Oh, I don't know. Must be quite emotional for you, the car and . . .'

I noticed then that it was almost dark. The dashboard clock said 18.46. 'Shit. Must've drifted off.'

'Haven't been sleeping well, honey?'

I brushed her question away with one hand, turned off the ignition, climbed out, checked the door was locked. 'Lucky you came out, Lis. I'm late for work.'

'Maybe you should –'

I shook my head, ran inside. I didn't feel rested, not at all. My phone flashed at me from the kitchen bench. Old Grey chasing me up, no doubt. I thought about calling in sick but then I saw the black garbage bag of Bella's personal effects. If I stayed home from work I'd have to go through it and I didn't feel ready for that.

'Best wait until you're feeling stronger,' Bella said. 'Maybe even ask Nate to do it with you.'

It was good advice. I rushed to get dressed for work.

I called Nate during my break. Voicemail. I left a brief message telling him I'd got Bella's stuff back, would like his help going through it before he left town. I suggested he come around either late tonight or tomorrow morning before he hit the road.

Near closing time I started thinking about that bag sitting there and then the clarity of Bella's voice in my head telling me to leave it. I got the shivers real bad then. It wasn't so much that I'd heard her, but that I'd responded like it was normal. I didn't know if I was going nuts or just spending too much time alone or what.

I tried Nate again; still voicemail. It was a quiet night, none of my regular sleepover pals around. There was one bloke who'd propositioned me a few times over the years but I'd not much liked the look of him and so I'd put him off until he stopped asking. Lingering with my Chux wipe near where he was playing pool I confirmed that I still didn't much like the look of him. I'm not talking about whether he was hot or not; to be honest he was in better nick than most of the blokes who come through here. But there was something sneaky about him. A way of smiling that made you think he was covering something up. A way of flicking his gaze away just at the moment of connection.

On the other hand, he was, as I said, in pretty good nick and the closer it got to home time, the more I thought about the garbage bag and the voice telling me not to go through it yet, the less and less I minded the look of him after all.

I didn't ask him outright; that's not my way. But I did make it as clear as I could that I was looking at him anew, that I found him worth undoing an extra button for. He read me loud and clear, pointed out the likelihood of rain, offered me a lift home. So I got what I wanted, yeah.

Look, I'll say this much: my intuition is bloody unreal. If you ever see me about to go against it again, slap some sense into me, will ya? The sex was fine the first time. The problem was I'd planned for it to be the *only* time. In my mind the deal was simple: I'd give him a good screw and a comfy bed; he'd give me a warm, strong body to shield my back from I don't know what, and living breath – snores and all – to silence any voices. Most of all, he'd give me a reason not to go looking through that damn bag.

Couldn't tell him all that though, could I? So not his fault, you know. Misunderstanding. He'd emptied his wallet of a good stack of twenties before he even got into my bed so I suppose he thought that was his end of things taken care of.

Not that he forced me. Not saying that at all. You know how it is though, sometimes easier to let a man do his thing than go through the trouble of explaining why not, of kicking him out, of having a big scene. So, yeah.

When he finally went to sleep I couldn't get away from him fast enough. I showered, rugged up in my ugly flannelette PJs and settled myself down on the sofa. Tried to settle myself. Every snore from my bedroom was a razor nicking my nerve endings.

Around 4 am, exhausted from trying to sleep, I grabbed the bag and in one move, before I could talk myself out of it, emptied it on the living room floor. Stared at the pile for a bit; couldn't see anything to be frightened of. I picked up her grey leather Guess duffel, revealed as a fake by the flaking on the handles. Inside, her wallet, emptied of cash but still containing all her cards and a picture of Mum and me. Clear lip gloss in a little tub. A straw-coloured hair band. Hand sanitiser. Tissues. Half-empty pack of tampons. *Who* magazine, dated the day of her death. Her phone, the screen smashed, the back caved in.

In a separate, smaller plastic sleeve was the gold ring me and Mum gave her for her twenty-first. It looked like it'd been buried for fifty years. I tipped it into my hand and the smell of old blood, the gritty texture, made me retch. I remembered her hands in the morgue, all . . . Jesus. Sorry. It's just the ring, her hands . . . It's impossible not to imagine her trying to fight them off, you know? Trying and trying until her hands, her ring . . .

The bag did not contain her clothes; I don't know what happened to them.

At some point I fell asleep. When I woke there was a pillow under my head, a blanket over my legs. I guess the man might've done it before he left. He did have some tenderness in him, I suppose.

Nate called. He was ropeable about me leaving messages for him the night before. Said that him being there for me when I needed would only work if I respected his boundaries and didn't call for every little thing. I tried to explain that it wasn't just a little thing, that it was Bella's stuff, but he cut me off with this stab of a sound and I understood he wasn't really angry, just frightened and sad and that he couldn't cope with it all any more and stay sober. I told him I was sorry for bothering him, and I meant it.

I saw that for everybody else – even people who loved her, like Nate – Bella's death was a thing to get over, to move on from. But Bella couldn't move on from it and so how could I? As had happened so often in our childhood, Bella and I had been abandoned in our suffering by all those claiming to care. But now as then we would be alright. I knew we would because we were strong and we had so much love and we were together.

■ ■ ■

May was in Sydney for twelve hours, her thoughts cycling between the pictures of Bella Michaels and the proximity of Craig the whole time. Spending the night at home would be asking for trouble on both counts so she headed back to Strathdee immediately after the march. For the first hour and a half she couldn't unclench her jaw or stop herself checking the rear-view mirror every ten seconds. Then JJJ split into static and she noticed it had been ages since she'd seen a shop or service station and she began to relax. Nobody knows where I am right now, she thought. She poked at the stereo buttons without looking until an Eighties pop song came through, turned the volume up all the way, opened the windows, felt alone and safe and more OK than she had in days.

Just after the Gunning exit her headlight beams bounced over a lifeless joey and May shuddered. No more than a hundred metres on, another, and then right away one more. Twelve dead bodies – joeys, wallabies, roos – in ten minutes and then she stopped counting. They seemed too intact to have been mown down by the road trains that thundered past every half hour or so. It was as though the slowly turning arms of the wind turbines on the nearby hills had struck a single heavy blow on each tiny skull. A few were stiff, their paws and pointy faces jabbing towards the sky, but most appeared soft, fresh. The blood on the hands of whoever had dragged them to the edge would still be wet.

Earlier that evening at her brother's house, a friend of his, Ollie, listened to her talking about Bella and said, 'Whoever did that needs to be strung up and gutted.'

'Eye for an eye makes the whole world blind,' Max said in a

singsong voice.

'Mate, tell me that if someone did that to your sister you wouldn't want him torn to pieces.'

'I wouldn't,' Max said quietly. 'More violence wouldn't be –'

'Of course, but it's not logical, is it? It's human nature. Someone does a thing like that to your sister, your blood, you can't help but –'

'I'm with Ollie,' May said. 'If someone did that to you, Max, I'd kill him.'

'You wouldn't.' Max topped up her wineglass. 'You might feel like it, but you wouldn't.'

'Women don't, generally, do they? Kill, I mean. Revenge or otherwise,' Ollie said, calm, interested. 'I used to think it was culture, socialisation, but the older I get, the more I think it's biological. I know we're not meant to say that, but, seriously. More and more I think there's something in it. Men are just more . . .' He took a small sip of his wine, waved his hand. 'I don't know. What do you think, May?'

'I have no fucking idea,' she said. She remembered being twelve and hearing in the canteen line that some kids in Max's year had wrenched off his shirt and tie and drawn tits on his little sparrow chest. She didn't hesitate. Went straight to the boys' toilets, where she'd been told they were boasting of their feat, while Max cowered in a stall crying. She ignored the gasps and jeering when she entered that stinking little domain. The boy with Max's tie wrapped around his head got a hard punch in the stomach. His mate, stunned, his pinched face turning red, let out a high-pitched 'No!' when she grabbed his hair and bashed his forehead into the toilet door. The boys ran away and she rescued her weeping brother, took him up to the office, where he was given a replacement shirt and a private place to sit until their mum could come and get him.

The boys were suspended. So was May. Grounded, too. 'I know they were shits, but they were *little* shits,' her mum said. 'You can't bash people smaller than you.' May felt shame. Or talked herself into a feeling like that, anyway. Now, all she remembered was the pleasure of it. The thrill of feeling that boy's stomach squish in around her fist, the satisfying clunk vibrating through her arm when skull met wood.

Was that what the truckies felt when their bumpers met a roo mid-bounce? A clunk both deeply satisfying and easily shaken off? A joey would dent her shit-box, a full-grown roo write it off, kill her even, if it hit the windscreen. If only she had a truck, a bus, a goddamn tank. No. That wouldn't do it. A vehicle, a gun – it wouldn't be the same, would it? All gore and no connection.

Is that all it is? she wondered. You realise it feels good to sink your finger pads into a neck, your elbows into a spine, your cock into a resisting hole? You realise it feels good and that, barring unfortunate timing or poor choice of victim, you realise you can?

Right before Strathdee she swerved to miss a giant crow devouring the innards of a split-open roo in the middle of the road. If there'd been oncoming traffic, she would've had to drive right over it. The bird, she was sure, wouldn't have seen her coming, so absorbed was it in its fresh feast.

Thursday
16
April

AustraliaToday.com

WHAT HAPPENED TO BELLA?

May Norman
16 April 2015

For the past few years, Sarah Loome started almost every work day with a cuppa and a chat with her colleague Bella Michaels in the staff tearoom at Strathdee Haven, a private aged-care facility in the NSW Riverina town of Strathdee. The two women, both aged 25, both single, both Strathdee-born-and-bred, would look out over the small enclosed courtyard not yet crowded with residents getting some air. Sarah would sip extra-strong Nescafé, Bella a herbal tea as they talked over the sounds of the night shift packing up and preparing to hand over.

Today, Sarah's small, freckled hands shake as she prepares a coffee for herself and taps her fingers on the variety box of tea that Bella Michaels will never again riffle through looking for the perfect blend for that day's challenges. On a noticeboard above Sarah's head, in the centre of the usual workplace notices about keeping the kitchen clean and remembering to fill out a timesheet each Wednesday, is an A4 sheet of paper. Across its top in bold print: WHAT HAPPENED TO BELLA? Underneath that, a photo.

She is in front of a Christmas tree hung messily with bright, chain-store baubles. A pair of these same baubles hang from her ears, peeking out cheekily from within her frizzy blonde hair. Her face is free of make-up. The glint in her eyes and open mouth suggest she's on the edge of laughter. She's wearing her pale blue nursing uniform, the top slightly-too snug, drawing attention to her small, high breasts and finely muscled biceps. She's strong, but feminine. Pretty but not glamorous. Everyone's stereotype of a typical young nurse.

Underneath, the same bold print, but smaller: *Taken from us Friday 4 March*. This is followed by a simple plea for information and a phone number.

'She was beautiful, wasn't she?' Sarah asks, running her fingers over the photo. 'I think that's why no one believes she didn't have a boyfriend. She didn't though. I'd have known. We talked all the time about our sad single lives.' She laughs then to make it clear neither of them was sad at all, not before.

It's true that many refuse to believe Bella didn't have a lover, that her death wasn't the result of an affair gone wrong. It may be, as Sarah suggests, that Bella's attractiveness leads people to believe she couldn't possibly have been single. It may be that the blend of sexiness and innocence evident in the photo on the poster is exactly the kind we imagine driving a man to extremes.

Or it may be that most of the time when a woman is murdered, it's at the hands of a partner or ex.

But Sarah, as well as others close to Bella Michaels, are adamant that there was no boyfriend. As for rumours she was involved with a married colleague, Sarah thumps the tabletop. 'Absolute crap. For one thing, this is a small, gossipy little place. We'd all know if anyone was sneaking around with anyone else. And for another, I knew Bella. She was the most moral person you could imagine. No way in the world she'd mess around with a married man. No way.'

Sit long enough in any of Strathdee's four cafés, six restaurants, two hotel lobbies or four pubs and you'll hear about the unidentified married man along with any number of darker rumours. In the last few days, there's been talk of satanic rituals and racist gangs, of a hidden pregnancy and an illegal prostitution ring. To Bella's friends, these would be laughable if they weren't so offensive. More importantly, they are each without a single scrap of evidence. All seem to have bubbled up fully formed from the black hole that opened in this town the moment Bella's naked, violated body was found beside the road a few kilometres outside of town on the 6th of April. Each day that passes without an arrest, the rumours get wilder and the atmosphere in town thickens with menace and unfocused suspicion.

Local police claim they have no suspects, but sources confirm that they have repeatedly interviewed Nate Cartwright, the former husband of Bella's sister Chris Rogers, a local barmaid twelve years Bella's senior. 'I feel for Chris, I really do,' Sarah says. 'They were closer than any sisters I've ever known. They'd talk every day. I don't know anything about this ex-husband, but if he's supporting Chris through all this, then that's good.'

Cartwright, 40, was sentenced to twelve months' jail for the violent assault of a woman in 2000. Now of Sydney and, reportedly, in a new relationship, he works as a driver and tour guide for a major coach company whose tours regularly pass through Strathdee. While no charges have been laid and there's no evidence that Cartwright had anything to do with his former sister-in-law's death, his constant presence at Ms Rogers' side since the murder, and the interest with which police seem to be treating him, are notable.

Indeed, a striking photo taken immediately after Bella's funeral shows him in an intimate moment with his ex-wife; in the background several police officers can be seen looking on. According to witnesses, moments after this photograph was taken Cartwright reportedly struck out at photographers and had to be restrained by police. 'He was like a rabid dog,' one witness says. 'And he's a big fella, too. He could've snapped that photographer in two with one hand, I reckon.'

The sight of Cartwright entering Strathdee police station earlier in the week showed a different side, however. He is indeed a large man with dark shaggy hair and a long, unkempt beard. On this day he wore tight, faded black jeans, a black heavy-metal t-shirt and scuffed black boots, looking for all the world like a member of a biker gang. But those big hands the witness imagined snapping a photographer in two were being used to gently steer the comparatively tiny Chris Rogers into the station. At one point, Ms Rogers hesitated, appearing to lose her composure, and Cartwright stroked her face with the gentleness of a small child patting a baby rabbit. Ms Rogers responded by squeezing her ex-husband's hand and flashing him a smile. Arms linked, the two entered the station. Whatever else may be true in this terrible, dark mystery, the bond between these two can be in no doubt.

Meanwhile, at the Haven, Sarah and her colleagues get on with their work, pausing every now and then to glance at Bella's picture. 'I don't like the wording on that poster,' a nursing aide tells me as she passes through the tearoom. 'I mean, I get that they had to keep it simple, but it's the wrong question, isn't it? We know what happened to her. We need to know who.'

'And why,' Sarah adds. 'Just, God, why?'

Anyone with information related to the murder of Bella Michaels should contact Crime Stoppers or the Strathdee police.

■　■　■

May knew that leaving the TV on all night was a bad habit, but listening to the twenty-four-hour world news channel seemed to be the only way she could avoid crying herself to sleep and waking up with a red-raw throat and punched-closed eyes. Late-night comedy and infomercials weren't strong enough to stop her mind flashing up a slideshow of Bella Michaels' body in between thoughts, sometimes accompanied by the sound of Chris Rogers' roar. And by the third or fourth repeated loop of news stories the wording and order became familiar and she could drift off.

Still, waking to voices in the room discussing bomb blasts in Syria or a massacre in Kenya was not the most pleasant way to start the day. Almost as awful as being jolted into consciousness by her damn phone.

'Andrew. Hi.' She checked the bedside clock: 6.28. Christ. 'What's up?'

'This piece you filed overnight? Not your best work.'

May reached for the remote, muted the TV, swallowed her panic. 'Can you be more specific?'

'Tabloid as fuck, not to mention clearly milking a dead cow, at this stage. But look, I've been outvoted on this one so we're going to stick it up this morning. Simone's putting together a package with an interactive map of Strathdee, a rundown of the events so far, slide show of pics and all that jazz.'

'Great. Thank you.'

'And that *will* conclude our coverage of Bella Michaels. If they catch someone, if there's another body, you go back. But save that, the story's done.'

'It really isn't. You have to trust me –'

'No, it really is. Even if something new did happen there – which it won't – we just got a tip-off that a woman's been found raped and strangled right here in Sydney. Jim's on his way out there now to get the prelims, but this is your beat. So see you here at eight, right?'

'Andrew, come on. It's a five-hour drive and I did it in both directions yesterday. I'm knackered.'

'Christ, May. I told you to pack up and come home on Tuesday. I assumed you'd filed this from up here. Jesus.' He huffed. 'Alright, get a move on and I'll see you here around one. OK?'

'Yeah,' May said. And then, after a pause just long enough to allow the Bella Michaels photos to flash behind her eyes, 'No. Actually, no. I stay on the Strathdee beat or I quit.'

'There is no Strathdee beat. There was a story and now it's run its course. More than run its course.'

'I know it seems like –'

'Jesus, Norman. You got yourself a boyfriend there or something?'

'Yeah, so, OK, I quit.'

'Don't be stupid.'

'I'll email my letter of resignation and my final expense claims this afternoon.'

'You're fucking nuts.'

She hung up, heart racing. She was fucking nuts. Shit. She dialled her brother.

'Max, I've done something, um, dramatic.'

'Oh? Sounds exciting.'

'I quit my job.'

'That is not exciting. That is . . . Why? I thought it was your dream job?'

'It was. But . . . It's not like I thought it would be.'

'In what way?'

'I don't know, I guess I had delusions of heroism or something. I thought I'd be able to look at all the ugliness and write something beautiful about it and that people would . . . I don't know. But as it happens, looking at the ugliness is sending me mad and my writing about it is kind of shit.'

'Your writing is not shit.'

'"Tabloid as fuck" is the totally fair review my latest effort received.'

'Yeah, well, tough story in a shithouse locale where everything's a cliché. It'll be better when you get back to Sydney.'

'No, that's the thing. My editor wanted me to come back and I said I wanted to stay here and keep reporting this story and that's when I quit.'

'Wait. Did you quit because you're not cut out to be a crime reporter or because you want to do more crime reporting but only from that specific town?'

'I don't know. Neither. Both.'

'You do realise you're not making any sense, right?'

'I know . . . It's like, OK, don't laugh or roll your eyes or whatever, because I know how this sounds, but I feel kind of traumatised by something that happened. Something that happened and something I saw. I can't get it out of my head, pictures flashing up when I close my eyes and all that.'

'Why would I laugh at that? That sounds horrible. Sounds like another good reason to come home, but.'

'No, listen: it's like the way I'm feeling is why I know I'm not cut out to be a crime reporter. But now that I've seen and heard what I have, I can't just leave. I need to follow through until the end. Make it right somehow.'

'May, I don't want to be harsh, because you're obviously in a lot of pain but –'

'No, be harsh. That's why I call you, to tell me how it is.'

'You can't make it right. No one can. That's why it's so awful.'

'But the fear, the injustice. If I write stuff that helps catch the killers, then those things will be made better. And if I can write about Bella properly, like really write about her life and who she was, not just what happened to her, then that's something, isn't it? It's leaving something for her to be remembered by rather than . . .'

May saw the photos again.

'If the police think you writing about it all will help catch whoever did it, then, yeah, I can see the value. But all that other stuff? Honestly? I think you're equal parts naive and egotistical if you think anything you write will make a difference to people who've lost someone they love in this way. If it were you, there's not a writer alive who could make even the tiniest smudge of difference to how I felt. Not a smudge.'

'You're right, I know.'

'But?'

'I need to see this through.'

'May, hon, some cases never get solved.'

'So I need to work really hard to make sure this isn't one of them.'

'It might be beyond your control.'

'And it might not. Look, thanks. You've helped. I feel much clearer now. I'm going to go and make some calls, get things happening.'

'Would you consider doing any of that from Sydney?'

'No, but I'll be back soon. The police will find who did this and I'll be here to report it and then I'll be home gloating about how wrong you were.'

He sighed. 'Do you at least have someone to hang out with there? Someone to do non-murder-investigation related stuff with?'

'No, but then I don't in Sydney either so –'

'Nice to know I'm chopped liver.'

'You know what I mean.' She felt tears coming. 'Hey, listen, I need to go. Freelance hustling to start. Thanks though. You always make me feel better.'

'You know what would make me feel better? You coming home.'

'I know. Soon. Promise.'

She called Chas, told him she'd be in all day. He came in his lunch break, high-vis shirt and thick navy work pants covered in concrete dust. He only had half an hour and was starving, he said. They fucked quickly and then walked across to the pub, where Chas ordered two steak pies to take away, eating one of them in three bites while May sipped her beer and smoked on the verandah.

He passed the remaining pie from hand to hand. 'Sorry to love ya and leave ya, but I've gotta get back before the boss has a shit attack.'

'It's cool. I'm going to hang around here a bit. See what I can dig up.'

Chas held his pie still, looked over her shoulder. 'Be careful, hey?'

'Of what?'

'You know. Girl hanging around a pub on her own.'

'Yeah? How I met you wasn't it? Turned out alright.'

'Not everyone's as sweet as me. Next time you mightn't be so lucky.'

'I'll take my chances. Thanks for your concern though. I really appreciate it.'

'Yeah, I can tell.' He started down the verandah steps, stopped, turned only his head back towards her. 'Glad you called, hey.'

May watched him cross the road, climb into his truck, pull out onto the road and disappear onto the highway. She finished her cigarette and headed back into the dim cool of the pub, ordered another beer and settled herself at the bar. Everyone knew who she was by now, no point lurking in the shadows.

A middle-aged man in footy shorts and a white singlet leant against the bar an inch from her elbow. 'How's it goin'?' he said to her thigh.

'Yeah, good. You?'

'Yep, yep.' He ordered a beer, turned so he could look directly into May's face. He was close enough she could've counted the broken blood vessels on his swollen nose. 'You one of them light-skinned Abos or something?'

May held her nerve the way she knew a woman with a near-stranger's semen turning her undies stiff who had just quit her job in order to follow a nothing story in a shithole town would do. 'Or something,' she said.

'Huh.' He backed off a little but kept staring at her as he necked his beer, putting it down every so often to check his dick was where he left it.

When he finished his drink he ordered another, pushed his hip against the outside of her leg while he waited. When she didn't react he picked up his glass and shuffled to the other end of the bar where a trio of drunks leant and gulped and mumbled. 'Thinks her shit don't stink, that one,' he said, settling into the group, his back to May.

'Pro'ly bottles her piss and tries to sell it as perfume,' one of the others said, and they all cackled.

The old bloke behind the bar glanced across at May with a small apologetic smile. 'They're harmless,' he said in a low voice.

'Them too, hey?'

He looked at her blankly.

'Listen, do you think you could do me a favour?'

'Mmm?'

'I really need to get in touch with –'

'Nah, love.' He held his hands up. 'Can't be having reporters sniffing around. I'm alright with ya drinking here or hanging out with your bloke or whatever, but there'll be no reporting business. Gotta be firm on that.'

'Of course. Sorry.'

He nodded and moved along down the other end of the bar, leant into the group of men and talked low the way he had to her. She strained to hear. Was he saying *Chas*? There was laughter and more mumbling and she heard it clearly this time: *gash*.

Her throat constricted. A word overheard her first year of high school, spoken with thrilled disgust. A moment of puzzling over its use in this context and then the sick surge as she understood. She felt it now, the subterranean hatred. Gash.

Chas had warned her. He knew those men, probably joked with them just like that when no women were around. He had fucked her sweetly but the words must be in his mind. Must be in his like they were in hers. However sweet it was, there was always after and after there was remembering – being reminded – of what you are. Gash, slit, axe wound, cunt.

She felt it again, the craving for the feel of flesh folding around her fist, the vibration up her arm as skull hit wood. She left her half-drunk beer, slid off the stool. Heard the snickering. Stuck up her middle finger as she walked out, feeling like a coward. Like a wretched bloody pussy.

Friday
17
April

Imagine it from my point of view. All week I've had journalists knocking on my door, pushing cards into my hand. More each day it felt like, and I didn't know if that was because they knew Nate was gone or what, but it was getting so I was never not on edge at home, always waiting for the next knock. Old Grey had promised to personally boot out any reporters who bothered me at work and Suze told me he'd been gathering up all the flowers and teddy bears and prayer cards and other useless, heartfelt shit that people left for me and dropping it at the hospital before I arrived each day. God, I appreciated it. Made me feel that, despite it all, I could relax a little there, just be Chris. Ironic, I'd say, yeah, feeling on display at home but nice and private surrounded by mouthy drunks and gossips.

Anyways, that was where my head was at when I answered a call at the pub and this sweet little voice goes, 'Chris! At last!', as though the two of us are old friends who've been playing phone tag all week.

I ask who it is and the little voice says, 'It's May Norman and I am truly sorry to call you at work but it's so important that I speak to you,' and I'm about to hang up but that man I stupidly took home the other night is heading for the bar and so I turn my back on him, phone in hand and I say, 'Important why?'

'Because, Chris, I'm sorry to say it but the police aren't getting anywhere and the longer this goes on the less likely it is they'll find who did this and, you know, I really think more can be done.' Such a sweet, sweet little girl's voice. I suspect you know that. Something that can't be helped but can be put to good use. Girlish voice, the reporter's version of the barmaid's big tits.

'Yeah, like what?'

'Better news coverage. More publicity.'

'Fucking hell, you listen –'

'Chris, I can help you. I can. Sit down with me for one –'

'You have a hide calling me while I'm here and –' In my rage I'd turned back around, raised my voice. The man was leaning in close, listening, frowning like he had a right. I dropped my voice, tried for a calmer tone. 'I just want to be left alone, OK? Please.'

'Chris, I understand, I do, but one really good, strong, detailed interview that lets the people of Australia really *know* Bella could make all the difference. I wouldn't be bothering you like this if I didn't think so.'

I guess my face showed more than I'd've liked because the man leant right over the bar and touched my elbow and mouthed, 'You OK?' I pulled back like he'd burnt me and I said, into the phone, but to him really, 'OK, yeah, all good.'

And the man watched while I faked a goddamn smile and said, 'Yep, great,' while Little Miss Sweetie-pie gushed that she'd see me the next morning at eleven.

I rang Nate at home, because I was really trying to respect his boundaries and only call his mobile in an emergency (as though life itself wasn't one). Renee answered and so I did the totally-over-it adult thing and asked how she was, how the baby was growing and she said it was all wonderful and I'd have to come up and meet him when he was born, and then she said in this extra-low, concerned voice, 'And how are you, Chris?' And I was like 'fine, fine' of course, but she wouldn't let it go, she made a little tutting noise and she said, 'No, really, Chris, listen – I've had a lot of experience with grief and I know how fierce and confusing and overwhelming it can be. You don't have to say you're fine if you aren't.'

I did consider what she said and then considered what a more honest answer to her question would be and then I was torn in half and turned inside out. Sitting there in the back office of the pub with the phone in my hand I became a gaping hole of horror and blackness and despair and Renee said, 'Chris? You there?' and I flipped back into my skin the right way again and I said, 'Yeah, sorry, I can't talk much now, that's all. But listen, is your old man there? I need to ask him something, real quick.'

The rest of the night went OK, especially since Grey stayed back to do the accounts, and so I could honestly tell that man who was hanging around that I was working late and getting a lift with the boss. I didn't think much about what had happened when Renee had told me I didn't have to be fine, nor really about what I'd gotten myself into for the next day. I just thought about how Nate had sounded OK about me calling and he'd said he'd try to get down here early tomorrow, and that was the nicest thing he'd said to me in a while and it felt good.

At home, though, the good feeling leaked away. Not all at once, but drop by drop as I showered and changed and listened to the radio and drank some tea. Bella's things were still on the living room floor and so I avoided that room all together, but I knew they were there and it got so the thought of going in and picking them up made me shaky. But then I remembered there was going to be a bloody journalist here in the morning and maybe Nate, too, and so I couldn't leave it all out there like that and it'd be better to move it tonight or else I wouldn't get a bit of sleep just from thinking about it and so I steeled myself and marched in there.

I sat on the floor meaning to scoop the bits and pieces back into the bag and then throw the bag in the linen cupboard until I could decide what to do with it properly. I can't say what happened except that when I came to it was after three and my hair and nightie were stuck to my sweaty skin and I was shivering hard enough to shatter bone, and all the stuff was laid out there just as it had been.

I didn't think, just did what I'd meant to two hours earlier – shoved it all back into the bag and then shoved the bag into the cupboard. I showered for the second time that night and then crawled into bed. I thought, *I am going mad.* I said it out loud. Then I said, 'Talking to yourself; way to prove the point.' And that made Bella laugh and laugh.

■　■　■

(Unpublished)

STRATHDEE ANIMAL DEATHS UNRELATED TO BELLA MICHAELS

May Norman
17 April 2015

Strathdee police are appealing to the public to help them find the person responsible for at least three cases of animal cruelty. In the most recent case, a dead tabby cat with its muzzle taped shut was yesterday found behind Strathdee football oval's toilet block. Local vet Dr Melody Nicholson said that the cause of death was 'asphyxia and strangulation'. Dr Nicholson also confirmed that both a cat found in the flower garden of the Memorial Park on 3 April and a dog found behind the post office on 12 April were killed in similar ways, although the dog also suffered a head injury.

'These appear to be incidents of deliberate cruelty carried out on innocent, defenceless animals and we are taking them extremely seriously,' said a spokesman for the Strathdee police. All three animals are believed to have been strays, but police have issued a warning to all pet owners to keep their animals inside or safely secured until the perpetrator is found.

Police say there is no reason to believe that the animal deaths might be connected with the unsolved murder of Bella Michaels. 'At the moment we are treating them as unrelated, but again we urge anyone with information about these crimes or any others to come forward and tell us what they know.'

Saturday
18
April

On the page, the TV and from a distance, Chris looked nothing like her half-sister, but in person, up close, the resemblance was there. The smile Chris flashed when May complimented her cherry-red boots was the same as the one beaming out from every photo of Bella. The accompanying crinkles around the eyes were the same, too, though Chris's didn't smooth all the way out when the smile dissolved the way May imagined Bella's would have. Chris was a little taller than Bella, as far as May could tell, and as top-heavy as her younger sister was pear-shaped. When she said, 'Come on in,' it was with the same broad country accent and deep, husky voice as that in the short nursing home video clip the TV news played over and over. That voice coming from sweet, young, blonde Bella was a surprise, but out of Chris it was perfect.

'Have a seat if you like.' Chris gestured to a round table covered in a rose-print cloth. In the centre of the table was a box of tissues, next to it a jug of water and two glasses.

'Is it OK if I record our conversation?'

'Ah, just wait a sec, OK? I'm not sure if I even want to do this. I mean, I'm not keen on –'

'I know you've had some rotten experiences with the media, Chris, so I do understand that you're wary. But the recorder is there to help me get things right, which is what you want, yes? To have someone write the truth about Bella?'

Chris smiled again, but it was the smile of a barmaid about to tell a boozed-up patron he'd be served no more. 'I don't want that at all. I don't want anything written about Bella.'

'Why did you agree to meet with me then?'

She sighed. 'Because I know you lot don't care what I want and that you'll write your bloody articles anyway.'

'And you want to make sure –'

'I want to remind you that there are real people who get hurt all over again every time one of you decides to dig your dirty little fingers into the wound.'

'I know that, Chris. I really do. The last thing I want to do is cause you more pain.'

'I know you don't want to. But you're willing to.'

May poured a glass of water, took a sip. 'I am, yes, I suppose that's true. But it's also true it'd upset me greatly if that's how this turned out. I want to make sure Bella isn't forgotten, that the police, the public, the politicians, the bleeding-heart protestors and hard-arse law-and-order lobbyists – all of them – remember what happened to her, remember that whoever did it is wandering around free, breathing easier and easier with every day that goes by. That's what I want to do, Chris. If reminding the world of all that hurts you, then that's regrettable, but I still think it's worth doing.'

Chris tapped the tabletop with her soft, chewed-up fingertips. 'I want to believe you, May.'

'Why would I lie?'

'Because I'm the golden get. I'm the source that'll make your reporting stand out from the others.'

'Who are these others, Chris? Who's given you this idea that there'll be some kind of journalist showdown?'

She leant back and opened a drawer behind her, pulled out a short stack of business cards, splayed them on the table in front of May. 'Six of them in the last two days. You lot have calendar alerts that go off if a terrible crime isn't solved within two weeks, hey? Now's the time to get the next of kin.'

'No, but we do all understand that when a big new case hits the headlines, the last one is likely to slip from people's thoughts.'

Chris let out a sharp, vicious laugh. 'You all think I'll spill my guts now, because I'm jealous of the attention given to poor bloody Kate Bronson.'

Kate Bronson, forty-one-year-old mother of five kids under ten, wife of a reasonably prominent businessman, grabbed while putting the garbage out after midnight, on the street outside her large, high-security home in a small, old-money suburb north of Sydney Harbour. Her body found a mere six hours later, lying right out on the footpath three streets away. Her photo and those of her small, stricken children and shell-shocked husband were everywhere the way Bella's had been a week earlier.

'Of course not. But you know how these things go. The nation is grieving. Australia is outraged. Australia is scared. We'll never forget. Until the next photogenic victim comes along. Some of us aren't ready to move on and we know that the victim's family will be feeling the same way.' May picked up the business cards, flicked through them, recognising the names. One of them had recently written a bestseller about a jailed gang of pack rapists. 'Have you talked to any of these people?'

'I've told 'em all to bugger off if that counts as talking?'

'You took their cards though.'

Chris shrugged one shoulder. 'Easiest way to get rid of some people is to pretend you'll think about what they've said and get back to them.'

Yeah, but then you chuck the card in the bin right after, May thought. She slid one of the cards to the top of the pile. 'Bet this bloke was hard to shake off.'

Chris squinted at the name. 'Don't know if he was trying to fuck me as a way to get the interview or interview me as way to get me into bed.'

'Hasn't changed then.'

Chris raised her eyebrows; May saw her opportunity.

'Nine or ten years ago, when I was a cadet reporter, he was my mentor. Which meant, basically, sending me out to do the reporting, meeting me at the pub to take all my notes and write them up into a story under his by-line, and if the story came together quickly, screwing me in the back of his Camry before dropping the copy off at the office.'

A smile. Slight, but real. 'We've all had a mentor like that, I reckon.'

'God save twenty-year-old girls from slightly-older men bearing bullshit world-weariness and hard-ons for giving advice.'

'God save us all. I've met more than my share these last weeks. Most of them coppers. Least I know to tell 'em to fuck off now. Doesn't make listening to their bullshit any easier, but.'

'The cops give you advice? About what?'

Chris's face hardened. She shook her head. 'I haven't agreed to an interview.'

'Personal interest in the ways and means of mansplainers only.' May held up her hands. 'No notebook, no tape recorder, see.'

'Yeah. That grub tried to get in my pants, you're trying to become my BFF. Form a bond, make me like you, trust you.'

'Chris, look, of course I want you to like me and trust me and speak to me on the record. But that doesn't mean I'm bullshitting you here. Not everything a reporter says is part of an angle they're working. I'm still a person.'

'Nice angle.'

'Fuck.'

Chris snorted. 'The cops think I shouldn't talk to any reporters not screened by their media unit. They think I should do another press conference but only if I stick to their script. They think I should stop drinking so much, leave my job at the pub, incriminate my ex-husband by spilling my guts about every cross word he's ever said, and they especially think I shouldn't bring blokes back here for a tumble. When I don't take their advice – which is always, because to hell with those useless pricks – they tell me I'm making their jobs harder or hurting the case or putting myself at risk or, my favourite, making myself and therefore Bella *look bad*.'

'Cops told you you're making Bella look bad? That's disgusting.'

Chris let out a deep sigh. 'Thank you.'

They sat looking at the table while somewhere nearby a motorbike revved to life and a dog barked its distress.

'If you talk to me – on the record and in detail – I can write the kind of in-depth profile piece that'll get national attention and of a different kind than the case has had so far. I think we can get it into one of the big women's mags. *Women's Weekly* would be my first pick. Large, totally engaged audience on its own, plus they have fantastic PR, which means it's likely to get picked up and reported on in some of the papers, too. You're a warm, charismatic woman, Chris, and middle Australia is going to be heartbroken for you. They'll be talking about you and Bella at work, at the school gates, at the hairdresser, over dinner. We'll make it so the whole nation is outraged by the fact the bastards haven't been caught.'

'It's a good sales pitch, I'll give you that, but here's my problem.' Chris reached back to the drawer again, slammed a piece of paper onto the table.

May's stomach clenched as she recognised it as a print-out of her *Australia Today* story about Nate Cartwright's assault conviction.'

'Chris, listen, when someone close to a case –'

'Do you have any idea what it might feel like to be grieving someone you love and have to read shit like this? Did it cross your mind how that'd be for him? Having the worst thing you've ever done dragged up in the middle of the worst pain you've ever felt?'

May could feel the heat rising from her chest, soon to humiliatingly flush her face. She breathed through it, focusing on her fingertips pressed into the tabletop. When she was reasonably confident her voice would behave, she met Chris's eyes. 'Have you read any of my other stories about Bella?'

'No.'

'OK, well, I think you should read how I've covered Bella's story in entirety before you decide –'

'Won't make a difference. I've read enough trashy crime writing in my time. I know what you're about. Get the housewives of Australia to gasp over my sister's gorgeous corpse, stir up the gossip about who might have killed her. If you can find a way to accuse the bloke the slutty sister's boning, all the better.'

A thrill surged through May. Slutty? Still sleeping with her ex? Gold.

'I get it, Chris, I really do.' She concentrated on keeping her tone calm. 'I get what you hate about these kinds of stories. But you need to think about what they can achieve.'

'Big sales for the magazine, big payday for the writer.'

'Maybe, but that's not what I'm in it for. I swear to you. I want to bring Bella to life for a broad audience, make those readers fall in love with her, think how she's just like them, could be their best friend, their sister, and then – bam – they get hit with the horror, have to go through the grief. Yes, it's a small, momentary grief, but it's there.

They feel it: the loss, the outrage. They'll remember.' Chris's gaze hadn't shifted from May's face. She was breathing heavily, twisting a tissue into a mess of white splotches. May pushed on. 'Next time they see some douche-bag politician ranting about law and order because some rich prick got knocked on the head and robbed of his watch or hear some blow-hard at the pub ranting about how feminism's gone too far and women have it easy, the women who've read my story will remember Bella, remember she's had no justice. They'll stand up, they won't let it go.'

May had started speaking in desperation but as the words came she realised she had once believed all of this about the power of a well-written story. The quaver in her voice told her that maybe she still did.

'Good speech. I'll vote for you even if this cranky old sow won't.'

May's head jerked toward the doorway where a behemoth of a man in a tour company t-shirt and obscenely short shorts held a loaf of bread in one hand and a white paper bakery bag in the other.

'My ex-husband likes to drop in and insult me from time to time.' Chris's expression was as hard as ever, but there was a softness in her voice May hadn't heard before.

'Insult you *and* bring you teacake.' The man crossed the room in two huge strides, put down his packages, leant against the sink, looking right at May. 'You're the reporter?'

May nodded.

'You came to the house before. I told you to get lost.'

'Yes, I –'

'I read all your articles.'

'Oh?'

'Yep, every one I could find.' He turned, grabbed a glass platter from the draining rack and slid the teacake onto it. Without looking, he opened the second drawer down to his right and grabbed a knife, then reached to his left and picked up three bread plates with one hand. 'I liked 'em', he said, bringing the cake and plates over to the table. 'Nearly all of them.' He winked at May and handed her a bread plate with a too-big piece of cake spilling over the sides.

'Of course you did,' Chris said. 'They're written for thickheads.'

'Easy, you.' His huge hand alighted for a millisecond on Chris's head and then flew up to scratch his beard. 'Nah, you're a good writer. Not that I'm an expert, but I do read a bit and I reckon you're good.'

May felt herself breathing more slowly, became aware that her cheeks were cooling. Chris, too, seemed calmer. Nate's presence had altered the energy of the room, made it feel relaxed, almost. This despite the deep thrum of shame she felt knowing this man had read the things she'd written about him.

'Not an expert, that's an understatement.' Chris rolled her eyes. Her phone rang and she glanced down at it, then pressed her lips together. 'Brandis,' she said to Nate. She answered while walking out of the room. A door clicked closed somewhere in the back of the house.

'Look, thanks for –'

'Once Chris realised you were the bird who wrote that shit about me she wanted to cancel your visit. I had to talk her out of it, convince her to hear you out.'

'Thank you.'

'It's not for your sake, trust me.'

'OK. So why –'

'You're right. We need to keep Bella in the public eye. Someone must know something and they must be getting all eaten up inside. Not the scum who did it. I don't expect they feel bad at all. But they live in the world, right? Someone they know suspects something. Someone saw or heard something weird. So we need to keep the pressure on for them. We need to make it so anyone who's trying to forget or ignore their suspicions about their mate, or whatever, is in hell whenever they turn on the TV or go to the supermarket. They need to be tortured.' A thin, mean note had crept into his voice and May saw that he noticed. He adjusted his posture. Gulped water from Chris's glass. 'So, I'm going to try and get her to talk to you, right? But don't you go manipulating and screwing her over like you did to Julie Atkins.'

'Julie – is that what she thinks?'

'Well, yeah, because you did. But like I said, this isn't about me and the shit you've written before. You promise to do right by Bella and I'll help you get Chris on side.'

Chris came back into the room and Nate went to her. She murmured something too low for May to hear and then, loudly, 'Look, something's come up so you need to go. But I'll think about what you've said, OK?'

'OK. That's great. And if you want to talk through anything, ask me any questions –'

'Yeah. Leave your card or whatever on the table and we'll get back to you,' Nate said.

May took out a card, hesitated at the sight of all those other cards. 'Um, so this is from the place I worked at before but I'm not working for them any more. My mobile's the same though, so you can . . .'

They weren't listening. Chris was squeezing her phone like a stress ball and Nate was rubbing her arm. May was desperate to ask the question, fire guesses at them until she got a confirmation one way or the other, but she knew she was on shaky ground. Patience, respect, gentleness would be what got her in with these two. She propped her card up against the cake platter and thanked Chris for her time. Resisting the urge to crouch under the kitchen window and listen in was painful.

■ ■ ■

Detective Brandis slapped a photo on the table. 'Familiar?'

'No.' I kept looking even though I knew right away I'd never seen him. 'Is he local?'

'Yeah. Name's David Hunt. Ring any bells?'

I didn't want to seem too hasty. Didn't want to be too hasty. I thought hard, turning it over in my mind, thinking David Hunt. Dave. Davo. His mates'd call him The Hunter, Grunter, Munter, Munt, Cunt. 'No,' I had to say. 'Never heard of him.'

Brandis kept watching me. I waited. Looked some more at the photo. The upper half of a thin man in a dark green shirt with a pocket logo I couldn't make out. Mid to late thirties, sandy hair flopping down onto his forehead, eyes all creased up with laughter.

'Is it him? Is this the –'

'Chris, I need you to stay calm.'

'I am.' I was. Sitting there, my hands in my lap, looking at that man. Looking.

'Now, I need you to listen to me carefully. This man is a person of interest. We have him at the station right now and we're questioning him. We're searching his home and place of work, but we can't hold him if we don't come up with something concrete, you understand? So I need you to think really hard about whether you've seen him, heard Bella mention him, anything that could help us pin him down.'

It was hard to think clearly. I couldn't stop looking at his face. He had a good smile. I would've bent extra low over the bar for that smile. I'd have worked at getting a laugh from him. His hands weren't in shot. If they were, maybe I'd know. I'm such a sucker for a sweet smile, but hands never fool me. If I could see his hands I'd know what he was capable of.

'Did Bella ever mention a delivery guy at work, maybe?'

I had a clear image of Bella at work, hauling herself up from the lunch table to answer the delivery bell. 'No. She'd bitch sometimes about how deliveries always seemed to come when she was on her break and since the delivery door was at the back of the staff room, she'd end up spending half her break standing by the door, supervising the delivery, checking the bloke in and out. I know it sounds petty, but they only got half an hour for lunch and the job's so exhausting. She said she wanted to cry some days when she heard that bell go just as she'd sat down. Once she dropped tuna all over the delivery log. She thought she cleaned it off OK, and hung it back by the door. But the brine must've soaked into the clipboard underneath and her manager went mental about staff eating while working. Bella was ropeable that day. "Working while eating, not eating while working!" she kept saying. Only to me though. She never made a fuss or bitched at work. She wasn't like that.'

'No. But she never spoke about any of the delivery men specifically?'

'I don't think so. You should ask the others at the home, though, they –'

'We've spoken to the other staff.'

'And?'

'You know I can't tell you everything about the investigation, Chris. You understand that, right?'

'Yes. I just . . . Can you tell me why him? I mean, did someone see him? Was there, like, DNA or something?'

'We've taken samples from him. They're being tested against the little we got from the scene. I can only tell you that we were led to him by a call from a member of the public.'

'Someone called with information?'

'Chris, hundreds of people have called and we've checked out every lead. This one seems promising.'

'But –'

'I can't tell you anything else right now, but if you think of anything, the tiniest thing that Bella might have said about a delivery man or someone called David or Dave, you call me right away, yeah?'

'OK. When will we –'

'I'll be in touch, Chris. Soon as we have anything concrete, I'll be in touch. In the meantime, well, I know you won't go blabbing to the media, but best if you don't tell anyone at this point. Even that fella of yours. All quiet, yeah?'

I nodded. Watched him leave without getting up from the table. When I heard his engine starting up I popped over to Lisa's to use her computer. I typed in the man's name, which was obviously hundreds of other men's name, too. I spent over an hour clicking through. None of them were him, the man with the nice smile and unseen hands who might have raped and tortured and murdered my baby sister.

Sunday
19
April

I told Nate they had a lead, but not that they'd given me a name, shown me a photo. If he knew, he wouldn't be able to help himself. As I couldn't.

It took me a while to figure out where to start. I've never needed to find anyone who wasn't in the White Pages or on Facebook. I wandered around the house, talking it through, aware that if anyone saw me they'd think I'd finally cracked it. I was drifting off to sleep when Bella finally chipped in with some advice. *Use what you've got* she told me and I said *What? Big tits and a broken heart?* and she said *People'll always help the busty and broken hearted, Chrissy, you know that.* Which is true.

First thing in the morning I walked up to the nursing home and asked about collecting any of Bella's personal effects she'd left there. The girls were so incredibly lovely. They'd made a kind of shrine on top of the fridge in the staff room: Bella's staff ID, a pen with a bright pink troll doll on the end, a 'Crazy Cat Lady in Training' coffee mug, a half-empty box of lemongrass and ginger teabags, lavender hand cream, lip balm, a copy of *The Fault in Our Stars* with a United Voice Aged Care Union bookmark poking out halfway through, a local newspaper photo of Bella dressed as a clown in front of a cluster of old people laughing so hard I worried that some of them might not have survived the photo shoot. All this placed carefully on her pale blue cardigan. So she wasn't wearing that when they took her. No wonder she was cold.

My plan had been to ask for a bit of privacy to make a phone call, but as it happened the moment overtook me and the darlings handed me tissues and told me to take as long as I needed gathering up her things. I was a bit of a mess, to be honest, but I stayed focused on my task, went straight to the clipboard hanging by the delivery door. There were six pages, each with a date at the top and between five and ten entries down the page. Company name, a description of the delivery, time, delivery signature, staff signature. My eyes were all blurry so I took out my phone and snapped photos of each page. It was a trick Carrie taught me for when you wanted to finish an article you started in the checkout line without having to buy the magazine.

Phone back in my pocket I went to the fridge shrine and carefully placed each item in my bag. It felt wrong to be shoving them in with all my everyday shit, but for all my plotting I hadn't thought to bring anything special to carry her things in. I had thought to bring a framed photo of Bella at her TAFE graduation, grinning like a loon, holding up her Aged Care Certificate IV. I put it on top of the fridge and stood back. Right away I could see it getting knocked down every time someone slammed the door. One day someone wouldn't pause and prop it back up and it would lay face down gathering grime, becoming another invisible bit of staffroom clutter.

'What a great photo!' Vicky bustled into the room, gave my arm a quick pat. 'Is that for us to keep?'

'If you want it, yeah, I thought . . .'

'Of course we want it. God, look at that smile, will ya? But if you don't mind I might move it into the rec room? Put it on one of the bookshelves? That way the residents can see her as well.'

I nodded, so grateful and guilty and sad I could barely stand.

Tuesday
21
April

May spent two days on the internet documenting every rumour, supposition and slanderous accusation relating to Bella's death. Every couple of hours she'd stop to take a walk around the block, have a coffee and ciggie on the narrow verandah or stick her head in the shower with the cold water on full. By Monday night she had a long, cross-referenced, colour-coded spreadsheet, and relentless nausea.

Tuesday she called Constable Matt Drey and asked him if he was free for dinner that night.

He said yes straight away, then, 'Oh, but, listen, d'ya mean, like… 'Cause you know I can't talk to you about –'

'If I wanted an interview I'd've asked for one. Dinner, you and me.'

'Seriously?'

'Seriously, but…'

'Yeah?' His voice flat.

'I do have some stuff I'd like to get your opinion on. Not police business, I swear. Just because you're a local and you've got such good insight into how everything works here.'

He was quiet for long enough she worried she'd lost him, but then he said, 'Righto. Imperial at seven, OK?'

May forced herself to spend the entree (massive serving of garlic prawns and another of salt and pepper calamari 'to share', he insisted) asking about his family and his footy team.

When the mains arrived she told him about her internet trawling, asked if he'd mind telling her – off the record, of course – if there was anything worth following up. He shook his head like he'd never been so disappointed in his life, but she held his gaze, doing her best to appear irresistibly impish and after a bit he half-smiled and nodded for her to go ahead.

May pushed her untouched chicken parma aside, pulled out her notebook and pen. '"My dog was strangled and hung in a tree only a few minutes from where this girl was killed."'

Matt swatted the air. 'Nothing like that's been reported. We had those three strays smothered, but no hangings.'

'So it's bullshit?'

'It's not been reported to the police is all I can say.'

May crossed it off her list. 'OK, how about this one? "I saw something that looked like a woman's thigh floating in Strathdee Creek. I told the police and when I went back it had gone."'

'What? A woman's thigh? How would you even be able to tell?'

May watched his face as he thought the question through. After a minute he flicked at the air again, shook his head. 'Whatever. No body parts in the creek. Guaranteed.'

'Right.' She put a line through the entry. 'So, there are a few versions of this one, but the general gist is that Bella was seeing someone she shouldn't have.'

Matt speared a piece of carrot, swirled it through gravy, raised it to his mouth and, as he chewed, gave May the slightest nod.

'Yes? That's a yes?'

He finished chewing, swallowed, nodded again. 'What else you got?'

'OK. Ugh. This one's nasty, so don't get defensive, OK? "I was raped not far from where she was found. I have told Strathdee police about the man who did it to me but they did not seem interested."'

Matt looked hard at May while he finished chewing a mouthful of steak. She tried to keep her face neutral. 'Listen,' he said. 'I don't know what kind of crazy internet den you're crawling through but that's just straight-out lying. Someone comes in and reports a rape it's taken seriously.'

'By you, of course, but what if someone else was on when –'

'May.' He laid his knife and fork down, lifted his right hand and pointed at her. 'I said I'd help you sort the crazy from the possible and I will, but I won't sit here and listen to you casting accusations on my colleagues.'

'OK I'm sorry. If you say that it can't be true then I believe you.'

He nodded, held her gaze for a few seconds, then went back to his steak.

'So what about –'

'Enough now, I think.'

May flinched at his tone. She closed her notebook and slid it into her bag. After a couple of minutes of silence she attempted to start a conversation about the talent show playing on the overhead TVs but he put his cutlery down again and gave the table a small thump with his fist.

'I saw what they done to her, May.'

'I know.'

'Nah, I don't reckon you do, because if you did you couldn't ask me questions like that, like . . . like . . . like inferring that we're not taking it seriously, that we're ignoring reports of rape and body parts.'

'Matt, I'm really sorry. I can be insensitive sometimes, I know.'

He bit his lip. 'I don't want to do this any more. This internet rumour bullshit. It's disrespectful.'

'OK, of course.' May reached across, gave his hand a quick squeeze. 'Again, I'm really sorry. Let me buy you another beer to make it up to you.'

'No need for that. It's all good. Eat your chicken before it goes cold.'

May tried, but the feel of the flesh in her mouth was repulsive and it was all she could do not to gag.

Back at the hotel she went through the remaining list of rumours ruthlessly, crossing off any that failed the eye-roll test. These included that Bella was a virgin and had been killed in a satanic ritual requiring virgin sacrifice; that she was a devout Christian and been killed in a race hate attack perpetrated by Muslim youths, and that she had been fond of hitchhiking and sometimes did it in one direction only to get out and return the same way just for kicks.

She couldn't get Matt's anger out of her mind. She knew all the Strathdee cops a little by now, couldn't imagine any of them turning away a woman alleging rape. But what did being able to imagine it matter? She couldn't imagine anyone doing most of the nightmare shit she'd been reading about these last few days and yet someone had, hadn't they? Even if the specific instances on the message boards and forums were bullshit, animal torture, human dismemberment and rape were real things that happened in the world.

May remembered reading how Ted Bundy insisted on walking his friend Ann Rule to her car each night after work. He worried about her going alone because he knew what men were capable of. Or more accurately, he knew what he was capable of and feared other men might be, too. So maybe it's the people who can imagine others committing atrocities that we need to be afraid of? They're not so much imagining as extrapolating.

But then she'd hardly known a man who hadn't at some point warned her of the need to be careful and always in a thick, low voice suggesting that they knew something about the ways of men that they hoped she'd never find out.

Had Craig ever done that? She was sure he hadn't. He'd never shown much concern at all about what she got up to when she was away from him. But she was the same – had to be or it wouldn't work. They spoke for hours about their childhoods and planned their shining future but the present reality outside of her bedroom was unspeakable.

Fuck. Why did everything come back to him? She typed his name into her web browser, spent a few minutes desperately clicking through the links knowing from experience that he had no web presence, except a single line on the council website, but not being able to help herself from looking anyway. He'd never let her take any photos of him and that was something else to hate him for, because she was sure if she could just see his smile she'd feel better, be able to sleep.

Holding her breath, she typed his wife's name, found her Facebook page. It was mostly locked-down but a handful of profile pictures were public. May saw at a glance that he wasn't in any of them, but she scrolled through anyway hoping for comfort in the way of cellulite and wrinkles. She found those, plus chubby arms and grey roots and a smile which made her eyes almost disappear. Rage rocketed through May's body. She hit her pillow over and over and when that gave no relief punched herself in the leg until her eyes watered. If she was in Sydney she'd drive over to Craig's place and scream down his front door. She'd knock him to the ground and kick him until he couldn't get up and then she'd let Carmel do the same to her.

She jumped out of bed, put on tracksuit pants and sneakers, got as far as the car park edge before Bella's body flashed up. She kicked the curb as hard as she could, swore at the pain shooting up her leg. She could hear a truck approaching from the highway exit and a second later its headlights cut the dark. She ran back inside, wrote a long rambling message telling Carmel she'd be better off without the treacherous prick who had phoned her, May, over a week ago while she, his wife, was at yoga, but hadn't phoned back or even texted since then, and how was it possible to love someone and miss them and also think they were utter scum who deserved to be kicked to death in the hallway of their own house?

Fuck. Fuck. Fuck him. She deleted the message without sending, grabbed her phone and *fuck him fuck him fuck him* blocked his number and deleted him from her contacts.

She splashed her face with cold water, opened a beer and toasted herself in the mirror, then sat down to make a list of people to call for interviews the next day, starting with all of the male staff at Bella's work.

Wednesday
22
April

Interview transcript

22 April 2015

Glen Goodes, Strathdee Haven Nursing Home

Thanks for agreeing to speak to me, Dr Goodes. Can you tell me about your relationship with Bella Michaels?
It was warm. Friendly. Same as with any of the staff here. We're a pretty happy bunch.

Same as with any of the staff?
More or less, yeah.

So you weren't having an affair with her?
Jesus! What kind of a –? Who said that?

Is it true, Dr Goodes?
No. For God's sake. I'm married. My wife is very ill, as it happens. If she were to hear any of this . . . Not to mention the insult to Bella's memory. I mean, Christ.

I'm sorry for upsetting you. I hope you understand why I need to ask these questions.
No, I don't understand that at all.

I'm trying to gather as comprehensive a portrait of Bella as possible. As someone very close to her –
You've been speaking to Chris Rogers, I assume. That woman is unreliable to say the least. Forgive me, I know she's grieving, but if you know anything about her it must be that you can't trust a word she says.

Why's that?
Oh, no, I'm not going there. Do your job. Ask around.

I'm asking you.
And I'm done with this interview. Next time get your facts straight before you [inaudible].

■ ■ ■

Interview transcript

22 April 2015

Carrie Smith

How long have you lived next door to Chris Rogers?
Oh, I don't know, love. I've been here my whole life. Inherited the house from my mum. So, however long Chris's been here, we've been neighbours.

What kind of neighbour is she?
Lovely. Quiet.

What about her ex-husband?
Nate? Oh, he's a darl. We all miss him around here. He'll do anything for you, that man.

Were you aware of any conflict between them?
No.

Really? They had quite a fiery relationship from what I hear.
Look. You're not going to hear a word against either of them from me, so if that's what you're after you might as well chuff of right now.

Is Chris seeing anyone now, do you know?
If you're writing about Bella, how come all your questions are about Chris?

I'm trying to gather as comprehensive a picture of –
Sounds like you're digging for dirt if you ask me. I told you: I don't have a bad word to say about her. No one who knows her properly

will. All that nasty gossip is just jealousy. She's a good-looking woman, Chris. People get jealous that she's still got so many fellas chasing after her.

Does she have a lot of –
That'll do now, love, if you don't mind. I'm not comfortable talking about her like this. No, no, really. I'll see you out.
[ENDS]

■   ■   ■

There was something about Chris that everybody thought – or knew – and nobody would say. May went back to her spreadsheet of internet rumours and considered the cluster related to prostitution: Bella worked part time as a prostitute; she had been a prostitute when she lived in Sydney a few years ago; she discovered her sister was a prostitute and the sister killed her to keep her quiet; someone mistook her for her sister the prostitute and then got enraged when she refused to put out.

May called Chas and asked where Strathdee's sex workers hung out.

'Geez, love, if you can wait until I finish work I'll sort you out for free.'

'Very kind of you, but I'm interested in the professionals right now.'

'Hang on a sec, I'm stepping away from all the big ears around here.'

May listened as the *beep beep* of a reversing truck was replaced by vague whooshing sounds and then Chas's voice at almost a whisper.

'Yeah, look, there's no brothel or anything in town. A couple of places in Wagga will send girls here, but only if you pay for an overnight in a hotel. Some fellas make the trek out there, but most just go for a quickie with one of the cheapos working the northbound truck stop. And before you ask, no, I don't know all this from personal experience. Blokes share info, that's all.'

'I appreciate you passing it on. What about, um, independent contractors? Women working privately out of their homes?'

A pause. 'Might be a bit of that.'

'Care to share any names?'

'Wouldn't know. That's the thing with people doing stuff privately. It's private.'

'Fair enough. So the rumour I heard about Bella doing it?'

'For fuck's sake. Just stop right there with that. It's off the fucking planet.'

'OK. Any idea where the rumour might've come from? Is it because her sister –'

He sighed. 'Listen, you're a great girl and I've enjoyed spending time with you, but you need to pull your bloody head in.'

'I'm sorry. I shouldn't have –'

'Anything else? I've gotta get back to work.'

'No, that's –'

He was gone. May was glad she was alone in her hotel room, because her face and chest burnt with shame. At least half her shame was due to how upset and shaky she was from being scolded. Not cut out for this at all, at all, at all.

Saturday
25
April

Soon as I got back from the nursing home I went through the photos I'd taken, noting down the company names and, where I could make it out, the name of the driver. All that week at work, I chatted up a storm with the few blokes whose names I'd recognised and made it my mission to find out where everyone I served worked. We get a lot of delivery drivers coming in, stopping for a quick beer before returning to Wagga or Albury or wherever, and it didn't take long before I'd connected a face and name to almost every company that made deliveries to the nursing home.

To be honest, I'm not great at this cloak-and-dagger undercover investigative shit. You'd have been horrified at how clumsy and obvious some of my questioning was, I'm sure. But if a man thinks you might want to root him he'll interpret any question you ask as flirtation. Especially if he's had a few beers and so is already inclined to believe he's God's fucking gift and who wouldn't want to know every detail of his life?

Friday I struck gold. A young frozen food delivery driver called Rick mentioned he'd worked double shifts all week thanks to his slack-arse workmate Dave taking unexpected leave.

'You're not talking about Dave Hunt, are you?'

'Aw, what? You know The Hunter, do ya?'

'A little,' I said, heart racing. 'Long time back. Don't know we'd recognise each other now it's been so long. Still got that mop of hair over his forehead? Smile like a cheeky kid?'

'Yep, yep, that's him.' Rick gave a dirty laugh. 'Shouldn't be surprised. Hear he got all the best-looking birds back in his day.'

'Come on, he's not that old. My age, I think.'

'Yeah, nah, didn't mean offence. Not like you're past it or anything.' He spent a long, meaningful moment considering my cleavage. 'Just meant he's settled down these days. Well settled. His missus is a scary one, keeps him on a tight leash, she does. Yep, yep, yep. The Hunter is well and truly retired.'

'Shame. He still living in that rundown joint out near the Wagga exit?'

Rick frowned. 'Nah, nah. He's been on Topia Street for, God, I don't know, three years or something? Ever since I've known him anyhow. Might be his missus' place come to think of it. Pretty nice, actually. White picket fence and all that shit.'

'Ah, well, white picket fence. That's a Danger Keep Out sign for a girl like me.'

Rick laughed, real dirty this time, and went to speak, but I was urgently needed out back.

It was good timing, me finding him the day before Detective Brandis called to let me know they had the wrong man. I asked him how they knew but he said he couldn't give out those details, I should just trust him that Hunt was not involved in my sister's murder.

I do trust Brandis, more or less. I mean, I think he's done his best. I believe he cares that whoever did this is caught and punished. But those relentless visions I get whenever I lie down to sleep and sometimes when I'm standing at the bar or at the grocery checkout or sitting at the kitchen table, those surround-sound, full-colour, fucking IMAX-quality visions I have of Bella's last hours, well, for almost a week those visions had been starring David Hunt and so however much I trusted Brandis I felt like Hunt's guilt was a witnessed fact.

Topia Street is short and a good chunk of one side is taken up by a council reserve. There used to be a public pool there when I was small. I can't remember when it disappeared, but I do recall that we all stopped going there after a little boy drowned. It must have been the early Eighties. I was still a kid myself but Mum told me all the details, as was her way, and next time I went in the pool I kept thinking his little hands were going to grab my ankles. I refused to go there after that, think I even had a couple of nightmares about these little ghost hands pulling at my legs. I suppose others stopped going for the same reason. Oh, not ghost hands, but the thought of the boy. Worries about safety and all.

Now there was no trace, just a wide, long expanse of buffalo grass. I walked the length of it in five minutes that Saturday morning. The stink of charcoal and grease from barbecues not used since January reminded me it was Anzac Day. By the time I got to work at six every man in the place would be maggoted, half of them sloppy and maudlin, the rest bristling for a fight to prove their patriotism.

None of the houses on Topia had white picket fences but two had white timber slats and one dark green pickets. I went door to door asking about a lost cat. I described Bella's old kitten, Mopey, for believability and, though I know this sounds stupid, for luck. To avoid suspicion I went to every door. Three people told me they'd spotted Mopey in the neighbourhood that week, which only drove home how fucking useless the general public are when it comes to finding the missing.

The sixth door I knocked on was opened by David Hunt. He was paler and thinner than in his picture, than in my visions. His hands were large, bony, mottled with sun damage. The left one had a tattered, beige-coloured bandage wrapped around it. 'Yeah?' he said.

I gave my spiel, thankful I'd started at the other end of the street so that I'd repeated it enough times that it came out smoothly despite the fact my insides were trying to slam their way out of me.

'Nah, sorry, love,' he said, and went to close the door.

'Wait, can you just –' I held out my hand, took hold of the door edge of the door.

He swung it fully open again, looked at me like I'd kicked him in the shins.

'Sorry, I wonder if I could quickly use your loo? I've been walking all morning and I'm totally busting.'

He looked at me hard for a couple of seconds, then stepped back and waved me in. 'End of the hall, let yourself out.'

I thanked him and rushed down the hall as if I was about to pee all over myself. I sat on the toilet, concentrated on slowing my breath. I hadn't planned past finding out where he lived, hadn't thought through this bid to get inside. There was nothing in this room apart from the dunny and a half-basin with a squirt bottle of soap. I riffled through my handbag for a weapon but there was nothing remotely useful. Why did I not carry a gun, pepper spray, a fucking Swiss army knife even? Why did I walk around like I was made of goddamn steel?

I entered 000 on my phone, locked the screen without dialling and then slid it into my front jeans pocket. Two touches and it would dial. Not that it would come to that. What he'd done to Bella he'd done far away and out of sight. He wouldn't risk anything in his house, on a bright Saturday morning, while all his neighbours were home and had spoken to the woman door-knocking the street.

I flushed the toilet. Washed my hands and face. I would say thank you. Leave. Knock on the last few doors. Go home and figure out what to do now I'd found him.

I walked back out into the hallway. 'Thanks,' I called, heading straight for the front door.

'Wait a sec.' He stepped out from a room to my left, stepped right in my path. 'My missus reckons she's seen a cat hanging around the bins.' He nodded his head towards the room he'd come from. A girl of eighteen or so with a baby of close to nine months pushing out her belly lay on her back on a brown velveteen sofa, a stack of multi-coloured cushions behind her head.

'Oh,' I said, trying hard to sound pleased, interested, stepping only very slightly towards the girl, away from the blessed front door. 'Little grey tabby? Barely more than a kitten? Blue-and-white collar around his neck?'

'Yeah, I think –' She blinked at me. Pushed herself up to a sitting position. 'How do I . . .?' I saw recognition rush over her. 'Fuck, Dave, fuck, it's her. Bella Michaels' sister.'

I spun on my heel, but he was right there in front of the door. He didn't touch me, but he made it so I'd have to touch him to get past. I held up my hands, think I said, 'please' or 'sorry' or something. Cursed myself for holding up my hands because now it would look sus if I shoved one into my pocket to get my phone.

'Fuck, you're thick,' the girl was saying. 'Her face's been all over the news. How could you not fucking recognise her?'

He didn't answer, just looked right at me with this hurt twist to his face. I made myself hold eye contact, same way I've done when an angry dog's been running and barking at me. Hold eye contact, don't show your fear.

He looked away first, over my shoulder. 'Call the cops.'

'You sure? We just got rid of the cunts.'

His eyes on mine again. 'I got nothing to worry about. Done nothing wrong.'

She muttered something under her breath and then I heard her speaking in a put-on voice, like the one I use to answer the phone at the pub. Hunt nodded towards the living room and not knowing what else to do I slunk in and sank into an armchair a metre or so away from a big-screen TV showing a silent game show. To be honest, the way my legs were feeling, it was actually bloody good to sit down.

It was young Matt and Sally who turned up. Sally took me out to the car and sat with me there while Matt talked to the Hunts. After about ten minutes he came out and stood on the lawn talking on his phone then slid into the passenger seat.

'Righto, Chris, we're going to take you down the station now, alright?'

I asked what I was being charged with, since as far as I knew it wasn't illegal to use someone's dunny with their permission.

'Not being charged, but I've just spoken to Detective Brandis and he has asked that you come in and have a chat.'

'Good,' I said. 'I can't wait to hear what he has to say about letting that raping, murdering monster go.'

The cops exchanged the look everyone who's ever worked in a pub knows. *Crazy but harmless enough*, it said. *Least we can do is be kind to the poor old bugger*, it said. In return I gave them another practised barmaid look: *Fuck you and the horse you rode in on, you big steaming pile of cow shit.*

Brandis explained it all, and I suppose I have to as well now, make it plain that David Hunt was fair-dinkum cleared. No DNA matches and a hell of an alibi. Hell of an alibi. That's why I say 'cleared' and not 'innocent'. He's far from that, believe me. See, the reason the police picked him up in the first place was because a doctor rang them and said that a few days after Bella was taken this bloke came into emergency with a super-infected wound on his hand. He said his dog had bitten him a few nights back and he'd thought it would heal up OK, but instead it'd turned crimson and started spewing pus. Thing is, the doctor reckoned the teeth marks were human, plus he also had scabbed-up scratches on his face. Anyway, the police looked him up, saw that he had a delivery route which included Bella's nursing home and a previous assault charge, and that was that; they brought him in.

His alibi, though. Yeah. His wife. Older than I thought, all of twenty-four. When the police interviewed her she was sporting a fading shiner and puffy lip. Broke down under police questioning and confessed that Hunt's bite marks and scratches were from her. They'd had a 'little fight' the week before and it had got 'a bit out of control'. She explained that he had started drinking at four in the afternoon and when, around nine, she suggested he stop, he'd belted her. This was not the first time an argument had got out of control. Probably wouldn't be the last, either, given she refused to press charges. None of the cops' business, she reckoned. She could look after herself. She'd fought back and got him good. That infected bite was causing him hell.

So, yeah, they let him go, because he might be a pregnant-wife beating shit bag but he didn't kill anyone, so that's alright then, hey?

Me, I was warned to stay away. As if I had to be told. Run into enough useless arseholes in this life without seeking them out.

Sunday
26
April

May lay on her hotel bed and tried to think of a reason to get up. It had been over a week since she had spoken to Chris. In that time she'd talked as in-depth as they'd allow with everyone she could find who'd had the slightest relationship to Bella or Chris. She had almost thirty hours of interviews recorded and had started a second spreadsheet just to keep track of who worked where and knew Bella how and was related to/fucking/in a feud with whom. And none of it gave her anything new to write.

Fuck it. She would give Chris Rogers one more day and then call her again, give the pitch everything she had. If it was still a no she would have to crawl back to Sydney and start begging for a job at some community paper where she could report on new school halls and local chess comps instead of trying to dig up details of a dead woman's sex life. Either that or try to make it as a glossy-mag freelancer writing 'How to tell if your husband is cheating' and 'Flirt your way to the top' articles for seventy cents a word.

Her phone buzzed. Chris. Holy God, like she had willed it into being. 'Hello?' she said, hearing the entirely inappropriate joy and excitement in her voice.

'Yeah, look. I've decided to do it. The interview.'

May fist-pumped her reflection. 'Oh, that's great. I'm so pleased. When would you like to start?'

'I've got today free up till five.'

May sniffed herself. It'd been days since she'd showered. 'Give me twenty minutes to finish up this thing I'm working on, then I'll be right over.'

Chris invited May through to the living room. It was small and simply furnished. There were two framed photos of Bella on the TV, one each on the stereo and the coffee table and three on the deep windowsill. May wondered how many had been displayed before and whose photos had been replaced, but it was too early to ask about anything that had happened since Bella died. Today's plan was to get Chris talking about herself, her early life, her beliefs and dreams, start getting a sense of her as an individual rather than a dead woman's sister.

The first hour went smoothly enough, though May had the sense that Chris was on high alert. She paused before each answer and then spoke softly and quickly, the words sometimes running into each other or even switching places. But when May asked how she'd met Nate, Chris visibly and audibly relaxed. As she spoke of their first meeting and early relationship the tight lines on her forehead and around her eyes all but disappeared and her mouth softened, seemed to become fuller. The hands she'd been knotting together in her lap gestured emphatically and gracefully. *Her eyes filled with love,* May scribbled in her notebook, then added: *Literally, which I didn't know was possible.* She wanted to ask Chris what the hell had happened to ruin this true love story, but she sensed that the pain there was almost as big as the pain of losing Bella and so resolved to hold off until their rapport was stronger.

'You obviously really like men,' she said when Chris had finished an anecdote about the send-off the staff and regulars at the pub gave her before her wedding.

'Yeah. I s'pose so. I mean, I like people. Mostly.'

'Sure, but I mean, you surround yourself with men. Spend so much time in their company.'

'Nature of working in the kind of place I do, I reckon.'

'You choose to work in the place you do. You're good at your job, well-presented as they say. If you wanted to you could get work in one of the more upscale places. I think you like the Royal because it's so blokey. I watched you there one night. There was an energy. Between you and all the blokes. Sexual, for sure, but not only that. They like you – not just your body or whatever – but you. And you like them.'

'People are nice to me, I'm nice to them. Nothing worth banging on about.'

'That's just it,' May said. 'It's so unusual and you don't even realise it. You don't realise how much most men dislike women. And knowing that, most women can't relax around men the way you do. Can't let ourselves show that we like them even if we really do.'

'Ah. That's a different thing, though. I like 'em fine, but I'm never relaxed, not fully. It's like with dogs. All the joy in the world, but once you've seen a labrador rip the face off a kid, you can't ever forget what they're capable of.'

May leant forward. 'Is that just a metaphor? The labrador thing?'

'I wish. When I was a little tugger, three or something, I don't know – how young can you remember things? I was tiny, anyway, couldn't get up onto a kitchen chair on my own. That's what I remember trying to do. Climb up on the chair because the dog was going at my cousin. It was her house. We'd been playing and the dog just sitting there like a slobbering stuffed toy and then suddenly it was ripping into Kylie's face. We were both screaming, dog growling, me trying to get up on that chair, get away. Probably shoulda kicked the damn thing, tried to help, but like I said, I was a tiny thing.'

'Was your cousin OK?'

Chris stood, left the room. May wondered whether to follow.

Chris shuffled back in, handed May an unframed photo. 'Taken a few years back. That's her on the left.'

May didn't need to be told. Chris, Bella and four other women squinting into the sun in front of a table set with red and green paper plates and golden crackers. Six women squinting through eleven eyes. Five women smiling and one grimacing through lips that looked freshly sewn on.

'Look at Bella, will ya?' Chris hovered over May's shoulder. 'Talk about a rose between thorns.'

'They all your cousins?'

'Yeah. My uncle Fred's kids. Kylie and Kim have the same mum, Jess and Rae different. There's a son, too, Jason, but we never saw him much.'

'You still in touch with the girls?'

Chris sat back down across from May, ran a hand through her hair. 'Yeah, little bit. They're up in Brissie, all got kids. Even Kylie. Face like that and she still managed to hook a fella. He's not much to look at himself, of course, but he's nice enough.' She shook her head. 'Nah, I don't know actually. If he's nice or not. It's just something you say, isn't it? Someone not much to look at you have to say he's a good bloke, but he mightn't be for all I know. Plenty aren't.' A smile, thin and mean.

'You've known some not-nice blokes then?'

'Jesus, haven't you?'

'I guess.'

Chris crossed her arms, held her gaze.

"Course I have. That's why I asked in the first place, about you liking men, you know. Because most women don't. Because we know most of them are shits."

'And most women aren't?'

'It's different.'

'How?'

'Chris. Really.'

The shock of it passing over her face. May itched for her camera. You can't be there for every significant event but you can extrapolate. That look, Jesus Christ, that look. Like seeing her hear the news for the first time.

■　■　■

Interview transcript (excerpt)

26 April 2015

Nate Cartwright

The way that you – that everyone – describes Bella, it's very difficult to imagine but I need to ask: is there anyone you can think of who would want to hurt her?
Her specifically? No.

What do you mean not 'her specifically'?
[Sigh] I was talking to my missus about it all, when it first happened.

She never met Bella but she'd heard all about her, even before all this. She knew I thought the world of her, saw her as a sister and that. And I said – it was the first or second night after they found her and I was a bloody wreck – and I said to Renee, 'Who would do this?' you know, 'Who would ever want to hurt someone like her?' And Renee, she looks at me real serious and she says, 'Plenty of people. She was a woman, wasn't she?'

Do you agree with that?
Yeah. Wish I didn't. But, yeah. No other way to understand all this.

What do you think Bella would say about that?
About?

The idea that plenty of people want to hurt women just for being women.
Fucked if I know. Sorry, but . . . It never came up, right? Why would it? Before this happened it never occurred to me to even think about why someone would . . . Yeah, gotta say, mate, it's a stupid question, it really is.

Fair enough. It's just I'm trying to get a sense of how Bella herself would think of all this. If it had happened to someone else, I mean.
Yeah, but it didn't. It didn't.

I can see I've upset you. I'm sorry. It's just really important to me that Bella's voice comes through in all this. That her views, her opinions are –
You don't get it. Bella's voice is gone. Gone. We don't get to hear it, don't get to find out what she thinks of anything any more.

But we can –

No. We can't. Not ever again.

■   ■   ■

I'm sure everyone knew about what had happened with Dave Hunt. I kept catching blokes looking at me from under their caps, women giving me the side-eye then flashing fake smiles. No one said a word about it, which is how I knew that I'd done something really bad. Do something a bit shit, like getting in a fight outside the TAB or getting a DUI, and people around here will bag the hell out of you. But something beyond the pale – beat your wife, hurt your kid, stalk a bloke because you think he murdered your sister – those things go unspoken.

Trust that this night of all of 'em, the fella I'd last taken home – the one against my instincts – he was there, eyeing me up and down openly instead of on the sly like everyone else. Late in the night he came right on up to me while I was cashing out the second register since Suze had just clocked off. 'Chris,' he said, 'been a while since we caught up.'

'Crazy busy lately.'

'Yeah. Been pretty flat out myself.' He ran a hand through his hair. 'Be really sweet if I could crash at your's tonight.'

'Yeah, listen, mate. Not really up to visitors at the moment.'

'You've had a shit time of it, I know. Might be a bit of company's just what you need.'

'Appreciate the offer, but I'd really rather not tonight. Now stop gasbagging so I don't have to count these notes a third time.'

He dipped his head and swaggered away. Took all I had not to keep on looking up to see if he was watching me.

I finished cashing out the till and took the proceeds into the back office, locked them in the safe and, on my way back to the till I stopped by the kitchen and asked Nadine if she had her car tonight. She didn't, as luck would have it, but when I told her there was a bloke I was a bit worried about she held up a hand at me and told me she'd give her old man a call and have him pick us both up. My impulse was to tell her not to worry about it, but then I thought again of the last time he'd been in my house and I nodded, thanked her.

The man left without bothering me again and soon after that I called last drinks. By the time Nadine's husband turned up I felt like a knob. Silly woman scared of nothing, needing to call someone else's husband to rescue her from the Big Bad Wolf. Felt even worse when I told him my address and he said, 'Yeah, I know.' I wanted to ask if it was sex or death that'd made my address common knowledge, but I didn't, of course, just climbed into the back seat of his Commodore and strapped myself in like the fragile little child I was.

'Want me to come in with you?' Nadine asked when we were out the front.

'Nah, I'll be right,' I said, even though I really kind of did. I hadn't left the front light on and the porch and front door were in shadow. I jogged up the path, trying to look light rather than rushed. I had ice in my guts, I tell you, and it felt crucial I get the door open and light on before that car took off. Nadine must've picked up on it and told her husband as much, because I heard the engine purring until I got inside and a second after I lit the kitchen up and locked the front door I heard two cheerful honks and then the car roaring away.

It was so quiet inside. Quiet and very, very cold. Yeah, it was middle of autumn and all, but this was different. It was like the air touching my skin was ten degrees colder than anywhere else. I know that doesn't make sense and there's no way I could know, but I'm just saying it's what it felt like. Like cold was clinging to me.

I had a hot shower and then got in my flannelette pyjamas and into bed. I was cosy as could be, started drifting off to sleep and then *whoosh* the cold was all over me again. I sat up, shivering and shivering. I called her name, softly, feeling mad and on the edge and in a minute I was warm again. I sank back down and on the verge of sleep there it was again, like someone had opened a freezer right over my bed. I started to cry. I said her name over and over. Asked her why she was doing this. But all that happened is I got colder and colder and colder until I couldn't lie there any more. I needed to move or I'd freeze to death, honestly, that's how bad it was.

I got up and started towards the hall cupboard to get the fan heater. I flicked on the light. For a second the room was bright and then the bulb sparked and all was dark. I was crying hard now, and, listen, you know how silly it sounds, me crying and carrying on because it was cold and a lightbulb blew? Well I knew that at the time, I really did, I was saying it to myself, *Get a grip, woman*, you know, but the feeling on my skin . . . Cold as a grave, that's what they say, isn't it?

I felt my way into the kitchen. The light in there worked fine. I put a mug of milk in the microwave and while I was waiting for it, I plugged in the heater and then took a slug of bourbon right from the bottle. There was a low boom and the heater shot sparks and whirred to a stop. My hands shook so hard I had to steady one with the other in order to put the bottle safely on the table. The microwave stopped its turning and the light overhead flickered on-off-on-off-on-off. I sat in the dark and howled like a bub. I asked her again why she was doing this and again felt my blood icing up.

Then this rumbling noise started and I about wet myself before I realised it was a car coming. Not a car; a truck. I ran to the window and watched as it stopped out front and the man climbed out of the cabin, moved up my driveway slow and easy. It occurred to me I should drop to the floor, pretend I wasn't there, but I couldn't move.

He knocked on the door and my face got all hot and then the warmth spread down my neck, to my chest and arms and stomach and legs. He kept knocking. I reached for the light and turned it on and it didn't flicker. I opened the door and he walked in, not smiling but not angry or anything, just normal, like he did this every day. He said hello and I said it back.

His touch left me cold, but only metaphorically. And that was better. Or it seemed so at the time.

I woke in the night to the sound of crying. It was soft, like she was trying to muffle it with a pillow. The man beside me snored so loud, too, it made it hard to hear anything else. But I heard and I knew it was her. I told her I was sorry and there was a little pause and then she started up again. I lay awake listening until she cried herself to sleep and then I did the same.

In the morning I gave him back his money. I don't know why.

No, I do.

He shrugged, pocketed the notes, left the way he'd come, few words and no expression.

Monday
27
April

When May arrived, Chris was waiting on the porch, huge sunglasses covering half her face, her white patent-leather tote bag at her feet.

'You going out? I thought we were going to talk some more this morning.'

'Yeah, really need to get out of the house, though. Can we go somewhere?'

'Of course.'

Chris picked up her bag and started down the driveway. May followed, unlocked the car, watched from the corner of her eye as Chris strapped herself into the passenger seat. The woman's hands seemed electrified. Not shaky. Jolting sharply, without pattern.

'Everything alright?'

'Oh, you know. Bad night.'

'Sorry to hear that. It's a beautiful day, though. We should sit outside somewhere. Is there a nice quiet park nearby or –'

'I wanna see where she died. Was found. You know the place,

right?'

'Are you sure you're up for it?'

Chris swallowed, pressed a hand to the base of her throat. 'Feels like something I have to do.'

'Sure. Of course.' May started the car. This was so fucking perfect she couldn't believe it. 'Hey, I wanted to tell you,' she said, keeping a calm unexcited tone as she drove towards the edge of town, 'I've spoken to a couple of editors. *Good Weekend*, *Australian Magazine* and *Women's Weekly* are all interested. Each would want it angled a slightly different way, of course. My preference would be *Women's Weekly*. Circulation's excellent. It's a monthly, so much longer for the physical copy to be hanging around places getting picked up. And they'd be wanting more personal focus, less about the crime itself, more about who Bella was as a person, how her loss has affected you. What do you think?'

'Yep, sounds OK.'

May glanced across. 'Did you want to call Nate, see if he wants to come along? Might help to have some support.'

'Nate's back in Sydney.'

'For good?'

'More or less. He'll pass through but . . . They're having a baby. Him and Renee. So he obviously needs to be around a lot more. Around her.'

'I'm sorry.'

'Nothing to be sorry for. How far is it?'

They'd passed the Melbourne exit sign a minute ago. Chris had become supernaturally still.

'Coming up on the left in a sec. But listen, if you change your mind at any point we can leave. Just say the word, right?'

'Yep.'

May spotted the enshrined tree up ahead, braked too quickly, half skidded to a stop at the verge.

'So this is it, eh?' Chris didn't wait for an answer, just opened the car door and strode out across the gravel, over the grass. She stopped short about a metre from the tree with the misspelt signs and deflated balloons and dead flowers. When May caught up with her, Chris held out her palm: a warning. Stop here.

'You OK?'

'Yeah. Yeah, I just . . .' She shook her head, dropped her hand. 'I thought I heard something.'

'Something like . . .'

'I dunno.' She shuffled forward a few steps, stopped again. 'There. There. Did you hear that? Like a whooshing sound?'

'Um, maybe. It's windy.'

Chris laughed, fake, awkward. 'Yeah, geez, I'm all spooked. Silly.'

'Spooked how?'

Chris waved her off, stepped closer to the tree, sucked in her breath. 'It's nice, I guess, that strangers'd do stuff like this. Weird, too, but.' She pressed a finger to a faded photocopy of a newspaper reproduction of Bella's photo.

'Weird how?'

'Well, have you ever done it? Read about some terrible crime and then driven out to the shithole where it happened and left a little handmade sign or whatever? Don't get me wrong, I think it's sweet, but I don't get it.' Chris squatted and picked up a long-dead bunch of roses. Once-yellow petals scattered and she brushed them away. 'Woulda cost a fortune, these ones. My favourites, you know. Wish I'd seen them when they were fresh.'

'Did Bella like roses?'

'Fucking hated them.' Chris barked out a laugh, stood, brushed her hands together. 'Any flowers. She liked them all right in gardens, but bunches, bouquets, all that – bane of her life, she said. People'd send them to the home for birthdays or anniversaries or, I don't know, out of guilt. Staff have to take the deliveries, bring 'em in to the patients, half the time poor old dear doesn't have a clue what she's supposed to be celebrating, so the staff explain. Then they've gotta find a vase if the cheap relos didn't send them in one. Find the vase, arrange the things, get pricked by thorns, bits of leaf everywhere. Put it somewhere it won't get knocked over. Few days later chuck 'em out, rinse the vase, explain to the old dear why her flowers are gone. "Two minutes on the phone for the guilty relo, a whole damn rigmarole for the staff," Bella used to say. Some of the other aides'd just chuck the flowers soon as they came in or leave them in the reception area, but Bella always made sure the patients got them. Whinged about it after, but always made sure Old Mrs Whatever had the fucking roses the son who's never visited her in a decade sends.' Chris picked a clingy petal off the front of her shirt. 'See what she meant now. Bloody messy business. Oh, wait!' Chris's hand flew to her throat as she looked up into the skeletal branches overhead. 'This tree isn't − The police didn't say anything about −'

'No, no, this isn't the place where − I guess it was just the most convenient place for people to leave . . .'

'So, where?' She spun on her heels, squinted toward the line of gums. 'Just, like, in the middle somewhere or . . . ?'

May nodded, started walking. Chris strode out in front a little, looking back over her shoulder and adjusting her trajectory as May closed in on the place.

They stood shoulder to shoulder over the patch of dirt. May saw it as in the photos, had to close her eyes to clear Bella away.

'Here? Yeah, OK, this is more what I . . .' Chris squatted, patted the dirt. 'Yeah, OK.' She looked out towards the road with a worried frown and then back over her shoulder to where the bush began. The creases softened. She breathed out and patted the dirt again. 'It's peaceful in a way, isn't it? Like, listen. Couple of birds, cars, but that's not a bad sound if you know how to think about it. It's a thing she'd do when she was little. Her room was at the back of the house, highway behind us, over the fence. She'd pretend that whoosh whoosh sound was the ocean. Once I was sitting with her – Mum and the boyfriend were fighting, I suppose – and I was sitting in with Bel while she went to sleep and she was saying how it was nice to hear the ocean and some hell-big truck's gone past just then and blasted its horn and she didn't skip a beat, just went, "Ah, there's the old tugboat coming through." Funny little . . .' Chris wiped her forehead and the back of her neck, seemingly oblivious to the tears streaming down her cheeks, the snot dripping from her nose. 'Bloody hot out here. She'd be red as a lobster in seconds, sun like this. But it was night, wasn't it, so that's all right. Woulda been dark though.' She looked up and out, then back at the tear-splotched dirt. 'No lights for ages, hey? Yeah, dark, no birds, but some cars maybe, she would've thought of the ocean thing, I bet.'

May turned away, watched a clump of grass shaking a few metres away. A sound ripped through the day. A banshee wailing with the force to shatter God's skull. Impossible that such a sound could come from a lone woman. But there she was, heaving and wailing, spraying snot and tears and sweat. *Like a creature possessed*, May wrote in her mental notebook. No. Bullshit. Like any one of us would. *Like all of us should when we think about what happened here.*

■ ■ ■

After I'd been out to see the place it happened I walked into my house and felt like I was still outside. Where I sat at the kitchen table, I was an easy target. Anyone could walk up the driveway see me through that huge window. Closing the curtain made it worse.

The entire outside world became an ever-moving shadow.

I stood against the front door and heard the wind pushing leaves along the road. I pressed the lock button in and out, in and out. What use is a lock if it's installed in a piece of bloody cardboard?

I walked down to the hardware and bought a galvanised steel-core door with a deadlock and chain and paid extra to have it delivered and installed that arvo. I also ordered stainless-steel security-mesh screens for all my windows, which the fella promised would be installed within three days.

By four o'clock the workmen had left and I was sitting alone, looking at my new door, thinking that I better get off my arse and get ready for work. That's when it started. She started.

First was the cold. You'd think I'd have been used to it by now but it's not the kind of thing you can get used to. It's like someone's slit your skin at the top of your spine and poured coldness in. 'I don't know what to do,' I said aloud and for a moment nothing happened. Then the smell of wet earth filled the kitchen. It was so strong and thick, I started to gag. Just like that it went away and so did the cold.

I ran to my room and started undressing, ready to chuck on my work gear and get out of there, but as soon as I pulled on my shirt the most terrible screaming started in my head. I know it was in my head, because I fell onto the bed and pulled the pillow over my face and stuck my hands over my ears and it just got louder and clearer.

I don't know how long I lay like that, wishing for it to stop, but at some point it got quieter and I could hear the little girl's voice underneath, *I'm cold, Chrissy, I'm cold I'm cold I'm so so cold*, and the wet earth was in my mouth and throat again. I threw the pillow off my face, overbalanced and crashed to the floor. The voice and the scream stopped instantly.

I crouched there, panting, waiting for something else or for enough nothing to know it was over. A shadow was spreading out on the wall in front of me. Spreading and darkening. I pressed my hand to it and was relieved at the heat, because that was a predictable thing. In the midst of it all here was something familiar. But when I brought my hand away it was covered in blood. I ran to the kitchen and turned on the tap, but my hand was clean and dry. I noticed the house had become quiet and I was warm. I also noticed my work shirt had a big rip along the left seam.

Breathing as calmly and deeply as I could I went back to the bedroom. The wall was normal. I took off my ripped shirt and pulled on another. The world tilted. It wasn't that I fell or got dizzy; it was like the wall and floor switched places and I was suddenly sliding backwards. I slammed into the dressing table and my little ceramic make-up tray crashed down on me, spilling perfume and eyeshadow all over my clean shirt.

I didn't move for a long time. When I finally did it was only because I was frightened I'd freeze to death if I didn't. Moving felt difficult. I've never felt exhaustion like it. I made it to my phone on the kitchen table and called in sick to work. The second I hung up the exhaustion and the cold were gone, just like that, and I thought, well, OK, Bel, message received.

I put on an old Madonna CD and walked through the house spraying the vanilla deodoriser she loved. I stripped the sex-stained sheets from my bed and took them and the bathroom bin holding the condoms and threw the lot in the outside garbage. I came back in and secured my new locks. I made a stack of toasted cheese sandwiches and smothered them in tomato sauce and then we snuggled under a blanket and watched three Julia Roberts DVDs in a row. Before the end of the third, I felt her head on my shoulder and heard her whispery snore.

I felt OK about having a couple of drinks then. I knew she felt safe and would sleep through the night.

Tuesday
28
April

May was woken by her phone. She answered blindly, heart hammering. Chris's voice. No hello, just a child's question floating out into the TV-lit room. 'Do you believe in ghosts?'

'What?' May fumbled for the remote and muted the news. 'Chris, it's the middle of the night, why are you –'

'It's barely past two. But, listen. Listen, I need to know –'

'You're a bit pissed, hey?' May found the lamp switch; the room turned dusky pink and her heart slowed.

'Yeah, a bit, but, listen, May, do ya?'

'Believe in ghosts? Um, not really. I don't think so.'

'Oh.'

'Chris, what's wrong? Has something happened?'

'Yeah, nah. I mean, I thought something did, but it can't have, hey? I just . . . Nate said it's grief. Like I'm seeing her because I need to, because I miss her too much.'

May's heart sped up again. 'You're seeing Bella?'

'Yeah. No. I saw her once, at the window. But that was a while back. There's been other stuff happening. I don't know. Sometimes it feels like she's here. Her smell, her hands. But sometimes it's just . . . scary. So it can't be her then, can it? She wouldn't want to scare me.'

'I don't know, Chris. Look, is Nate with you?'

'Nah, he never stays with me overnight any more. As if we can't fuck just as well during the day.'

A vision of Craig slamming into her while the midday sun turned the living room into an oven, the sharp, shocking pain of the memory making her gasp.

'Don't you act all shocked, not after what you've been getting up to with Chas. Who's no more single than Nate, thank you very much.'

'I'm not shocked, I was just . . . How'd you know about that?'

A cackle. 'It's not exactly a secret. Babin' young reporter from out of town; nice-looking root-rat constantly on the hunt for fresh pussy. It was only a matter of time, hey? Though from what I hear it didn't take much of that. Didn't even buy a beer before – woo – off you went.'

'Shit.'

'Ah, don't worry about it. No one cares.'

'Really?'

'Oh, they talk. People talk a lot of crap about everyone here. But it doesn't matter. It doesn't change anything. You're still a reporter. People won't tell you any more or less than they want to just because you've joined the sisterhood of Chasfuckers.'

May sipped from the water glass on the bedside table. She was a Chasfucker. Brilliant.

'Seriously, but. Do you think Nate's right? Is it a grief thing?'

'Oh, I don't know. I suppose it could be. I mean, it seems more likely than . . .'

'Yeah. I know it does, but . . .' A swallow, a glass connecting with a tabletop, bottle unscrewed, soft splash. 'Not doing the job of comforting me right now, you know?'

'Look, Chris, do you want me to come around?'

'Nah, it's cool. I shouldna called so late. I'll see ya tomorrow, yeah?'

The line went dead. May switched off the light, lay back down, pressed hard on the bruises inside her thighs, blood surging at the memory of Chas's stabbing hipbones. Fucking whore. Him, her. What was the point? The hunger for flesh, the crazed greed that made everything permissible, and then the shame. Not shame about the fucking, but about the need for it. Shame that in the lead-up moments it felt so important and now, lying alone in her shitty hotel bed, it seemed as exciting and urgent as double-stitching the dropped hem of her suit pants.

It hadn't felt like that with Craig. The urgency never left, the shame never came. Until the end – hell, until right now – having his flesh on hers seemed a necessary thing.

May punched the bed, sat up and drank some more water, punched the bed again. She forced her mind to the phone call. When was the last time she'd heard anyone talk about ghosts? At uni, a story about a woman who'd suicided from a top-floor window and whose ghost would sometimes push books and papers to the floor during exams. Teenage sleepovers, silly, gory stories about axe murderers who wouldn't die and children who refused to leave the place they were killed.

Further back, family stories saved for those nights when a summer storm or forgotten bill had shut the power off. May and her brothers snuggled together in Mum's bed or spread out on the back verandah fanning each other with pieces of stiff card, the wind firing warm water bullets at their feet, and Mum would light a candle or let the darkness be, and she would tell of the old lady at the end of Aunty Kay's bed when she was eight, the teenage murder victim who cried invisibly in the old Parramatta cinema toilets, the spirit who would untuck Grandma's sheets and warm up the bottom of the bed for her and sometimes switch the radio to Classic FM while Grandma was listening to talkback.

A memory long-abandoned flooded back: May was sixteen, on a history excursion to Old Government House. A middle-aged volunteer in a flouncy dress and mob-cap led the teenagers through the building telling dull stories about early colonial governors and their wives. May was up the front of the group as usual, in an effort to escape the attentions of Vaughan Tanner and his mates up the back. It was the height of summer, and when they stopped in a long stone corridor to hear yet another tale of an old English dude recreating the place he'd sailed for two years to get away from, May leant back against the stones and luxuriated in feeling cool for the first time that week. She was wide awake, though bored out of her mind. She closed her eyes for a second, but no more.

When she opened them there was a girl of twelve or thirteen standing behind the guide. She wore a long pale blue dress, a matching bonnet, a white apron and a short white cape over her shoulders. May wondered if she had missed the introduction of a child performer into the tedious colonial pantomime, but even as she thought it she knew it wasn't so. The girl flickered as though she was standing behind a translucent, fluttering curtain. Her arms were wrapped tight around her belly. Tears streamed down her face. The guide kept droning and Mr Wilcox kept nodding enthusiastically and the students kept whispering and jostling all around her. May locked eyes with the girl. She flushed with heat and was told later she made a 'weird squeaking sound' and then fainted.

She was only out for a second, but the guide uncovered a walkie-talkie from within the folds of her gown and called for first aid. May could only say she was fine so many times before the repeating of it became more embarrassing than the fainting. She was glad to follow the first-aid lady who came out of the hallway. As she passed she heard Vaughan and his cronies saying, 'I'm fine, I'm fine, just a little fainting spell, I'm fine,' in high-pitched voices.

Outside she felt much worse on account of the blazing sun and increasing understanding of how very, very embarrassing the incident was. She must've cried a bit because the first-aid lady, who was also the refreshments lady, patted her back and said, 'Don't feel bad, that passageway often freaks people out. I've felt queasy walking through there myself.'

'I saw a girl crying.'

'From your school?'

'No.'

'Ah.' The woman looked back at the building. 'I've never met anyone who's seen her. Only heard third or fourth hand.'

'Who is she?'

'Can't really say, love, but there are stories. Come back for the night-time ghost tour and you'll hear them all.'

'Can't you tell me?'

'Not really meant to tell students that kind of thing. Sorry. Maybe if you ask your teacher he can find out for you?'

May sank into silence. She wondered if you could get heat stroke in less than ten minutes. After a bit the class came trooping out into the gardens and she rejoined them while the first-aid/refreshment lady went off to haul out the juice and biscuits for morning tea. May accepted the class's judgement that she was a frail little fainting princess and after a while began to think of herself that way. She often insisted on sitting near windows and exits, for instance, 'in case I get faint again'.

Sitting up in bed and switching on the light again she grabbed her laptop and looked up Old Government House. There it was, exactly as she remembered it, an off-white Georgian mansion whose shuttered windows stared blindly out over the clipped lawns. She skimmed the historical and ghost tour info and then went back to the search page, added 'haunted OR ghost' to her search term and started to read through the dozens of pages of results.

Lots of references to the 'haunted atmosphere' and 'ghosts of the past', and plenty of bloggers reporting on the ghost tour, some of them with grainy, dark photos claiming to be of spirits. After half an hour she came to the page of a 'spirit-whisperer' who had visited Old Government House after hearing that 'there were many tormented spirits in need of a sympathetic ear'. Among them, May read with a rapidly increasing heart rate, was that of fourteen-year-old Maisie Noakes, a maid, who was gang-raped by 'persons unknown' in the passageway between the main house and the servants' quarters. She died soon after of internal injuries. 'Poor Maisie seems not to understand that her sad, painful life is over. She haunts the passageway clutching her stomach and crying, waiting, tragically in vain, for help to come.'

'Real good move reading that shit in the middle of the night,' May muttered. She got up and went to the bathroom, determinedly ignoring the impulse to check inside the cupboards and out the window. Coincidence coincidence coincidence, she repeated, until it turned into a mantra that eventually allowed her to fall asleep.

Before heading over to Chris's in the morning, May called Max. 'Weird question, I know, but . . . ghosts.'

'Not a question.'

'Do you believe in them?'

'Um, no. But only because I'm not six years old or mentally deficient.'

'Judgy much?'

'Oh no, May. Is this the next stage of your unravelling? You're being haunted?'

'I'm not unravelling! Is that what people are saying?'

'If you consider me people, then yes.'

'Obviously I don't, so that's fine. And no, I'm not being haunted, but this woman I'm writing about thinks she is and at first I was like, *pfft, she's a drunk, whatever*, but then I had this weird memory.' May told him about the school excursion and then the internet search.

'Oooooh, spooky.'

'It is, right?'

He sighed. 'Seriously? May, ghosts aren't real, but nasty shit that people's brains sometimes can't handle is and so is the power of imagination.'

'But the thing I read last night described the girl exactly.'

'As I bet the guide did during your tour. Seems likely you heard the story and all your teen angst emo combined with your excitable imagination and created this image which was not dissimilar to the image other people who have heard the story have imagined.'

'The guide didn't tell us that story. I'm sure of it.'

'Well, you heard it on the bus on the way in or from someone whispering up the back. Trust me on this, high schoolers adore local ghost stories. Especially ones involving sex and violence. That's always been true. Stories like that one would've been told and retold by generations of kids.'

'Yeah. Maybe.'

'Yeah definitely. Look, when are you coming home? We miss you.'

'Who's we?'

'Mum, Jason, me. Probably other people do too, but I don't know them so can't say for sure.'

'I'll be here a while longer. I'm just starting to build a real rapport with this woman.'

'And money? Are you building a rapport with some money?'

'Sorry, Mum, is that you?'

'We're worried about you. You know, the whole not having a job and therefore not getting paid thing.'

'I will get paid. I just have to put the work in first. Until then I have some savings. It's fine.'

'And so you put the work in and get paid for this article and then what? Hope there's an arrest? Hope there's a long drawn-out trial? Hope there's a twist and a new arrest at the last minute so you can get another long drawn-out trial?'

'Fuck you.'

'I'm just saying. It's not a life plan.'

'No, it's not a life plan, but it's not as scatty and nasty as you make it sound either. This is a story I care about. A lot, actually. I'm thinking of turning the article into a book, as a matter of fact.'

He was silent a second. 'A book. OK. That's interesting. Means you can apply for some grants, get some funding.'

'Yes, I know.' She typed 'book funding grants' into Google. 'It's in process.'

'Well . . . OK. I'm glad to hear it.'

'Good.'

'You can still come home though. Work on the book in between other work and hanging out with your brother?'

'I'll try to come and visit soon, OK?'

'Alright. You take care. And stay away from GhostHunter dot com or whatever the fuck it is. Crazy is catching, you know.'

■　■　■

Interview transcript

28 April 2015

Arthur Tomesberry, Strathdee Historical Society

When we spoke a few weeks ago you said you thought this area was haunted. Can you tell me more about that?
Yeah, well, there's the massacres. I use the plural advisedly. No written records, but the stories have come down and even if they hadn't it's common sense.

Common sense?
This was no *terra nullius*. This was inhabited land. Long inhabited. Deeply and well inhabited. And then, within a couple of years, it's like the blacks were never here. You think it's likely every last one of them just shrugged and wandered off, leaving it all to the new arrivals? Pull the other one. Read the official history and between each line of text is a paddock full of bodies.

And when you said the region is haunted, you meant it metaphorically?
Yeah, well, no. I mean, I'm not saying there's white-sheeted characters flying about. I'm saying there's rivers of blood soaked into the soil here and once you're aware of that you're aware of it.

What about more literal hauntings, Mr Tomesberry? Any reports of them around Strathdee?
White-sheeted characters flying about?

Or similar. I noticed there's a ghost tour on your brochure.
[Chuckles] Look, offer a historical cemetery tour and you get one

or two researching their family history. Call it a ghost tour and you get a busload. I only tell the stories that have a good amount of documented history behind them. And you know, it's not like I invent the ghosts, it's just I've never seen 'em personally.

You should come along and see for yourself, anyway. We only hold 'em every six weeks or so this time of year. Next one's third Friday night in May.

If I'm still in town, I'd love to come along. In the meantime, tell me your best Strathdee ghost story. The one that comes closest to scaring even you.

[Laughs into coughing fit] Sorry about that. Scares even me, hey? Well, I'll tell you there's one grave up in the old cemetery that – look, I've never seen or heard anything myself, but the reactions I've seen in some of the tourists, well, that's been enough to give me some real shivers, I'll admit.

The grave's sunken pretty badly and the stone can hardly be read. Sarah Harley or Hurley we think it was, but there were a lot of ladies with similar names around the time, living here and around and passing through. It's hard to know for sure who she was and so there's no story to this one. With the figures some folk see in the window of the Anglican church, say, I can tell all about the history of the place, how the priest's little boy died tragically there and all that, but this grave I have nothing to tell. It's not even on the official tour map. But time and again it's the one that gets the scares.

Some blokes – not all or even most, understand: some – say that as they walk towards her grave, within five or ten feet I'm talking, they hear this high-pitched scream. Woman's scream. Like I said, I've never heard it, but I've seen tough old blokes and slick city fellas alike turn heel and bolt, and afterwards they say that's what made them run.

Funny thing about this one is that it's always the men. I've never had a female hear the scream or get spooked there at all.

And you don't know anything about the woman buried there?
Ah, there are stories, but I can't find evidence for a single one of 'em, so I won't tell 'em.

Not even to me?
Not even to you. From me you get facts, that's all. If it's gossip and gruesome stories you want talk to Bev next door in the teashop.

■   ■   ■

Interview transcript

28 April 2015

Beverly Grant, Strathdee Historical Society Tea and Gift Shop

Arthur tells me you're the person to speak to about Sarah Harley, why her grave frightens people.
Well, I can't tell you why it frightens some gentlemen but I can tell you what I've heard about the lady herself.

Heard from where?
Arthur'd call it gossip. I call it oral history. There are people in Strathdee whose families have been here since before the town had a name. We're trying to record as many of the stories as we can before all that knowledge has passed. Arthur's a stickler, though. He

won't let us write anything up in the brochures or on the website unless there's independent verification. Me, I think we should have a little section on the website that's just for stories people tell, if you see what I mean. Not claiming it all as fact, just sharing the stories people tell and letting visitors and readers decide for themselves about it all.

And what are the stories about Sarah Harley?
Well, there are a few, and we can't be sure if they're all about the same woman – it was a common enough name – or if any of the Sarahs are the same as the one buried up there, but, anyway . . .

It's said that Sarah Harley or Hurley arrived in the colony on the *Friendship* in 1818, transported for stealing a pair of britches, or some say it was a shirt. She was seventeen or so. There was talk of licentiousness on board – licentiousness meant sex, I suppose. Whether willing or not we can't say. Once in the colony she was a well-behaved girl, served her sentence without incident and earned her freedom. Freedom from prison, anyway; she was married off as soon as she left the place. The husband was wealthy, don't know by what means. Sarah bore him eight children.

One night she was walking home – from where? Why? We don't know – when a gang of men set upon her. 'In a fit of lust' the men killed her, it's said. She was raped to death is what that means. Her body was dumped in front of her house for her husband and kids to find. That's one story.

Another story goes that Sarah was never a mother of eight, never a wife and never a convict, though her parents both came out on the convict ships. She was seventeen and so pretty you could choke. Even though her mum was a lady of the night and her dad a thief, Sarah thought she was Princess Mary. One night she was walking home – again, from where and why no one ever says – when a gang of men set upon her. 'In a fit of lust' they killed her. They left her body where it lay.

Now I don't know which is true, or if neither are, but the similarities suggest at least that whoever she was, and whatever the story of her life, her death was a terrible one.

I don't know what Arthur told you about the grave. He's an old sceptic, that one, but plenty of people around here will tell you that if you visit you might hear her screaming and you might run. If you are a man you will likely fall and get a mouthful of dirt. Some of them say they've felt for a second that this might be how it ends. After, they might say it was nothing, probably some kid mucking around, tripped on a root; the trees here are so old, they're bursting up from beneath. But some will insist they felt the cold of Sarah's hands around their throat.

I've also heard from some ladies who've seen Sarah perched in a tree over the grave. But if she's in the tree and there's a man there he won't see her but he might feel her nails on his cheeks or back, hear her screams and pleas for mercy. One young fella said he was knocked to the ground from behind and fell hard on what felt like a body.

Have you ever seen or felt anything there?
Nothing like any of that, no. But there's a feeling there to be sure. You go on up and you can't help thinking about the stories, can't help thinking... Well, it's awful to say but you can't help wondering what it would've been like. Raped to death. I do imagine her screams and fear when I'm up there, of course. If some people hear them for real, then I'm not surprised, not one bit.

Do you think Bella Michaels's story will resonate like Sarah's? Will you start to hear stories of her haunting people?
I think that is a very insensitive question.

I'm sorry. It's just that the similarities are so –
No, we don't know what happened to Sarah, we just imagine from stories. We do know what happened to Bella. She was set upon. To death. Her body left. [Sobs] I can tell you what will happen if you visit her grave. You will hear nothing but the birds and see nothing but stone and grass and sky and dirt, because that poor girl is dead and no amount of nasty poking and digging from the likes of you is going to change that.

■ ■ ■

I didn't want to risk another tantrum from Bella so I spent the afternoon at Lisa's, helping her bottle some pears, and then went on to work from there. It was an OK night. Good mix of regulars and travellers, busy enough to stop my mind going to dark places but not so busy I couldn't duck out to the kitchen for a sip of beer and couple of chips every so often.

Near closing time, I was chatting to Lynn about her grandson, who's just started uni down in Melbourne. I was behind the bar and Lynn was propped up against it, an empty glass in front of her. I always try and talk to her a bit in between drinks. Slow her down a bit, you know?

Anyway, out the corner of my eye I saw that man coming through the door and my guts dropped. I kept talking to Lynn and he kept walking in a straight line towards me. He sat beside Lynn and ordered a beer, which I got for him while managing not to look at his face. He kept sitting there, not saying anything, and after a bit it got so I couldn't stand it and I had to leave Lynn alone with a fresh gin rather than stay there a second longer.

I went out to the kitchen and I must've looked wrong, because Nadine stopped her pot scrubbing and came over, asked me if I was right.

'Just this fella hanging around again. Bloody pain in my arse.'

'Which one is it?'

I told her and she raised her eyebrows. 'He's a bit of all right, that one. You could do worse.'

'Yeah, yeah, just not up for any of that right now.'

'Not like you, Chris,' she said, but friendly-like.

'Ha. I know, right? Just with everything . . .'

'Yeah, I know, mate. I know.' She patted my arm, so stiff and awkward I nearly burst into tears. I plastered on a smile and went back out before I lost it.

He was waiting there. Definitely nice-looking. I can't explain why I didn't want him, only that I'd always had that feeling about him and being with him made it worse. It was like I couldn't hint or joke my way out of anything. Most blokes, you can make it clear you're not into them or what they're doing, but in a light way. They get it, they back off. Him, I felt it was fight or let it be and he put things in a way that made fighting seem an overreaction.

That night he stayed until close and when I said (smiley, jokey) that it was time to hit the frog and toad, he nodded and left and I hoped that was it but my guts knew different, and when I walked out into the car park there was his truck and him leaning against it. He turned, opened the passenger door and stood there like that, his hand on the door, just looking at me.

'Oh, hey, I'm actually off to a mate's place tonight. She lives near here so I'm going to walk on over, crash there. Catch you later, hey?'

He must've seen I was scared, tripping over my words and almost tripping over my feet. Maybe he didn't, maybe he did and didn't care. Or liked it. I don't know.

'Nah.' He took hold of my upper arm. Not hard. I could've pulled away. 'No point walking. I'll drive you.'

I made myself look at him. His lips made my skin crawl, firmed up my determination. 'Seriously, it's so close. I'll walk. G'night.' I stepped away and he dropped my arm.

'Come on, Chris. Not safe walking around here, you know that better than anyone. What if I let you go and then something happened to you? How'd I feel then?' His hand on my arm again, gentle, turning me around, walking me towards his truck. I could've kneed him in the balls and made a run for it, but that seemed extreme. See what I mean?

He helped me up into the cab of his truck. I strapped in and then pulled out my phone, texted Nate: *Tell Mel I need to crash at his place, explain later.* 'Just letting her know I'm on my way,' I told the man.

He scratched his face. 'Thought it was close? You'll be there before she has time to read it.'

My phone buzzed and he looked at me hard. The engine was running but we hadn't left the car park. I read the message: *I'm at Mel's now. U ok?*

Yep C U soon. I turned my phone to silent, told the man the address.

'Other end of town.'

'S'pose. Never seems far when I walk it.'

The drive was fine. He didn't touch me, didn't even speak. Bloody hell did I feel tense, though, holding my phone so tight I'm lucky I didn't crush it to bits, my other hand around the door handle, ready to squeeze it open the second we stopped. I don't think I took a proper breath until we turned into Melvin's street, but then I saw the brick outline of Nate beside the letterbox and my throat closed up.

'Ha,' the man said, bringing the truck to a stop. 'Funny. That's your ex there, innit?'

'Oh, yeah. His mate Mel's married to my friend Julie. Didn't realise he was in town, but.'

'Bullshit.'

'Thanks for the lift.' I unsnapped my belt.

His hand closed on my thigh. 'You coulda just told me you had plans.'

'I did. Plans to stay at my friend's house.'

He smiled, real nasty. 'Yeah. Righto. Whatever you say.'

'What I say is that I don't wanna see you again. Got it?' I opened the door, jumped to the ground in one go, came down hard on my ankle. Bloody Nate was charging over.

'You right?'

'Yeah, all good,' the man called down. 'Just a misunderstanding.'

Nate's attention was fully on the man. 'Yeah. What kind of misunderstanding?'

'Nate, leave it.'

'Ah, you know what she's like, mate. Mixed messages and that.'

'Yeah, well here's a clear message: get fucked.'

'Nate.'

The man opened his door, stepped down from the cab. Nate walked around to meet him on the road.

'Listen, mate, you should know she's not right in the head. Comes on to me, goes to town, yeah, then ice cold, plays hard to get, and then she's all over me again.'

'Please just leave,' I said as if either of them were listening to me.

'Messes with a man's head, you know?'

I saw Nate trying, God love him. I saw him try. His fists were clenched so hard by his side. 'Yeah, well, she's been clear now.'

The man raised his palms. 'Yeah, yeah, I'm going. Just, you know, don't shoot the messenger, but you should watch out for her. Most whores, if they give you a freebie and cling to you all night like white on rice, it means something. This bitch –'

Nate punched him in the stomach, then grabbed him by the hair and smashed the back of his head into the truck. I told him to stop but it was as though I wasn't even there. The dull thump of Nate slamming the man into the truck followed me halfway down the street and the sound of the man's flesh splitting open replayed in my brain for the entire forty-minute walk home.

Wednesday
29
April

May waited a full minute after knocking and then called Chris's mobile. She heard it ringing on the other side of the door and then Chris's voice coming through the phone and through the door at once.

'It's May. I'm at the door.'

'Hang on.'

Several seconds of clicking and fumbling inside and the door swung open. May recognised the tracksuit Chris was wearing from the press conference the day she arrived in town. She barely recognised the face of the woman wearing it though.

'You OK? You look exhausted.' Which was a polite understatement. Very polite. Extreme understatement.

'Yeah. That's one word for it. You want coffee?'

May nodded and watched as Chris took two coffee mugs down from a shelf above her head, dumped a spoonful of Nescafé in each and filled them from the apparently just-boiled kettle. Every movement seemed to hurt, but when May offered to help Chris shook her head – grimacing as she did – and carried on.

When they were both sitting down May told Chris she'd just come from the hospital. The man Nate had belted was a mess but there was no damage that wouldn't right itself in time.

Chris swallowed air. 'How'd you know?'

'Police tip. Listen, I –'

'Christ. Please, May. Please don't write about it.'

'It's news.'

'How is two testosterone-poisoned idiots getting into a fight news?'

'When one of them is related by marriage to a murder victim and the fight was caused by that victim's sister . . .'

'Excuse me?'

'Story I got is that they were fighting over you.'

'I didn't want them to fight. I didn't cause anything.'

''Course. Stupid choice of words. When the fight happened in the presence of –'

'Only the start and I had no choice in that.'

'OK, but you understand why people will be interested.'

'Honestly, I don't.' Chris closed her eyes. 'Is he pressing charges?'

'Seems likely.'

A tear leaked out of Chris's left eye; she swiped it away angrily, looked at May directly.

'Don't write about it.'

'Chris, I –'

'Please. If it's in the article his boss, his girlfriend, everyone will see it . . .'

'Why do you care?'

'Wish I knew, mate, wish I knew.' She stood, shuffled across to the sink, bent with difficulty and splashed her face with water.

'I won't mention it in the article.'

'Thank you.'

'But it'll probably need to go in the book.'

'The book?'

'Yeah. I wanted to talk to you about that. About the possibility of a book. What do you think?'

'About Bella?'

'About the case. I've been sounding out a couple of publishers. There'd be interest for sure, but we need, well, we need an ending.'

Chris looked at her blankly.

'An arrest, at least. Preferably a conviction. But that will happen. Only a matter of time.'

Chris's nod was barely perceptible. May couldn't bear to look at her.

'And in the meantime I can be researching and writing, getting the bulk of the story done. I'd need your cooperation, of course. No point in a book about Bella without you. What do you reckon?'

'I don't know. Maybe.'

'You've upped your security,' May said, taking note of a new deadlock and chain.

'For all the good it did. For all the bloody good anything does.'

May's phone rang. She excused herself and stepped into the living room to answer.

'Hi, May? It's Matt. Um, Matt Drey, from –'

'Matt, great to hear from you, what's up?'

'Um, just you asked me to call you if there were any, ah, developments that you might ...'

'Yes, of course. What's going on?'

'Can't say, but if you just happened to come down to the Imperial Hotel right now ...'

'On my way.'

May saw the police car before she'd reached the car park. By the time she pulled in she'd clocked the twenty or so people gathered in front of the blue-and-white tape strung from a corner of the hotel's verandah to the fence dividing the property from the tyre shop next door. Matt was standing up against the tape, chatting to the people he was clearly supposed to be dispersing. When he saw May his face lit up.

May winked at him and ducked right beneath the tape, rushing past him towards the uniform crouched at the end of the passageway, looking at something just around the corner. A hazy lens dropped over the scene and she realised she was in danger of passing out. She paused, pressed her palm into the brick wall to her right, concentrated on breathing properly. There was nothing in the world she wanted less than to see what it was the cop was looking at, but then Chris didn't want to be going mad from grief and fear and Bella sure as fuck didn't want to end up the thing that made others mad with grief and fear either. Toughen up, woman, get down there.

'Senior Constable Riley,' she said softly, stepping up behind him.

He turned, almost overbalancing as he quickly stood and moved forward to cut her off. 'Fucking Drey.'

'Oh, don't blame him. One of the onlookers was creating a fuss about something and I slipped by him. What've we got here?'

'May, come on, you know you're not meant to be here. Detectives will be here any second. We'll be done for if they know we let a reporter in.'

'I promise I won't write anything about this. I'll go wait out front for the official statement like everyone else, but just tell me, please, is it to do with Bella?'

The man's eyes went to the sky, he shook his head. 'Can't say.'

'It's a body though?'

The cop ducked his head around her, must have determined the approach a detective-free zone because he abruptly stepped out of the way, giving May a clear view of what lay in the grass. She looked away but too late not to see the small, withered yellow dog, its head at an impossible angle, its muzzle bound with grey tape.

'Fourth one in as many weeks,' the cop said.

May looked only at the wall behind the officer's head. 'Yeah. I wrote about the others. Couldn't get a run, though. Not much interest.'

''Cause they're strays?'

'No, I mean, outside of Strathdee. A dead animal isn't a national or state story, you know. Anyway, thanks. I better clear out before you get in trouble.'

'Yeah – hey, in case the detectives are out there already, go out this way, yeah?' He pointed along the back wall of the pub, towards the passage on the other side.

She looked at the dog as she stepped over it, the terror of feeling its skull crunch underneath her shoe stronger than the fear of seeing its face. But she underestimated the cruelty of her imagination, heard and felt that crunch for days.

■   ■   ■

Nate came around early afternoon. His eyes were tiny. As soon as he was inside my blood started icing up. I told him I was about to take a walk and he could come if he wanted. He looked ready to tear my head off but he agreed and the warmth came back into my hands and feet.

We set off without speaking. All along the street curtains and blinds flickered and flashed as we passed. By night the town'd be buzzing with the thrilling and important news that two people who used to be married took a walk together in the fading light of an autumn afternoon.

We rounded the corner and I started heading up towards the park, but Nate mumbled something about the creek being more private and so we turned left again, cut through the community centre's backyard and stepped over the half-down fence onto the creek bank. I stumbled a little going down the slope, grabbed Nate's arm. We used to come down here to fight or fuck when Bella lived with us but I hadn't been for years. It was the same, more or less. More wild vines growing around the sides of the creek; less light, less air.

Nate took his arm back and leant against a tree trunk. 'So?'

'So what?'

'What's the story? Who was the dickhead?'

I sat on a patch of dry, spiky grass and tucked my feet up beneath me. 'A mistake.'

'What does that mean?'

'I slept with him. A mistake, like I said, but then he wouldn't take a hint. Kept bothering me.'

'He called you a whore.'

'Yeah, well, men do that sometimes.'

'I don't think he meant it like that. It's not the first thing I've heard . . . I mean, people watch what they say around me, I think, but I've heard stuff . . .'

The vines on the opposite bank rustled as something slithered through them. One of the reasons Nate and me chose this as our private place was that the bustling, mostly invisible wildlife meant it had a reputation as dangerous, haunted even. When Bella was small some older kids told her that a bunyip lived down here, scared the living daylights out of her. She'd go around asking every adult she knew about the bunyip, trying to determine if it was real and, if so, how much of a danger it was. She had nightmares and everything. One time I found a picture she'd drawn of it, horrifying thing, like a giant croc with a bird's head, but standing like a man. I remember saying, 'It doesn't look that scary; no claws, no teeth.' And she looked at me like I was retarded and said, 'It doesn't need them. It *hugs* you to death.'

'Are you going to say anything?'

'What do you want me to say, Nate?'

'Is it true?'

'That I'm a whore?'

'Yeah.'

'You're seriously asking me if I'm a whore?'

He looked up and out at nothing.

'Sometimes, Nate. Sometimes I suppose I am.'

He didn't react right away, just stood there looking at the space in front of his face. 'Right,' he said at last. 'Right.' And then he took a couple of giant steps up the embankment and over the fence and left me there, didn't look back.

I don't know how I expected him to react. The strongest, most terrible feeling I had was that I didn't know him. We've loved and grappled and wept and torn at each other as much as any two people could, but when it comes down to it he's trapped in his own skull and I'm here in mine and thinking otherwise is a romantic daydream.

Maybe I should've tried to explain it to him like I did to you, explain how it happened accidentally and all, but I doubt it would've made a difference. I mean, it doesn't make a difference, does it? If I'd thought up the idea myself and put an ad on Gumtree would it change the meaning of what happens in my bed? I started whoring accidentally and teenaged Nate got into his first fight accidentally but we've both made a thousand choices since then and here we are.

Brandis called while I was walking home, wanted to know what the story was with the man whose head Nate had smashed in. I told him the briefest true version I could.

'Did he ever mention Bella?'

Everything stopped. My breath, my heart, the turning of the world. I flew back in time, went through every second I'd lived since she'd gone and then further, to see the things I'd only imagined again and again. I relived the night she couldn't.

'Chris?'

'No.'

'You know his mother is at Strathdee Haven?'

'No.'

'He's visited her once a fortnight or so for the past three years.'

I heard Bella sobbing while he lay beside me. Only in my head this time. Only in the torture chamber of my memory.

'Impossible that he wouldn't have got to know your sister at least a little bit in that time, I'd have thought.'

'He never said.'

'Which is a bit odd, for sure, but not necessarily indicative of anything sinister.'

'Isn't it?'

'He explained it by saying he thought you wouldn't want a reminder of her.'

'She hasn't even been gone a month.'

'Yeah, yeah, reminder's my word. I was trying to soften the . . . He's got a foul mouth on him that one. The stitches and broken teeth might be contributing to that, I suppose.' I could hear Brandis's approval – admiration, even – and relief and shame and fear churned in my guts. 'What he said, if you'll excuse the bluntness, is: "It woulda killed the mood to bring up her murdered sister, I reckon."'

'Right. Nothing sinister.'

'Look, he's a grub, no question, and we'll take a good long look at him, for sure, but . . .'

'Is he still in hospital?'

'He'll be out today.' Brandis went quiet and so did I. After a minute he said, 'He do something to you that I don't know about, Chris?'

'Nothing illegal.'

'I can tell him to steer clear of you. Make it sound official. But if you want an enforceable order you'll have to –'

'I know. It's OK. Thanks.'

'Have you considered getting someone to come stay with you for a while?'

I laughed a little then.

'Chris, it's important you feel safe.'

Like he couldn't even hear himself, you know?

I told Old Grey I was taking holidays until further notice. God knows I had enough owing to me. He said he needed to know when I'd be back so he could rework the roster. I told him to fire me if he wanted and replace me full time and he said, 'Don't be silly, love. I'll check in with you next week.'

I flicked through the stack of phone messages Lisa and Carrie had written out for me over the past few days. Most were from long-ago friends or distant relatives wanting to check in or pass on their love and I tossed them in the bin as I went. I found the message I was looking for. Lisa had mentioned it when she handed the pad over on, I don't know, whatever day it had been, twelve or so pages ago.

Barbara Stein: Bella's landlady. Needs to organise clearing out and return of bond etc.

'Alright, Bel,' I said, steeling myself for the call. 'Time to get you moved back in properly.'

Thursday
30
April

The invitation had surprised May but she managed to answer yes as casually and naturally as if she'd just been offered a cup of tea. She offered to drive and pretended not to already know the way.

Immediately on opening the door they were met with a putrid stench. Like rancid flesh, May thought. Chris had stopped three steps through the doorway and dropped the bucket of cleaning supplies and the stack of flattened cardboard boxes she'd been carrying. Her whole body seeming poised for attack, or for being attacked. May, carrying her camera, with her own stack of folded cardboard boxes under her arm stayed behind Chris's left shoulder, waiting.

The front door opened directly into a miniature sitting room with mismatched easy chairs, a coarse, bright striped rug, a dark wood coffee table and there, in the centre, the source of the foulness: a bowl of rotten fruit and a vase of long-dead flowers. At the far end of the sitting room was a vestibule crowded with a fridge, sink, microwave. On the floor to May's left was a wonky plastic shoe tree, yellow ballet flats and sequinned thongs and sensible black low-heeled court shoes neatly gathering dust. To the right of where Chris stood was an open door, through which May glimpsed the edge of a bed. A little past that was another open door, glossy white tiles peeping out over the edge of the grey carpet.

'Righto,' Chris said and strode over to the coffee table, then pulled out a black garbage bag and emptied the fruit bowl without covering her nose or gagging.

May ducked into the bedroom, her hand over her nose and mouth. Fucking soft. She concentrated on the details of the room, taking photos as she went. The faux-cast-iron double bed, made up with a matching quilt and sheet set of pale blue and yellow checks. A pine dresser, the type you could buy from a discount furniture barn for $79. A red velvet jewellery box, open to reveal a small collection of silver bracelets and chains, each in its own tiny compartment. At the back of the dresser, three bottles of chain store perfume, each used almost equally, lined up next to three lipsticks, two bottles of foundation, one tub of moisturiser, one of hair gel, a pale grey eyeshadow palette and a tube of dark brown mascara. Near the door, a small bookshelf, same pine as the dresser, holding several bestsellers from the past three or four years plus *Anne of Green Gables*, *Little Women* and the entire Harry Potter series. Four framed photos: Chris and Bella together; Chris, Bella and their mother together; Bella's dad Tony squinting into the sun, unsmiling; a tiny tabby kitten yawning up into the camera.

'Did Bella have a cat?' May called.

'A few years ago she had this little darling. Mopey, she called him, because he was such a sook, mewling or sulking in corners if she didn't pay attention to him every second.'

'What happened to him?'

A long silence. May held her breath and headed out to the sitting room where Chris was wiping down the glass coffee table with a rag soaked in what smelt like bleach.

'She had to get rid of him,' Chris said, not looking up. 'This bloke she was seeing, he was allergic.'

'Did he live here with her?'

'Nah. Used to stay here a bit though. I think he still lived with his parents, so this was the only place they could . . . Anyway, Mopey made him sneeze, I guess.'

'Shame. I used to have a cat. Couldn't take it with me when I moved into my terrace. My mum has her now. She loves her, so that's OK. I miss her, though, which is weird. Never thought of myself as a cat person, but I guess I must be. Or that cat anyway. Pixie.'

'Thing is,' Chris said, dipping her rag into a bucket by her side, squeezing it out, 'I don't think he had allergies at all. I think he didn't like Bella's attention being on anyone but him.'

'Jealous of a cat?'

'He was a particularly needy cat, that one.'

'And a particularly needy boyfriend by the sound of it.'

Chris rocked back on her heels. The sun through the front windows made her hair look auburn, her skin glow. May raised her camera and took what she guiltily, excitedly, thought of as the cover shot. 'Not particularly, no. Pretty nice guy. Maybe he did have allergies. I don't know. I find myself thinking the worst of everyone these days.'

With the site visit, the apartment clean-out and several hours of home interviews, May knew she had enough to close the deal with *Women's Weekly*. She spent the evening working on the pitch package, sent it off at 8pm. Called Chas and told him she was in the mood to celebrate.

'Yeah? They arrest someone?'

'Oh, no. It's just . . . It's stupid. A small work victory.'

'How small? Champagne or beer?'

'Beer. But the good stuff.'

'Right, VB it is.'

May laughed. Craig wouldn't have even got that joke, the elitist prick.

'Did you hear anything about the fight Nate Cartwright got into the other night?'

'No offence, darl, but your pillow talk could use some work.'

'Sorry. Oh, baby, oh, baby, you're the best I've ever had. Did the earth move for you too, etcetera?'

'Cold, cold woman.'

'Well, if you don't want to talk . . .' She sat up, made to get out of bed. He dragged her back down with one arm, not opening his eyes or changing position.

'We off the record?'

'If you insist.'

'I insist.' He wriggled his arm so she was tucked in against his chest. 'Word is that the Giggler –'

'Who?'

'The bloke got his head beaten in. Everyone calls him the Giggler 'cause that's what he does, but like, not when something's funny, just randomly. Nervous tic or something.'

'Well, that's creepy.'

'S'pose. Anyway, he thought Chris was his, which is fucking stupid because everyone knows she's Nate's and –'

'Chris is a grown woman. She doesn't belong to anyone but herself.'

'It's just an expression. Don't get your knickers in a knot.'

'Not wearing any, so there. And it's a shit expression. Say what you actually mean.'

'Chris does her thing and that's fine, a good time is had by all but everyone knows that's all it is. At the end of the day, she's Nate's girl and always will be.'

'Even if he's with someone else now.'

'Not saying it's good, just telling you how it is. Look, you'll hear some shit talked about Chris because of how she handles herself, but I reckon she goes about it just right.'

'Can we cut the coyness? She takes money for sex, yes?'

'Yeah.' He stretched the word out. 'That's my point. I mean, however good a time you have, however sweet she is to you, if you're paying her, it's pretty fucking clear she's not your girlfriend, you know?'

'I'm not your girlfriend and you don't pay me.'

'What do you call a six-pack of Coopers? Speaking of . . .' He slithered his arm out from under her, crawled to the end of the bed, gave her an eyeful as he leant down to the bar fridge and pulled out a couple of beers.

'So you're telling me that Strathdee rules are that if a woman has sex without accepting payment it means she's betrothed.'

He knocked her arm with the icy bottle. 'It's a little more complicated than that and that's exactly the problem in this situation because the Giggler is not a complicated man. One might even say he's simple. So, right, word has it that Chris let Giggler have a go without charging. Not unheard of. She's got her fuck buddies like anyone else, just usually they're blokes who know the difference. Like I said, though, this one's bright as a two-watt bulb. He got a freebie and thought it meant something. Chris took him around to Nate so he'd get the message that it didn't.'

'You ever been with Chris?'

He let out a small burp. 'Years and years ago. Pre-Nate.'

'Why not post-Nate? You and her would get on well I'd think.'

'We get on great, yeah. She's a top bird. Just a bit old for me, to be honest.'

'You're the same age.'

'And when I was twenty-five, that was fine.'

'Ugh.'

'It's biology. Men are drawn to youth. Not my fault if I'm not attracted to women over thirty.'

'This must've been really hard for you then. I appreciate the effort you've made to hide your lack of attraction.'

'You're not over thirty.'

'I'll be thirty-one next month.'

'Yeah, well, Sydney thirty-one is like Strathdee twenty-five.'

'I'm so flattered. No, wait, I mean, appalled and offended.'

'Sorry. What was it? Oh, baby, oh, baby, you're the best I've ever had ...'

'Alright. So tell me this: you live in a small town, you work your way through all the women in their twenties – then what?'

'Long as people keep having daughters there'll keep being women in their twenties.'

'So you have no problem with sleeping with the daughters and then granddaughters of former lovers? You are really, really gross, you know that?'

'I'm honest, is all.'

'And what happens when the twenty-somethings start screwing up their noses at the gross old man cracking on to them?'

'Come on. Can you imagine saying no to me? At any age? Never happened, never will.' He got to his knees, shook his dick in her face. She drank some beer, faked the lack of interest he deserved.

'I don't believe for one second that nobody has said no to you.'

'Well, OK, yeah.' He fell back against the pillows. 'My wife says it a fair bit.'

'Maybe she's attracted to young flesh.'

'Don't talk about her, OK?'

'You're the one –'

'Bella.'

May's breath caught in her throat. 'What?'

'Bella said no.'

'Um. Wow. What happened?'

'No "wow", no big story. She was a good-looking girl, of course I tried it on with her. She was sweet about it. Told me she thought I was lovely but she was seeing someone.'

'When was this?'

'I don't know. A year ago? About that.'

'Did she say who she was seeing?'

'Nah. I think she was making it up, to be honest. Not a good feeling, having a girl lie to let you down easy, like you're some sensitive little . . . Anyway, there you go. My story of shattering sexual rejection. Happy now?'

'She was seeing someone, I think. He was married so she couldn't say.'

'Yeah?' Chas took a long swig of his beer, shook his head. 'Good for my ego if that's true, but, gotta say, a bit disappointing. Married man. Didn't think she was like that.'

'Like me?'

'Don't take it personal. If you'd ever met her you'd understand.'

'And yet you, a married man, hit on her and was upset she knocked you back.'

He scrunched up his face. 'Yeah.'

'It's always different when it's you.'

'S'pose.' He sighed. 'I should go home.'

May kissed her way down his chest and belly. People who knew her would be surprised at what she was doing. Or no, not what, but to whom. People who knew her would say what Chas just had about Bella, she was sure. Nobody had known about Craig and nobody would know about this and so May got to go through life unscorned (except by the man she was doing it with) and she guessed that was why she didn't feel like she was the kind of girl who screwed married men.

Or maybe this was exactly what being *that kind of girl* felt like. It felt like being lonely and uncertain and excited and anxious about enjoying the company of a man who speaks frankly even while finding some of the things he says a bit upsetting. It felt like wondering if you were a bad feminist because the scent of a man's groin sends blood to your cunt and the way he grips your hair and groans gets you dripping wet and knowing you are a bad feminist and a bad person because there are more important things than wanting a man and wanting a man to want you, things like dignity and sisterhood and not wanting to cause harm in the world but you feel that there's something wrong with you that you can't help because when it comes to making the choice, the hands and the voice and the smell and the cock, yeah, be honest, the cock makes you ignore all that, wilfully just put it out of your head and that doesn't mean you don't know it all, wouldn't say it all to some other woman thinking this was an OK way to live, but it's different because you know it's not OK you just can't help it and that – this – climbing on a man who's begging you in the filthiest, most un-respectful way to do exactly what you want to do anyway while also thinking *I hate myself* but then coming so hard that the hate is replaced with certainty that there isn't actually any better thing in the world that you could be doing and knowing this is why you keep on doing it because this is it, the whole fucking point of all of it – and then that's over and you're sticky and shivery and he's closing the door behind him and you get up and shower and get on with your bloody day.

Is that how Bella felt when she was riding the man whose wife was at home dying of cancer? Did she fuck herself into self-loathing and out the other side again and call herself the names that no one else could because they didn't know she was like that? Like May.

And if May had been grabbed and pulled into a car and men did to her things that ended in police photos that scorch the brain and soul of some try-hard crime reporter, if that was happening to May would she think (she thinks it now and wishes it away no no no no) that the men had seen it in her, what she'd done, what she was, and this was what happened, what you had to expect?

Because if Bella was like May, if the same tracks had been laid in her deepest secret self, if the thoughts that sped through unstoppably in those moments of terror were these ones, then that was the most unbearable thing of all. I am – May thought, pulling on her running shoes, because what else could she do right now with this this this in her – unable to bear this.

Friday
1
May

It was getting harder and harder to leave the house. Every time I made a move to get dressed in something other than undies, pyjamas or a nightie she'd start me shivering or shaking, give me dizzy spells, make it so I couldn't breathe right. I had to say, out loud, very firmly, 'I'm only going to the supermarket,' or, 'I'm only popping across to Lisa's,' or whatever and then after a minute or two I'd feel normal enough to go. And the very thought of going to work or even into the pub for a quick beer and catch-up with Grey set her off something wicked. I mean, it would have been funny if it wasn't so frightening. The second I'd picture the place my insides would start trying to get out.

One time I tried ignoring it, just breathing and breathing and telling myself *you're fine you're fine you're fine* just like I used to when I'd drunk too much on a night out and got worried about throwing up in the taxi or some bloke's car. And it worked, too. I pushed myself through the feeling and made it as far as the front door. I opened it and, geez, that fresh night air, it was a wonder.

There was quite a wind up, actually, but I've always loved going out when the weather was on the edge of wild. The racing heart and flipping stomach were forgotten. I stepped out, ridiculously excited about feeling the wind lift my hair and whoosh past my ears. Somewhere at the end of a street a car backfired and I guess I was a bit jumpy. I sort of skittered back into the house and from there, just inside the doorway, as I was ready to head out again, I could hear her crying her little heart out. Made me start up too, of course.

I asked her over and over how I could help, what she wanted, but the only reply I got was dizziness and shooting pains and cold and hot flushes charging over each other every thirty goddamn seconds.

Exhausted, I stopped asking and gave up on the idea of leaving. I locked us back up inside and put on one of her old CDs and all was quiet in the house again but not in my heart. I never knew having her back with me would be so painful. That's a terrible thing to say, I know, but I don't mean I didn't want her there. Only that it was so hard to know how to live with her any more.

We do have a couple of biddies calling themselves psychics right here in town, but even if I thought any of them had genuine abilities I wouldn't've gone to them. The more my life is hung out to flap in the wind like bedsheets the more I cling to my privacy. The whole town might know every last thing about the parade of dicks through my house, about my stalking that shithead, about the drinking and Nate and all, but I was damned if they'd know I'd got desperate enough to visit a goddamn woo-woman.

I did tell Lisa, but. I trusted her to keep it mum. She called up her friend who knew about such things and after a bit of back and forth she booked me in with someone called Lorna, up in Sydney.

I got Lis to drive me to the station so there was no problem getting out of the house. I used to love catching the Sydney train. Used to do it almost every weekend in my early twenties. I had a bloke up there. I'd met him when he came through Strathdee on a footy trip. He hated the place. Hated it. So he'd never come down to visit me, always me up there to him. I didn't mind, but. That train trip was time out. Nobody barking orders, nobody asking questions, nobody feeling me up. Just me and my thoughts, the cattle and canola.

My thoughts aren't what they used to be, though. The whole way, this goddamn loop. Bella's poor body, Bella's voice, Nate's face, Nate's voice, that other man on me and Nate on him, David Hunt's hands and his girlfriend's belly and back to the start again. I dozed off at one point between Gunning and Bundanoon and had one of those thick, twisting nightmares that leave you feeling hurt and haunted but unsure why.

Lorna's flat was in Surry Hills, a hard walk uphill from Central. I was knackered and sweating like a pig when I got there. I wanted to stand outside a bit, catch my breath and cool off, but she must've been looking out for me because she swung the door open before I'd even thought of ringing the bell.

She was about the age my mum would be if she'd lived, and she had over-bleached fairy-floss hair like Mum, too. I'd been expecting her to be dressed like Lisa, all floaty skirts and bangles, but she was in pale jeans with a crease right down the front and a lolly-pink oversized t-shirt. The room she led me too was all done up like her. Light blue carpet and curtains, pink chairs with white trim, a table draped with a pale pink-and-blue-striped cloth.

I sat down in the chair across from where she'd sat herself, draping the jumper I hadn't needed since Yass over the back. When I turned to face her she was looking really bloody pointedly at my cleavage. I thought about putting my jumper on, but I was sick with heat as it was. Maybe if the bitch cracked a window or, God forbid, put on the ceiling fan, I could've covered up a bit.

Still looking down her nose at my tits, she told me how much and waited while I paid and then she started to give me instructions. I had to interrupt her and ask for a glass of water, I was that parched from the train and the walk uphill. Honestly, it's like I'd asked for a three-course meal, the look she gave me. But she went out of the room and I heard a tap go on and off and then she was back with a butter-yellow ceramic jug of water and a tall amber glass.

She waited for me to pour and gulp down some water and then refill the glass before she took up where I'd interrupted her.

'Take one of those.' She pointed to a stack of notepaper on the corner of the desk closest to me. 'Write down the names of the people you want me to reach. Then cover the paper with this.' She handed me a piece of thick black cardboard.

'There's only one person I –'

'More than one,' she said. 'At least two. Two people is the minimum you can write. Go on. I'll cover my eyes if that's what you're worried about.'

I wasn't worried about that. If I was worried about anything it was spewing up the water I'd just guzzled. I thought about telling her I felt sick and leaving, but while I was just sitting there she made this annoyed sound, this big sigh, and I thought, *Fuck you, I'm going to stay and see what damn bullshit you come up with*.

I scribbled down *Bella* and *Mum*, thinking of the ways I'd tell this cow off, tell her what a fraud she was, demand my money back. Just to mess with her I added Rosie and Clive. Rosie was my grandmother, who died when I was two and who apparently only saw me twice before then. Clive was Nate's dad who died last year. I saw him twice, too: on my wedding day and when he came to help Nate move his stuff out.

Lorna slapped her hand over the cardboard as soon as I'd placed it, slid it towards her and then spread both palms over it while muttering to herself like a meth-head. Every few seconds her closed eyes would flutter half open. My guts felt like I'd binged on Maccas after a big night drinking.

'Alright, love, Granny's here. Oh, yes, yes.' Lorna's voice was soft, gentle. Like she was talking to someone she cared about instead of a bosom-flaunting, panting, sweating, water-wanting country sow. 'Alright, alright. Darling, Granny says she's sorry for leaving early. If she coulda stayed longer she would have. She thinks things might've turned out differently if she'd been around. Says she never would've let any of you get hurt. Oh, love, she's crying. She's very distressed. Oh, I need to leave her be for a bit. There are others coming through not on the paper. Shouty bunch around you. Wait, wait, OK, here's Clive. He's happy at how things've come out. He says . . . Oh, well, that's not nice . . . I'm not going to repeat – Oh, go away, you nasty old – Yeah. OK, oh, love, oh, darling, I think I've got your mum. Yeah, yeah, it's her, but she's not speaking. Oh, love, what's happened? She's weeping. Oh, I don't like this kind of grief in the past. Oh, sweetheart, something awful, something dark has happened. Her and your gran both just . . .' Lorna started to move her head in long, slow, sweeps from side to side.

'What? What's wrong? Mum? Mum? Lorna, speak! What's she saying?'

Lorna opened her eyes. They were horribly bloodshot. Her cheeks slapped pink. 'I'm sorry, but I'll have to stop. The crying and shouting is too –'

'No, not yet. I need to hear from my sister. She's the one I came for.'

Lorna was quiet a long time. That feeling like I was going to chuck built and built and then, just when I thought I was going to have to run for the toilet, she gave a big sigh and shook her head. 'She's not there.'

'What does that mean?'

'It means she hasn't passed over.'

'She has. She has. We buried her. I saw her body.'

Lorna nodded. 'Not everyone who dies passes over right away.

I can only reach those who've gone to the other side. Explains why your other ladies were in such a state. They'd be wishing her with them.'

'Where is she then?'

'She's hanging around here, I'd wager.' She smiled kindly. 'Ah, that's why you're here. You've had contact?'

'I don't know. I think so, but I can't communicate with her. She won't tell me who did this to her, won't tell me what she wants. She just . . .' I broke apart. That's the only way I can put it. I told her everything and she nodded and handed me tissues. She said it sounded like Bella was confused. That happens with traumatic death, apparently. Just like a living person might block out things that have happened, terrible things, the dead do that, too. Block out their deaths. But death isn't like being fingered by your uncle in the back of the family station wagon, you know? You literally can't get on with your life afterwards. So, Lorna said, Bella is all confused and disoriented and so she's hanging out where she feels safest, where things are most familiar, she's trying to make everything normal.

'I'll make her at home,' I said. 'I'll talk to her, tell her about my day, reassure her everything's fine. Make her feel safe.'

'It doesn't work like that, love. You have to help her face up to the truth, help her accept that it can't be like that any more. Help her cross over.'

'I don't want to.'

Lorna shook her head and my guts churned again. 'I know, love, but this is hurting her. You know that, right?'

'She's been crying. I hear her at night.'

'Those ladies on the other side are crying for her, too. You can help make it better for them all, Chris. You can bring them peace.'

'How?'

'This is going to be tough, but you need to help her face up to what's happened. You need to make sure she knows that she's not of this world any more.'

I didn't cope with that very well, to be honest. I might have yelled a little bit. It was just, I didn't think the woman understood what it was she was advising. Like, bad enough hearing that news about someone you love, but having to hear it about yourself . . .

Lorna asked me to leave, which, looking back, I understand, as I may have been making her feel unsafe. But at the time it felt like the worst kind of cruelty. I stepped back out onto the Sydney street and I felt like an ant. It didn't seem possible to join the flow of foot traffic back to the station without being trod into the ground under someone's heel. I didn't know how I was ever going to get back home. Being alive seemed, at that moment, the most terrible and difficult thing.

I can tell her that, I realised. I can tell Bel, totally one hundred per cent honestly, that although she went through something awful to get there, she really was better off now. I could tell her that and I could – I tell you, I felt myself swelling up with courage as I thought it – I could join her there. Me and Bella, Mum and Grandma, and no one left to suffer.

Monday
4
May

When three days had passed without Chris answering or returning her calls, May grabbed her laptop, complete with PDF proof of the *Women's Weekly* story, picked up a six-pack of Coopers from across the street and some hot chips from DeeDee's Takeaway, and drove over.

She knocked on the door with her elbow. Waited. Put her laptop bag and the beer on the porch and knocked harder with her knuckles. 'Chris?' she called.

'She's not answering her phone either.'

May turned and saw the hippy-chick neighbour, Lisa, floating up the driveway. 'You've been trying, too?'

'Twice yesterday and again this morning.' Lisa reached May's side and glanced at the hot chips burning a hole in her arm. 'If the smell of those hasn't got her out here, there must really be something wrong.'

May knocked again, half shrugged at Lisa. 'I don't suppose you have keys?'

Lisa opened her hand to reveal a shiny new silver ring with two shiny new silver keys. 'Nate gave them to me.' Lisa grimaced. 'I don't think Chris knows. She wanted him to keep the spares, but he knew he wasn't going to be around as much and wanted to make sure someone nearby had them just in case.'

'Quite the benevolent patriarch, isn't he?'

'He cares about her. And he knows her. Shit. Should I ring him? See if he thinks we should go in?'

'Come on, he's not her dad, and even if he was she's a grown woman and so are you. You've got the keys – you decide what to do with them.'

'Normally I'd say give her her privacy, but . . . You know it's a month yesterday since she was killed? It feels like –'

Heat flushed through her. 'Lisa, you said Nate gave you the keys just in case. This is an "in case" situation, OK?'

'OK, yes, I think you're right.' Lisa nodded, pressed her lips together, stepped up to the door. She fumbled for a second, then May heard the click of a lock opening. Another second, another click. Then a push, a glimpse into the dark kitchen and a clunk as the door stopped.

Lisa looked back at May. 'The chain's on.'

'Shit.' May nudged Lisa out of the way and stuck her nose through the gap. 'Chris!' she yelled. 'Chris, if you're in there you need to tell us right now or we're going to have to call the police to come break your nice new door down. Chris! You hear me?'

May waited, her body pressed hard against the edge of the door.

'Can you hear anything?'

'No.' May stepped back. 'I'm going to try all the windows. You call the police, tell them we might need an ambulance.'

'Oh, God.' Lisa looked like she was about to pass out, but she was dialling.

May ran across the front to the kitchen window. The security blinds were down tight. Same with the bedroom windows, the living room at the back, bathroom, spare room. The place was sealed up like a tomb. She returned to the front, heard Lisa say the police were on their way, and restarted yelling Chris's name.

Minutes passed. May was aware of neighbours congregating in the driveway, Lisa trying to get them to go back into their homes, but doing it in such a way that made it clear something hugely exciting was happening and so the crowd grew. May's voice was wearing out but she kept yelling, kept dialling Chris's phone and hearing it ring out only metres away. By the time the cop car swung into the driveway, forcing the neighbours onto the grass, she was just repeating the one word over and over: Chris Chris Chris Chris.

'Alright, I need you to move aside, please.' She recognised the voice behind her as Matt's; at the same time, she was sure she heard something from inside. She pushed the side of her face harder into the gap.

'May, you need to step aside.'

'Shhh.' She waved a silencing hand. There it was! A small voice: 'Coming.'

'Chris? Shit, you hear me?'

'You're yelling loud enough.'

May could see her now, or at least a dark blob that spoke with her voice, creeping her way along the kitchen wall.

May spun on her heels. 'It's fine. You can go. She's coming.'

Matt crinkled his brow. 'No offence, May, but I need to see that for myself before I can leave.'

May turned back to the dark kitchen. The slow-moving blob was almost at the door. The unmistakable smell of shit sent May reeling back, then realisation pushed her to lean in again. 'Chris, before you open the door, just give a shout-out to Constable Drey to let him know you're OK.'

The blob stopped moving. 'Cops are out there?'

'Just the one and he's going to leave as soon as he knows you're alright. So give him a nice big shout-out, hey?'

There was a pause and then Chris's crackly voice shattered the silence of the porch. "Course I'm alright. Can't a woman have a bit of damn privacy in this bloody town?'

'OK?' May said to Matt, quietly, because Chris was close now.

He looked unsure, kept trying to get up to the door.

'Please. She's OK, you heard her. But she'll be mortified if she comes out and sees the audience. I really need you to get all these spectators off the lawn. Can you do that for me? Except Lisa. Ask her to come back up.'

He nodded, gave his goofy little smile, then turned to the neighbours on the lawn and started shouting at them to clear off. He sounded in no way threatening to May, but people here still had enough respect for the police that they quickly dispersed. Either that or they'd realised there really was nothing to see.

Lisa returned to the porch and May took her hand and pulled her into position so that if there were any busybodies still watching, they'd see nothing but Lisa and May's backs.

The smell was strong and close. The door closed, the chain glided along its track and then Chris was standing there, small and stinking.

'Oh, honey,' Lisa said, and she and May stepped inside, closing the door behind them.

Chris had taken enough sleeping pills to end herself, but fortunately she also took even more than her usual quantities of booze along with them and her body took care of what her mind was too befuddled and her heart too bruised to do and expelled every last bit of poison while she was unconscious.

Lisa helped her clean herself while May changed the bedsheets. They got her to drink some water and eat half a piece of Vegemite toast and then settled her into bed.

'OK, hon, you just stay right there. I'm going to dash across the road and grab all my dull work nonsense and bring it on over so I can work away right here beside you.'

'Lisa, I'm fine. Bugger off and do your work.'

'Just as easy to do it here as over there.'

May felt like she was eight years old again, standing stupidly in the hallway while her aunties and grandparents fussed over her mum. 'Go on and look after your little brothers,' her Grandma Bess told her and so she tried but Jason kept kicking her and Max kept crying and no one would tell her where her dad was or why her mum was howling like the wolf in the *Hundred Nights of Horror* DVD she'd watched that time at her friend Sasha's house even though it was rated M.

'I can stay,' she said, cringing at the weak trill of her voice. *Stop it. You shouted loud enough to wake the dead You screamed her alive.* 'Seriously, I've got nowhere else to be. I can hang here as long as necessary.'

May expected Chris to say it wasn't necessary, but she just nodded very slightly, pulled the blanket up over her shoulders and closed her eyes.

■　■　■

Bella took the news of her death better than I expected. There was no blood or bruised walls, no tilting floor. It didn't even get cold. Instead there was just this long, long silence and only when I called her name did I hear a soft little cry and then I smelt her antiseptic hands up close to my face. I waited for her touch but it never came. Eventually I realised the smell was gone and the room was still and silent and I was alone.

I thought I'd been in pain before but I knew nothing. The despair of her leaving, of knowing that I wouldn't feel her hand or hear her voice ever again, was just . . . It was complete. It made it very easy for me to take the pills. I didn't hesitate for a moment.

I know you'll say it was just luck or biology or whatever that stopped me from dying, but I know it was her. It was her last act of interference before she passed over to be with Mum and Grandma. I don't understand why she would condemn me to this suffering, but she has and I will try hard to respect her wishes, to hang around.

You tell me it will get better, but I don't see how that is possible. Something I learnt from my mum's death is that grief is unending. I was unprepared for that, fell into a deep hole seven or eight months after she went, wondering why I didn't feel better already, wondering why I still felt so sad. I mentioned it to Old Grey one night at work, not having big D&M's or anything, just he said, 'You've not been yerself lately,' and I said, 'Yeah, I'm still sooking about Mum. You'd think I'd be over it by now.' And he goes, 'I never got over me mum's death and that was thirty years ago.' He kept counting the till and I kept wiping the glasses and he said, 'Yer just always a bit sadder than before. Seems bad at first, but you get older, you look around, we're all a bit sadder. It's alright. You get used to it.'

It really helped me, you know, to think, *I don't have to get over this.* I'll just always be a bit sadder than before. Bella liked it, too, when I told her. She said she'd seen it with the old folks at work; they'd all lost more loved ones than you could count on two hands and they all got sad when they talked about them, even ones they'd lost decades ago. Grief is unending, but it's not life-ending. You keep on going. That's the thing.

But this is different. How I feel now, it's not grief. Or it is. I mean, what else do you call it? But it's so deep and thick and black that when I think about it as unending I think, nah, nah, can't do it. Not unending. Unsurvivable.

I'm not trying to be dramatic. For real, how do you survive it? How do you go on every day every day every day living your life, everything the same, except now you're doing it from the middle of this swamp of black blood? How do you drink your morning tea, chat with a friend, pour some beers, have a laugh, have a root, whatever, all of it while pushing and kicking and trying not to drown in blackness? Every breath is hard, because you don't know if it'll let more of that black shit into you or if something worse'll come spewing out. And everybody around you is clear of it, you know? The ones who know, they talk softly as though they understand that you're already nearly mad from it, and they touch you gently on the elbow, the shoulder, the cheek as though they can actually see the fresh wounds being ripped into you every minute. And the ones who don't know, they smash against your sides, make so much noise, laugh at everything and complain about nothing and you want to show them all your gashes, all the black shit oozing out, but you know that'll make it worse because you know that really they do know, not about you in particular, but about the hell that happens on earth, the torture and rape and killing of sisters, they do know that, like you knew it back when you barely paused in your laughing talking complaining to say *hmmm, how awful about some other sister*.

And the worst thing, the unsurvivable thing, is understanding that there exist people who know in their flesh the truth of all this. They know it because they created it, created hell with their bare hands and then just kept on living, kept on as though they never stopped a world. When you understand that, understand that there are men who butchered a girl and then went home to sleep and have slept and woken, slept and woken all the days and nights since, and that they'll continue on with those pictures in their heads, the memory of ripping her apart pressed into their skin, the secret knowledge of the look on her face, the sound in her throat in her last moment . . . All this inside them and they don't rip out their own hearts! There are men who can do that, remember doing that, know what it is to do that and still go on.

And there are men who don't cause quite so much damage and so are all too happy to publicise the worst so they can look mild in comparison, and men who do no violence and so don't see how it is their problem that others do, and there are men who want us to know about the bad and the worse and the negligent so that we go to *them* for protection and there are men – my heart wants to say it's most of them, but my heart is a battered, blood-soaked madwoman – who are pure and good of heart and intent and who want only to be our friends and brothers and lovers, but we have no way of telling those from the others until it's too late and that, perhaps, is the most unbearable thing of all.

But she chose for me to bear it and so I will try. I will try.

June

The story ran in *Women's Weekly* and, as May predicted, the newspapers ran excerpts or reports of the article, many of them reprinting May's photo of Chris on the floor at Bella's apartment, and the TV networks clamoured to get an on-camera exclusive with Chris. But Chris was unavailable to them and to the police who wanted to capitalise on the renewed public interest and hold another press conference with Chris front and centre. Chris was unavailable to anyone except May and, to the extent that she would exchange greetings and eat the soup she brought, Lisa.

'I seem to have accidentally become her guardian,' May told Max when he rang to congratulate her on the story. 'I might as well move in with her, save the cost of the hotel room.'

'That sounds like the worst idea yet in a string of terrible ideas. Look, May, the story is really fantastic. Even I shed a little tear, I admit, but it's only a story, you –'

'It's not though! Aren't you listening? This woman is falling apart.

Has fallen apart. She won't leave the house. I can't just abandon her now that I've got my bloody magazine exclusive.'

'But that's what journalists do. It's not nasty, it's your job. Like I have to let the kids I've taught all year go when December comes around. Some of them have tough stuff going on and when they're in my care I try to make a difference, but then the year ends and a new one starts and I get a new batch of kids to worry about. It's the job.'

'It's different though.'

'How?'

'I've only helped myself. Not her. Since she's known me she's only got sadder and crazier.'

'May, listen to yourself. The woman's sister was murdered. Recently. If she's a wreck it's only to be expected.'

With Chris's consent, May took on some of the TV and newspaper interviews in her place. She must've done all right, because offers to meet and 'talk about future opportunities' began to trickle into her inbox. Her former editor called and congratulated her on her 'breakthrough' and said he'd be happy to receive freelance contributions from her any time. She had her pick of publishers wanting the book about Bella. She chose the one which offered her enough money to live off for a year and a promise to publish at the end of that time even if the killer had not been found.

The day after May had signed the contract, four weeks after the *Women's Weekly* article was published, the police charged a thirty-two-year-old Strathdee housepainter with Bella's rape and murder. They had found him after a tip-off, searched his home and found a piece of Bella's clothing. DNA was conclusive.

Chris had called May with the news and invited her over. Together they drank whisky and watched the 7pm bulletin. When the footage of police leading the man, whose face was blurred, out of a nondescript red-brick house came up, Chris gasped and said, 'Fuck.'

'What? You recognise him?'

'No,' Chris said. 'But . . . I mean, look at him. He's so . . .'

May looked. He was average height, slim, with short light brown hair. He wore jeans and a dark blue t-shirt. 'Yeah,' May said. 'I know.'

Seconds after the broadcast finished, May's publisher texted her: *We have an ending! Let's talk tomorrow about a fast-tracked schedule. Seize the moment!* May read it out loud to Chris, who smiled and said, 'Congratulations. It's a big day for you.'

'Chris, you know I can't write this book without you, right? I need you with me or it can't work.'

'I'm with you, I am. It's just . . .' She muted the TV, tucked her legs up on the sofa, closed her eyes. 'Like your publisher said, you have your ending. But I don't. She's dead and that doesn't end.'

May could think of nothing to say to that, so she refilled their glasses instead.

'I've watched enough *Law and Order*, read enough true crime. I know it's how it has to go. Finish with a last memory of the pretty dead girl and the sound of the jail door slamming shut on the monster who killed her and everyone can feel like the world has been set to rights. The grief and fear can stop. I know it has to go that way, I do. But it's bullshit.'

'I don't think it's bullshit. Justice, punishment, an end to this man's ability to do this to someone else, that's real. That's really happening.'

'I'm not saying that isn't true, I'm saying . . .' Chris looked to the ceiling, took a large slug of whisky. 'All that's ended is one man's freedom to hurt people. Bella's death isn't fixed and neither is the world that she died in. The idea that locking up one man could do that, could make everything OK . . . that's bullshit.'

'OK,' May said. 'I think I get you, but . . . I can't think about it right now. I need to get to work. I'm going to head down to the station and get my little mate Matt to fill me in on what he knows. Then I'll –'

'You're not going anywhere, you drunk. You've had a quarter bottle of whisky.'

May looked at the half-empty bottle. 'Have I really? Shit.'

'You better stay here.' Chris took a deep breath. 'This sofa's pretty comfy.'

'Are you sure?'

'I'll get you a blanket.'

The next morning Matt told May that the man they arrested had only lived in Strathdee for a year. Detectives were looking into the possibility he was responsible for cases throughout the state going back a decade. May spent a few hours online familiarising herself with ten years' worth of unsolved rapes and murders. She read about bodies burnt beyond recognition, decomposed, dismembered, shoved in suitcases, dumped in rivers, stashed in freezers, partially dissolved in chemical drums. She read about stab wounds, blunt-instrument trauma, strangulation, suffocation, shots through the heart, stomach, throat, head. She saved details of those that seemed closest to Bella's murder. It was a long list. The list of those she disregarded was twenty times longer.

There was nothing in this research especially new to her as a reporter, a news junkie, a viewer of crime dramas and serial-killer films. But when she tried to sleep that night her closed lids opened caverns of horror. Immense dark spaces in which time rolled back and the shattered, smashed, melted, desecrated bodies showed her their faces and limbs and beating hearts and screaming mouths.

Against her will she remembered something from her first year of high school. A round-faced, quiet boy used to stare across the class at her. Her friend Bethany asked him if he had the hots for May and he admitted he did, but instead of asking her to go with him he began to leave drawings of her imagined naked body in poses undreamt of in her locker. In one, she hung upside down, her hair pooling on the ground, blood seeping from beneath whatever it was encircling her ankles, her arms wrapped lovingly around her waist. In another, she lay between two trees, a dog wearing a studded collar frothing at the slit between her wide-open legs; a disembodied hand in the process of releasing its hold on the dog's chain.

There were others but those two were the first and the only ones she remembered clearly. The boy was expelled after Bethany showed them to the school counsellor. May didn't know what happened to him after that, but she remembered his cow eyes sizing her up in Year 7 maths every time she saw one of those dog collars.

This had nothing to do with what happened to Bella and what happened to Bella had nothing to do with Tegan Miller and none of it had to do with the rich Sydney housewife left out to rot in the street, which had nothing to do with the Nigerian girls stolen as sex slaves or the Indian woman eviscerated on a bus or the man grabbing women off the streets of Brunswick.

None of it connected, she knew, and yet, and yet, it felt like it. It felt, to May, that there was a thread connecting it all, and if she could find it she could follow it back, see where it began. Rip it out and examine its source.

It seemed to May that Max was right: Chris's madness was only to be expected. An entirely rational response to what had been revealed to her about the world. What's surprising, May thought, is that more of us don't lose our minds, become lock-ins, scared of shadows. It was why her own mind skittered away from her when she tried to connect the horrors.

It was why she wished it was not the middle of the night so she could call Chas and have him come into this room and have every opportunity to hurt her and yet not, because that would be proof that the thing her mind skittered from wasn't true, not entirely anyway.

She almost did it. Instead she called Chris, who answered right away.

'Tell me if I'm being too forward, but what do you reckon about me coming to stay with you for a while? Until I finish the book, I mean. I'd pay of course. Same as what I'm paying here at the hotel?'

'No you won't, because I'm not running a bloody hotel. You chip in for bills and groceries and that and don't expect me to clean up after you and make the sofa up for you each night.'

'Sounds good.'

'Alright then. Hey, how'd you go with it all today? Researching that bloke and all. Find out much?'

'Yeah, but, listen, I'll tell you about it later. I can't think about it any more tonight.'

'I hear you.'

'I know you do. Goodnight.'

'Night, mate. See you tomorrow.'

After

People say I wouldn't talk to the media because I'd signed some lucrative exclusive deal. Such a laugh I had at that. A house guest who records everything you say and sits up till all hours tapping at her keyboard and never, ever leaves. Some lucrative deal.

People assumed I didn't sit in court and watch Bella's killer tried and sentenced because hearing him describe what he'd done would have been too much for me. Well, I didn't laugh at that one but I sneered, I snarled. There's not a thing that man could say that would touch me. He did all the damage he was ever going to do when he ended Bella's life. He's harmless now. He's nothing.

People wonder why I left Strathdee. They guess I can't stand to be near the place where Bella died, but that's not it at all. Strathdee is the place she lived and every square inch of the ground is soaked with memories of her life. I could've happily stayed there until the end of my days if the ghouls and tourists hadn't decided that the places she lived and worked should become permanent reminders of the worst and shortest day of her life. Forgive me, Strathdee. I don't blame you and will always love you but I can't live in my sister's tomb.

If you keep your word and tell this story as I told it to you, people will mock me for speaking of ghosts. In the same breath they'll talk about monsters, of how my sister died because she had the misfortune of meeting one. As though that bunyip slithered from its underwater cave and hugged the life from her. As though the drowned child's zombie hands grabbed her ankles and pulled her below. They talk as though little girls grow up being warned not to talk to goblins and women are cautioned to not get drunk around werewolves and battered wives got that way by marrying Freddy Krueger.

People ask if what I've been through has made me afraid and of course it has. But not of monsters. Only of those who insist they exist.

Acknowledgments

An Isolated Incident was written over several years in all kinds of places. Special mention must go to the Keesing Studio at the Cité Internationale des Arts, Paris, where this novel was finished during six transformative months. I am so grateful to Nancy Keesing and the Australia Council for the Arts for the incredible gift of this residency. Thank you, too, to Varuna, the Writers' House, and to the NSW Writers' Centre for providing writing space closer to home.

I am enormously thankful to Emma Rafferty, Ali Lavau and Libby Turner for their thoughtful editing, to my agent, Charlie Viney, for his continued support and guidance, and to Pam Newton for reading, talking it all through and urging me on. Thanks, too, to Alex Craig and the Pan Macmillan Australia team, and to Scott Pack and the Lightning Books crew for their enthusiasm and commitment.

Big love and gratitude to the incredible, never-flagging cheer-squad that is my family. I got so, so lucky with you lot. To my girl gang, thank you for walking the talk and giving me the strength and courage to go to the dark places. And always, always, thank you Jeff – you make everything brighter, better and more hopeful.